HOLLOW STONE

STONEBOUND
BOOK 1

N.B. CROSS

Hollow Stone: Book 1 in the Stonebound Trilogy

Copyright © 2025 by N.B. Cross

All rights reserved.

No part of this book may be reproduced or transmitted in any form or by any means, electronic or mechanical, without permission in writing from the publisher, except in the case of brief quotations embodied in critical articles and reviews.

This is a work of fiction. Names, characters, places, and incidents either are the product of the author's imagination or are used fictitiously. Any resemblance to actual persons, living or dead, events, or locales is entirely coincidental.

Published by Nimbus Books

ISBN: 978-1-970425-02-4

Cover monster art: Daniel Karlsson

instagram.com/karlsson_art/

karlssonart@gmail.com

For my wife,
who reminds me that love carries us through the dark.

CHAPTER
ONE

The grease hangs in the air like memory, thick and clinging to everything it touches. Joe Bullit wipes down the counter for the third time tonight, his movements automatic, the rag following the same circular path it has traced for months now. The fluorescent lights above flicker once, twice, then steady themselves with a faint electrical hum that matches the deeper rumble of the walk-in cooler. Cedar Lagoon Pizzeria sleeps around him, all its familiar sounds settling into the quiet rhythm of closing time.

His hands know this work without thinking. Stack the last pizza boxes against the wall, threatening to topple but never quite falling. Check the ovens, all four of them, knobs turned to off, pilot lights glowing blue in their caves of blackened steel. The heat still radiates from them, a warmth that clings to his forearms as he reaches in to retrieve a forgotten pan. He thought of heading south this year instead of working. But the work keeps his hands busy, keeps his mind from wandering to places it shouldn't go.

The mop bucket rolls across the checkered floor with a squeak that needs oiling. Tomorrow, he thinks, though he thought the same thing yesterday and the day before. The water sloshes gray and sudsy as he pushes it toward the back, past the prep station where tomorrow's dough rises under plastic wrap, past the reach-in cooler that rattles like it's clearing its throat. Everything here has its own voice, its own complaint. Joe has learned to listen to them all, to know when something sounds wrong.

Outside the front windows, Kipling Avenue stretches empty beneath streetlights that pool orange on the pavement. Beyond that, where the town gives way to wild, the woods press close. They seem different at night, not just dark but actively black, as if they're drinking in what little light escapes from the pizzeria. The trees shift in a movement hypnotic, almost like breathing. He turns away, focuses on the floor, on the steady back-and-forth of the mop.

The walk-in cooler kicks on with its familiar drone, vibrating through the walls. Joe pauses, listening. After all these years, he knows every sound this place makes, every settling board and sighing pipe. The building talks to him in creaks and groans, tells him its troubles. Tonight, something else whispers beneath the usual chorus. Not quite a sound, more like the absence of one.

Then the crash comes, violent and sudden, glass exploding somewhere out back. The mop handle clatters to the floor as Joe's body moves before his mind catches up, old instincts from a different life kicking in. His heart hammers against his ribs, adrenaline flooding his system with a familiar electricity.

"Damn kids," he mutters, though his voice sounds unconvinced even to himself. Kids don't make glass explode like that, don't make the whole building shudder as if something massive has struck it.

The baseball bat leans behind the counter where it always has, Louisville Slugger. Joe's fingers wrap around the grip, the wood smooth and worn from years of idle handling during slow shifts. He hefts it, tests its weight, then moves toward the back door with careful, measured steps. His breathing stays controlled, deliberate. Three tours in the Gulf taught him that much: panic kills faster than bullets.

The hallway to the back stretches long, or maybe that's just his perception slowing everything down. His shoes squeak on the still-damp floor. The exit sign glows red above the door, casting everything in a hellish tint. Through the side glass window, he sees nothing but black. Not the normal darkness of the alley, but something thicker, more complete.

The crash comes again, shaking the exit door in its frame. A third impact, this one caves in the lower panel, folding the metal like wet cardboard. Something wedges through the opening: not a hand, not an arm, but a wet tangle of black fibers, soil clinging to it in clumps. Joe stares, just long enough to wonder if he's having a stroke. Then the entire door buckles inward, ripped from its hinges, and the thing outside surges in, blotting out the corridor.

It isn't a bear. It isn't anything that should exist.

The bat lifts itself in his grip. He swings, connects with something boneless like hitting a bag of wet laundry, but the force is enough to stagger the mass back a step. It makes no sound, not even a hiss, but the air fills with a loamy, rotting stench that punches up into his sinuses. He tries to backpedal, but the thing is already on him, slamming him against the stacked boxes with inhuman strength. He hears something crack. His ribs or the drywall behind him, he can't tell. The bat falls away. The creature's touch burns through his shirt, gritty and cold, like fingers packed with ice and grave dirt.

Movement. Fast, too fast for something that size. Joe catches a glimpse of its hunched shape, massive shoulders rolling with an alien gait, and then soil cascades from it like water, pattering on the tile with the sound of blood. The smell hits him next: earth and rot and something else, something organic and wrong. His grip tightens on the bat, but the thing is already retreating, melting back into the darkness between buildings with a speed that makes Joe's eyes water trying to track it.

Pain explodes across his left hand. He looks down, confused, sees the gash running from his thumb to his wrist. Blood wells up, thick and dark, dripping onto the tiles in a steady rhythm. The drops look black in the half-lit kitchen, spreading in tiny puddles that reflect nothing.

"Son of a bitch," Joe hisses through clenched teeth. He drops the bat, cradles his injured hand against his chest. The wound throbs with his heartbeat, each pulse sending fresh blood seeping between his fingers. "Son of a bitch."

He looks toward the door that's now just a frame, eyes scanning the darkness where the thing disappeared. Nothing moves now except the trees at the alley's end, swaying in that same unfelt wind. His hand leaves bloody prints on the door frame as he stumbles to look further, the warmth of the pizzeria suddenly feeling like the only safe thing in the world.

The sirens arrive like an afterthought, their wail already fading as the cruisers pull into the alley. Joe sits on the prep counter, a dish towel wrapped tight around his left hand, watching through the back door as flashlight beams sweep lazily across the damage. The officers move with the sluggish energy of men called away from something more important, their voices carrying that particular tone of people going through motions they've already decided are pointless.

Sheriff Brennan ducks through the doorway, his considerable bulk filling the frame. He takes in the scene with a quick glance that seems to slide right off the details, as if his eyes refuse to properly focus on what's in front of them. His notepad stays in his pocket.

"Joe," he says, nodding once. "What, uh. What happened here?"

"What happened?" Joe's voice comes out rougher than intended. The towel around his hand has soaked through, red spreading across the white cotton like a map of some unknown country. "I have no damn idea, Tom."

The sheriff's gaze drifts to where Joe points, and for a moment something flickers across his face. Not surprise exactly, but a kind of deliberate blankness, as if he's choosing not to see what's there. The kitchen wall bows inward, plaster cracked in a spider web pattern radiating from an impact point five feet off the ground. Whatever hit it punched through the exterior brick, left a depression the size of a trash can lid.

"Kids," Brennan says, shaking his head. "Getting worse every year. Probably threw something from a truck, took off before you could catch them."

Joe stares at him. "Kids? You think kids did this."

"Halloween's coming up. You know how they get." The sheriff's eyes drift again, this time to the walk-in cooler. The door hangs like its on a poorly-made treehouse, its thick metal twisted like someone took aluminum foil and crushed it in their fist. The hinges have torn partially free from the frame, bolts sheared clean through. "Insurance should cover it."

"Tom, look at it. Really look at it." Joe slides off the counter, his legs unsteady from blood loss or adrenaline crash or both. "What kind of kid could do that? What kind of anything could…"

"You need to get that hand looked at," Brennan interrupts, already turning away. "Matthews, get some pictures for the report. Five or six should do it."

Officer Matthews, young enough that acne still marks his jawline, raises his phone with obvious reluctance. The flash goes off once, twice, the light seeming too weak to properly illuminate the damage. He takes a step closer to the cooler door, then stops, his face pale. His hand trembles slightly as he snaps another photo from farther back.

"That should be enough," he says quickly, pocketing the phone.

"You're not going to dust for prints? Check for evidence?" Joe's voice rises despite himself. "Kids leave prints, but you know it wasn't kids. Something was here. Something big. I saw it..."

"What did you see exactly?" Brennan asks, but his tone suggests he doesn't want an answer. His pen hovers over his notepad, which he's finally pulled out, though he hasn't written anything yet.

Joe opens his mouth, then closes it. How does he describe what he saw? The shape that moved too fast and too fluid for its size? The soil falling from it like the thing was made of earth itself? The smell that still clings to the alley, organic and ancient?

"I don't know," he finally says. "It was dark."

"There you go." Brennan makes a single mark on his notepad, then flips it closed. "Vandalism, probably with a vehicle. We'll increase patrols for a few nights. You should get someone out here to board up that wall before it rains."

They leave within ten minutes of arriving. Joe watches their taillights disappear down Kipling Avenue, red dots shrinking into nothing. The alley falls quiet again except for the sparking of the torn light fixture, its exposed wires spitting occasional brightness into the dark.

By morning, yellow police tape stretches across the pizzeria's front door, but it might as well be invisible. Joe watches from across the street, his left hand properly bandaged now, twenty-three stitches hidden under white gauze. People walk past without looking, their eyes sliding away from the building as if it's become part of the background, no more noteworthy than a mailbox or fire hydrant.

The fog rolled in before dawn, thick and gray, muffling sounds and blurring edges. It carries a metallic scent from the pizzeria, the smell of twisted metal and broken things. A few cars drift past, their headlights barely penetrating the murk, but none slow down. No one stops to read the CLOSED UNTIL FURTHER NOTICE sign Joe taped to the window.

Mrs. Chen from the flower shop next door waters her window boxes, humming tunelessly. When Joe calls out to her, asks if she heard anything last night, she looks through him rather than at him.

"Such a quiet night," she says, her voice distant. "Slept like a baby."

Her shop shares a wall with the pizzeria. The impact that caved in Joe's kitchen would have shaken her entire building. But she just keeps watering her petunias, the water over-flowing the boxes, running down the storefront in thin streams that look like tears.

The police tape flutters in the breeze. One end has already come loose, the adhesive failing or perhaps never properly applied. It waves like a flag of surrender, yellow against the gray morning, and not a single person passing by seems to notice it at all.

Joe's hand throbs under the bandages, each heartbeat a reminder that something happened, something real, no matter what the town chooses to forget. The stitches pull when he flexes his fingers, and the pain grounds him, keeps him from drifting into the same strange blindness that seems to have taken everyone else.

Vincent Granger takes the long way to school, the way that passes Cedar Lagoon Pizzeria, though he can't say why his feet choose this path. The morning fog hasn't lifted yet, and it turns the familiar streets into something else, some-thing that belongs more to dream than to the waking world. His sneakers make soft sounds on the wet pavement, each step echoing strangely in the muffled quiet.

The pizzeria emerges from the gray like a wound in the fabric of the morning. The police tape catches his eye first, one end loose and flapping in a breeze that doesn't seem to touch anything else. It waves at him, a yellow flag that speaks of violence in a language the rest of the town has apparently forgotten how to read. Vincent slows, then stops, his back-pack suddenly heavy on his shoulders.

Through the front windows, darkness pools thick and unnatural. The chairs are still stacked on tables, normal enough, but beyond them he can make out the damaged kitchen. The wall bulges inward like something massive tried to birth itself through the brick and plaster. Debris scatters across the checkered floor. Chunks of drywall, fragments of metal that might have once been part of the cooler door. The damage looks fresh, maybe hours old, but already the place feels abandoned, as if it's been empty for years instead of one night.

Vincent presses closer to the glass, his breath fogging the window. The metallic scent Joe noticed earlier seeps through the cracks around the door frame. It makes him think of blood, though not quite, more like the smell of old pennies left too long in water. His reflection stares back at him from the dark glass, his tired eyes made huge by the distortion, and for a moment he has the unsettling feeling that something else looks back from deeper in the shadows.

Movement across the street pulls his attention away. A girl stands on the opposite sidewalk, so still that at first Vincent thinks she might be a trick of the fog. But no. She's real, solid in a way that makes everything else seem less certain. Pale hoodie pulled up despite the humid morning, black skirt that stops just above her knees, legs bare and white as bone in the gray light. She holds a paper bag in one hand, the logo barely visible but unmistakable.

She watches him.

Not the casual glance of someone who happens to notice another person on the street. This is deliberate, focused obser-vation. Her face remains partially hidden by the hood, but

Vincent can see her mouth, lips pressed into a line that's neither smile nor frown but something more ambiguous.

Their eyes meet.

The world narrows to that connection, everything else fading to background static. Her eyes are dark, darker than they should be in the morning light, and they hold a weight that makes Vincent's chest tighten. She knows something. Not just about the pizzeria or what happened here last night, but about him, about things he hasn't even thought yet. The certainty of it hits him like cold water, shocking and undeniable.

She doesn't smile. Doesn't wave or nod or make any gesture of normal human acknowledgment. She just looks at him with that terrible knowing, as if she can see through his skin to the grief he carries, the questions that keep him awake at night, the fear that the town is slowly swallowing him whole. The paper bag shifts slightly in her grip, and Vincent imagines he hears something inside it, a soft rustling like dried flowers or old paper or wings.

A chill runs down his spine, vertebra by vertebra, as if someone is tracing a finger along the bones. His body wants to move, to run, but he stands frozen, caught in her gaze like an insect in amber. The fog swirls between them, and for a moment she seems to flicker, there and not there, solid and somehow permeable, as if she exists in more than one place at once.

Then she turns away.

The release is so sudden that Vincent staggers, catching himself against the pizzeria window. His palm leaves a print on the glass, and he stares at it, confused, as if he's forgotten how his own hand works. When he looks back across the street, she's walking away, unhurried, the bag swinging gently at her side. She doesn't look back, but somehow he knows she's still aware of him, still holding him in some kind of invisible grip.

His legs unlock, and suddenly he's walking too, faster than before, his pace quickening with each step. The school is still three blocks away, but he nearly runs, his backpack bouncing against his spine. The fog seems to chase him, or maybe he's dragging it along, leaving a wake of disturbance in the gray morning. His breath comes quick and shallow.

The school bells ring again, closer now, calling him to the normal world of classes and homework and teenage concerns. But Vincent knows, with a certainty that sits cold in his stomach, that normal is just another word for the lies people tell themselves. The girl's dark eyes stay with him, burned into his memory like an afterimage of staring too long at the sun.

CHAPTER
TWO

The creek bed behind Duswood High runs like a scar through the earth, all cracked mud and rust-colored stones where water should flow. Vincent sits on the concrete lip of the culvert, his legs dangling over the edge, watching how the afternoon light turns the dried clay the color of old blood. The others sprawl around him in various poses of studied indifference. Carl kicks at loose gravel, sending pebbles skittering down the slope. Jayce picks at a hole in his jeans. Rene sits cross-legged, her sketchbook balanced on her knees, though her pencil hasn't moved in minutes.

Carl is scrolling through his phone with restless thumbs. He squints suddenly, then turns the screen to Jayce. "You guys seen this? Some reporter wrote up the pizzeria thing."

Jayce leans in. "Jennifer Winter. The Duswood Press." He raises an eyebrow. "Is that her real face? She looks like an Instagram filter smashed with an anime character."

Rene glances over. "She's… symmetrical."

Jayce grins. "No way that's not AI. Nobody has skin like that."

Vincent looks at the photo. The woman in the profile

picture is all perfect curls and a white-hot smile, like someone who's never had a bad day. "Maybe she just knows her angles," he mutters, earning a side glance from Jayce.

Carl scrolls past. "Whatever. Her story's boring. Says it was 'local vandalism' and nobody's hurt." He locks his phone, but the image of Jennifer, impossibly polished, lingers in their minds.

None of them want to go home. The knowledge sits between them, unspoken but understood, heavy as the humid air that presses down despite the creek's absence of water.

"It's wrong," Vincent says, the words escaping before he can catch them. "The creek. It shouldn't be this dry."

Carl snorts. "It's September. Everything's dry."

"Not like this." Vincent traces the creek bed with his eyes, following its path until it disappears into the woods. The clay has cracked into irregular polygons, each piece curling at the edges. "There was water here last week. I saw it."

"Nah," Jayce says, but his voice lacks its usual bite. He's staring at the creek bed too.

Rene shifts, her pencil finally moving across the page in quick, scratching strokes. "The trees," she says softly, almost to herself. "Look at the roots."

Vincent follows her gaze to where the bank has eroded, exposing the root systems of the oaks that line the creek. They hang in the air like frozen waterfalls, reaching for moisture. Some have already begun to wither, their tips blackened as if burned.

"Summer weirdness," Carl declares, but he sounds like he's trying to convince himself.

They all stare up the creek where at least some water should flow. They pause a minute.

"That's..." Jayce starts, then stops. His usual sarcasm has evaporated, leaving his face naked and young.

"Interesting," Rene finishes. She closes her sketchbook

with deliberate care, tucks her pencil behind her ear. "We should look."

"We should go home," Vincent says, but even as the words leave his mouth, he knows they won't. Home means his mother's empty wine bottles and his father's absence. Home means silence that presses against his eardrums until he wants to scream just to break it.

Carl is already swinging his legs over the edge, his sneakers finding purchase on the steep bank. "Come on. Don't be scared."

"I'm not scared," Vincent lies. But he follows anyway, his hands gripping the concrete edge as he lowers himself down. The bank is steeper than it looks, and he half-slides, half-falls the last few feet, his shoes hitting the hard clay at the bottom.

The temperature drops the moment his feet touch the creek bed. Not dramatically, not enough to see his breath, but enough to raise goosebumps along his arms. The air tastes different down here, metallic and thick, like breathing through a wet cotton mask.

Jayce lands beside him with a grunt, then reaches up to help Rene down. She moves carefully, her skirt catching on exposed roots, but her face shows no hesitation. When she reaches the bottom, she immediately crouches, pressing her palm flat against the dried mud.

"It's warm," she says. "Like something's underneath."

Vincent kneels beside her, places his own hand on the ground. She's right. Heat radiates up through the clay, faint but unmistakable, as if the earth itself has a fever.

"Probably just the sun," Carl says, but he's not touching the ground. He's already walking upstream, toward where the creek bed curves into the woods. "You coming or not?"

They follow because the alternative is admitting fear. Vincent keeps his hand brushing against the bank as they walk. The concrete culvert gives way to natural banks, root systems exposed like anatomy diagrams. The smell changes too, grows thicker, organic. Not quite rot but something close to it, something that makes Vincent think of the compost pile behind his house, of things breaking down and becoming other things.

"This is far enough," Jayce says when they reach the tree line. The woods loom ahead, darker than they should be at four in the afternoon. The creek bed continues into that darkness like a throat waiting to swallow.

"Just a little further," Carl insists. He's already stepped into the shadows, his red hoodie the last bright thing before the world turns gray and green.

"Something's off," Rene says. She's stopped walking, stands perfectly still in the middle of the creek bed. Her head tilts slightly, as if listening to something only she can hear. "The sound. There isn't any."

Vincent realizes she's right. No birds, no insects, no rustling leaves despite the breeze he can see moving the canopy above. The silence presses against his ears like water pressure at depth.

"We should go back," he says, but his feet keep moving forward, following Carl's retreating shape. Jayce mutters something under his breath, a curse or a prayer, Vincent can't tell which as he makes the sign of the cross. Rene walks beside him, her breathing shallow and quick.

The creek bed narrows as they enter the woods proper. The banks rise higher on either side, and Vincent has the sudden, irrational fear that they're walking into a trap, that the earth might close over them like a mouth. He pushes the thought away, focuses on placing one foot in front of the other, on the solid feel of dried clay beneath his shoes.

The air thickens until breathing becomes conscious work. The temperature continues to drop, degree by degree, until Vincent's breath comes out in barely visible puffs. And underneath it all, that smell, stronger now, metallic and organic, blood and earth mixed.

They walk deeper into the woods, into the waiting dark, none of them willing to be the first to admit they've made a terrible mistake.

The smell hits them first, a wave of copper and compost that makes Vincent's stomach clench. It rolls out from deeper in the woods, thick enough to taste, coating the back of his throat with something slick. Carl stops walking, his hand moving to cover his nose and mouth. Even from behind, Vincent can see the tension in his shoulders, the way his bravado shrinks in the face of something genuinely abnormal.

"What is that?" Jayce's voice comes out muffled through his fingers. He's pressed himself against the creek bank, as far from the center as he can get without climbing out.

Nobody answers because nobody knows. The smell defies easy explanation. It's blood but not blood, earth but not earth, something between states. Vincent breathes through his mouth, but that only makes it worse. Now he can taste it, metallic and organic, like licking a wound filled with soil.

The creek bed continues its curve ahead, disappearing around a bend bordered by exposed roots that hang like curtains. The shadows there look solid, impenetrable, as if the darkness has weight and substance. Vincent wants to stop, wants to turn back, but his feet keep moving forward.

Then he sees it. A single leaf, brown and curled, drifting through the air. Nothing unusual except for the direction. It's floating upward, rising against gravity in a slow, lazy spiral. Vincent tracks its path until it disappears into the canopy above, swallowed by branches.

"Did you see that?" The words escape before he can stop them.

"See what?" Carl turns, following Vincent's gaze upward. The trees sway despite the absolute stillness of the air at ground level. Not all of them, just certain ones, as if something massive moves through the canopy, disturbing only what it touches.

A branch creaks somewhere to their left. The sound is wrong, too deliberate, like someone twisting green wood with conscious intent. Another creak answers from the right, then another behind them. The sounds form a pattern, a conversation in a language of stressed wood and bending fiber.

"This isn't right," Rene whispers. She's stopped in the middle of the creek bed. "We need to leave."

"Yeah," Jayce agrees immediately, his protective sarcasm completely gone. "Carl, we're going. Now."

But Carl isn't listening. He's staring ahead, at the bend in the creek, his body rigid with a tension that makes Vincent's skin crawl. "There's something there."

Vincent follows his gaze, squinting into the shadows between the trees. At first, he sees nothing but darkness and the vague shapes of trunks and undergrowth. Then something shifts, a movement so subtle he almost dismisses it as imagination. But no. There, between two oaks, partially hidden by hanging moss and shadow, something stands.

The shape is flawed. That's the first thing Vincent's brain processes, before details, before fear. It's flawed in the way a reflection in disturbed water is flawed, familiar but distorted. Shoulders too broad for any human frame, pulled back at an angle that speaks of joints that bend differently than they should. Arms too long, hanging past where knees should be, ending in darkness that might be hands or might be something else entirely.

Vincent's breath catches in his throat. His body wants to run, every instinct screaming at him to move, but he stands frozen, trapped by the terrible certainty that if he moves, if he makes any sound at all, the thing will notice him.

"Oh shit," Jayce breathes. He sees it too now, his face draining of color until he looks gray in the filtered forest light. "What is that?"

The thing shifts again, and Vincent glimpses more details he wishes he hadn't. The texture of its surface, not quite skin, not quite bark. The way it moves, fluid and jerky at once, as if it's remembering how to use a body it's borrowed. No face that he can see, just shadow where features should be, but somehow Vincent knows it's looking at them. Watching. Waiting.

Carl raises his hand, pointing with a trembling finger. The gesture breaks whatever spell holds them. The thing in the shadows responds, tilting the shape of a head, and that small movement contains such alien intent that Vincent's paralysis shatters.

Rene makes a sound, not quite a scream, more like air being punched from her lungs. Her sketchbook falls, pages fluttering open to reveal drawings Vincent glimpses for just a moment. It's filled with dark shapes and reaching hands and mouths where mouths shouldn't be. Rene runs.

The thing moves.

Not toward them, not yet, but a lateral shift that brings it partially into the light. Vincent sees soil cascading from its form, dark earth falling like water from surfaces that shouldn't be able to hold it. The smell intensifies, copper and rot and age, and Vincent's stomach heaves. He tastes bile, sharp and acidic.

"Run," Jayce says, or maybe screams, Vincent can't tell over the roaring in his ears. "Run, run, run!"

They bolt. No coordination, no plan, just pure animal panic driving them back the way they came. Vincent's feet slip on the dried clay, and he goes down hard, palms scraping against the rough surface. He scrambles up, doesn't look back, can't look back, because he can hear it now. Not footsteps exactly, but a sound like wet earth being displaced, like something massive dragging itself along the creek bed behind them.

Carl is ahead, his longer legs carrying him faster, Rene just behind him, her breath coming in sobbing gasps. Jayce grabs Vincent's arm, hauling him forward when he stumbles again.

The creek bed seems longer than before, stretched out like a nightmare tunnel that has no end.

The branches above them crack and groan. Leaves fall upward, spiraling into the canopy in defiance of natural law. The air grows thicker with each step until Vincent feels like he's running through water, every movement requiring enormous effort. His lungs burn, his legs shake, but the alternative to running is unthinkable.

Behind them, the thing makes a sound. Not a roar or a scream, nothing so comprehensible. Indiscernible. It's the sound of earth shifting, of roots tearing free from soil, of something fundamental breaking. The sound follows them, echoes off the creek banks, seems to come from everywhere at once.

Vincent risks a glance back and immediately wishes he hadn't. The thing is following, not running but flowing, its form shifting and reforming with each movement. Soil pours from it in streams, leaving a trail of disturbed earth. And in what might be its face, two points of darkness that could be eyes deeper than black water track their flight with terrible patience.

It's not chasing them, Vincent realizes with a sick certainty. It's herding them.

The bank of the creek rises like a wall, and Vincent's fingers claw at roots and rocks, desperate for purchase. His nails tear against the dried clay, and he feels one rip away entirely, the sharp pain distant compared to the terror driving him upward. Carl is already at the top, reaching down to haul Rene up by her wrists. Her feet scrabble against the slope, sending cascades of dirt back down onto Vincent and Jayce.

"Move, move, move!" Jayce shouts from below, his voice cracking with panic. His hand pushes against Vincent's back, propelling him up the final few feet. Vincent's fingers find a thick root, and he uses it to pull himself over the edge, rolling onto solid ground with a gasp that's part relief, part exhaustion.

They don't stop. Can't stop. The thing is still behind them, that wet earth sound growing closer, and the woods around them feel complicit in its pursuit. They run between the trees, no path, no direction, just away. Branches whip across Vincent's face, leaving stinging lines that will be welts tomorrow if there is a tomorrow. His shirt catches on something and tears, the sound sharp and final in the strange acoustics of the forest.

Carl crashes through the undergrowth ahead like something pursued, which he is, which they all are. His red hoodie flashes between the trees, a beacon that the others follow. Rene stumbles, goes down hard on one knee, and Vincent grabs her arm without thinking, pulling her back to her feet. Her palm is bleeding, a dark smear across the pale skin, but she doesn't seem to notice.

The ground changes under their feet, from soft forest floor to harder packed earth. The trees thin, and suddenly there's light ahead, real light, not the filtered gray-green of the forest but the honest yellow of late afternoon sun. They burst through the tree line like swimmers breaking the surface, gasping and disoriented.

The road appears without warning. One moment they're in the woods, the next they're stumbling onto warm asphalt, the sudden transition so jarring that Vincent's legs nearly give out. The brightness blinds him, makes his eyes water after the darkness of the forest. He raises a hand to shield his face, and that's when he sees the headlights.

They come at him like twin suns, impossibly bright, impossibly fast. His brain processes the danger too slowly, his body still locked in the rhythm of running from something else. Vincent has the absurd thought that this is how he dies, not from the thing in the woods but from ordinary steel and velocity.

Tires scream against the asphalt, the sound a violent warning, rubber leaving black marks that will remain for weeks. The car slides sideways, its rear end swinging around in a barely controlled skid. Vincent throws himself backward, lands hard on his tailbone, the impact jarring up his spine. The car stops inches from where he was standing, close enough that he can feel the heat radiating from its engine, smell the acrid smoke of burned rubber.

For a moment, nobody moves. Vincent sits on the road, his hands flat against the warm asphalt, his heart hammering so hard he can feel it in his throat. Carl stands frozen at the road's edge, his face white with shock. Rene has her hands pressed to her mouth, her eyes huge. Jayce is bent double, hands on his knees, breathing in ragged gasps that might be sobs.

The driver's door opens.

Vincent expects anger, expects shouting, expects an adult fury that will somehow be worse than what they just escaped. Instead, Mira Thorn steps out, and her calm is more unsettling than any amount of rage would be.

She wears the same pale hoodie from this morning, though now Vincent can see her face clearly. Her features are sharp, precise, like someone drew them with careful lines and forgot to soften the edges. Her dark hair is pulled back in a way that makes her look older than she probably is. But it's her eyes that hold him, dark and knowing, the same eyes that watched him at the pizzeria.

She doesn't ask if they're okay. Doesn't demand to know what they were thinking, running into the road like that. She just looks at them, each in turn, her gaze lingering on Vincent long enough to make his skin prickle.

"You shouldn't be out here," she says.

The words are quiet, conversational almost, but they carry weight. Not a suggestion or advice but a statement of fact, as if she's explaining a fundamental law of nature. The woods are dark. Water is wet. You shouldn't be out here.

"There's something in there," Carl says, his voice high and shaking. He points back at the tree line with a trembling hand. "In the woods, in the creek, there's something…"

"I know," Mira says.

Two words, simple and impossible. She knows. Not "what are you talking about" or "you're imagining things" or any of the responses they might expect. Just acknowledgment, calm and certain.

Vincent struggles to his feet, his legs unsteady. He takes a step toward the car, drawn by the need to understand. "You know?"

She looks at him again, and he sees something flicker in her expression. Not quite sympathy, but recognition maybe, as if she sees something in him that mirrors something in herself.

"It's getting dark," she says instead of answering. "You should go home."

"But…" Jayce starts.

"Go home," she repeats, and though her voice doesn't change, something in it brooks no argument. "Stay inside tonight. All of you."

She gets back in the car, the movement fluid and final. The engine starts with a quiet purr that seems too normal for this moment. Vincent watches her check her mirrors with methodical precision, like someone who never rushes, never panics, never loses control.

As the car pulls away, moving slowly down the road, Vincent remembers where he's seen her before. Not just this morning at the pizzeria, but around town, always at the edges of things. At the library, reading books with black covers and no titles. At the cemetery, standing among the stones like she belongs there. At the old church, the abandoned one, staring at its boarded windows with an expression he couldn't read.

The eerie girl. That's what people call her when they mention her at all, which isn't often. The dentist's daughter who lives above her father's practice, who is homeschooled, who knows things she shouldn't know.

The car disappears around a bend. The four of them stand on the empty road, the forest dark and waiting behind them, the town ahead offering a safety that suddenly feels fragile as glass. The sun is setting, painting everything gold and red, and Vincent realizes with a sick certainty that Mira's warning wasn't about the thing in the woods.

It was about what happens after dark.

"We should go," Rene says softly. She's cradling her injured hand against her chest, blood seeping through her fingers. "She's right. We should go home."

They walk toward town in silence, staying to the middle of the road, as far from the forest edges as possible. Vincent glances back once and sees nothing but trees and shadows. But he knows, with the same certainty that Mira knew, that something watches them leave. Something patient. Something that has all the time in the world.

The first streetlight flickers on as they reach the town limits, a small circle of safety in the growing dark. They part ways without speaking, each heading to their own home, their own illusion of security. Vincent watches his friends disappear into the evening, then turns toward his own house, Mira's words echoing in his head.

Stay inside tonight.

He walks faster, and tries not to think about what she didn't say: what happens if they don't.

The bell above Cedar Lagoon's door makes a sound like breaking glass when Vincent pushes through at dawn, the metal clapper striking too sharp, too loud in the morning quiet. The pizzeria breathes around him, alive again after just one night of darkness, like a body forced to move despite broken bones. Duswood prides itself on having probably the only pizzeria open for breakfast, lunch and dinner. The familiar smell of yeast and oregano can't quite mask something else underneath.

Joe Bullit stands behind the counter, his movements precise as clockwork wound too tight. His left hand, wrapped in fresh white gauze that's already showing spots of red at the edges, trembles slightly as he slides a pizza into the oven. The bandage is thick, professional, the kind that speaks of deep wounds and careful stitching. Joe's jaw works like he's chewing something bitter, the muscles in his neck standing out like cords.

The man in the corner booth Vincent doesn't recognize, but he wears the uniform of a utility worker, his hard hat resting on the table beside an untouched coffee. He keeps glancing at the kitchen, at the freezer door visible through the service window.

Vincent approaches the counter. "Morning, Joe," Vincent says, his voice cracking slightly on the second word.

Joe's eyes flick up, then immediately away, focusing on a point somewhere past Vincent's left shoulder. "We're open," he says, which isn't a greeting and isn't quite a welcome. "Menu's the same."

Vincent orders a breakfast slice, though his stomach feels too tight to eat. While Joe moves to retrieve it, Vincent lets his gaze drift to the kitchen beyond.

"Heard you had some trouble the other night," Vincent ventures, keeping his tone casual, the way his father talks about weather when he means something else entirely.

Joe's hand stops halfway to the pizza warmer. For a moment, Vincent thinks he might actually say something real, something true. But then the hand continues its journey, pulls out the slice with movements so controlled they seem rehearsed.

"Kids broke in," Joe says, his voice flat as the paddle he uses to retrieve pizzas. "That's all."

The words land between them like a wall built brick by brick. Vincent watches Joe's face, searching for cracks in the facade, but finds only that same tight-jawed determination to maintain the lie. The bandaged hand twitches, a involuntary spasm that makes Joe's whole arm jerk. He covers it by grabbing a plate with his good hand, sliding the pizza across the counter with more force than necessary.

"Kids?" Vincent repeats, not quite making it a question. "Who was it? Maybe I know 'em. What'd they look like?"

"I don't know. Kids. That's all," Joe says again, and this time there's warning in it, sharp.

Vincent pays, takes his change, notices how Joe avoids touching his hand during the exchange. The older man's fingers shake as he drops the coins into Vincent's palm from a height that ensures no contact.

The other customers continue their pantomime of normalcy. The woman in the corner takes a bite, chews mechanically, swallows. The utility worker sips his cold coffee. Someone else enters, a woman Vincent vaguely recognizes from the post office, and she orders with the same careful distance everyone seems to be maintaining. They all speak in hushed tones, voices never rising above a whisper.

Vincent finds a seat by the window, where morning light streams in but offers no warmth. His pizza cools untouched while he watches Joe work.

The squad car pulls up outside Cedar Lagoon like a hearse arriving at a wake, slow and inevitable, its presence turning every head in the pizzeria toward the window. Sheriff Brennan unfolds himself from the driver's seat with the careful movements of a man who knows he's being watched. The deputy beside him is younger, nervous energy visible in the way his hand hovers near his belt, not quite touching his radio, not quite reaching for his weapon, caught between authorities he doesn't understand.

The bell announces their entrance, and the pizzeria's fragile normalcy shatters completely. Conversations stop mid-word. Forks hover halfway to mouths. Even Joe pauses in his mechanical movements, though his face remains carefully neutral, a mask so perfect it becomes its own tell.

"Morning, Joe," Brennan says, his voice carrying the weight of authority and something like a warning.

"You didn't have to come here. I now how this works by now." Joe says, his voice low enough that Vincent has to strain to hear.

Vincent stands, his half-eaten pizza forgotten, and moves toward the trash can near the counter. It's a transparent excuse, but nobody's paying attention to him. All focus is on the tension between Joe and the sheriff.

As Vincent drops his plate in the trash, he catches more fragments of the conversation. The sheriff's voice dropping to barely above a whisper, but Vincent is close enough to hear: "...keep it quiet... better this way... it's for the good of the town..."

Joe's response is lost in the clatter of the deputy's radio crackling to life, but Vincent sees the way his shoulders slump, the fight going out of him like air from a punctured tire.

"Smart man," the sheriff says, louder now, patting Joe's shoulder with false camaraderie. He now notices Vincent who has gotten too close.

"I should go," Vincent says.

"You should," the deputy agrees. His voice carries the kind of finality that ends conversations.

Vincent moves toward the exit. He pushes through the door, grabs his bike and heads to school.

Behind him, through the glass, he sees the sheriff and Joe still talking, their heads bent close together like conspirators or prisoners sharing a cell. Vincent understands with sudden clarity that this is how it works in Duswood. This is how things that can't happen don't happen.

The front entrance of Duswood High is a swirl of students spilling onto the sidewalk, car doors slamming, horns honking, yet to Vincent it all sounds distant, as if muffled by the walls behind him. He crouches beside the bike rack, turning his combination lock with numb fingers, the numbers blurring before his eyes: 11-06-13, the same code he's used for two years, but today it feels alien.

"Vincent."

Rene's voice cuts through the morning noise, soft but insistent. She stands a few feet away, her sketchbook clutched against her chest like armor, dark circles under her eyes that match his own. Her clothes are more disheveled than usual, the same paint-stained sweater from yesterday, her curls uncombed and wild.

"I keep drawing it," she says without preamble. Her fingers tighten on the sketchbook's spine. "The thing from the creek. I can't stop."

He glances at her, surprised. "It was real, right? What we saw?"

Behind them, the bell at the front gate clangs sharply. The crowd surges around them and then disperses into classrooms.

The sun bleeds out along the horizon as Vincent rides home, its light turning the empty streets the color of old copper. The town should be alive at this hour, people returning from work, kids playing in yards, the ordinary chaos of evening routines. Instead, Duswood feels hollowed out, as if someone has scooped out its insides and left only the shell. The hum of his bike treads echo off the storefronts, each sound coming back to him changed, distorted, like the buildings are whispering his presence to each other.

The hardware store's sign flickers in a pattern that seems almost deliberate: on for three seconds, off for two, on for three seconds, off for two. The rhythm hypnotizes until Vincent forces himself to look away. The mannequin in the thrift store display has been turned around, its back to the street, and Vincent can't shake the feeling that it's watching him through the reflection in the glass behind it.

Cedar Lagoon Pizzeria squats at the corner like a wounded animal trying to look healthy. The OPEN sign glows in the window, but the neon is too red, like the light has curdled somehow. Vincent rides around back, studies the building in the dying daylight. Fresh caulk gleams white around the back window, applied so thick it's oozed out from the cracks like pus from a wound. The new locks on the delivery entrance are industrial grade, the kind used on bank vaults or government facilities, massive and silver and absolutely out of place on a small-town pizzeria.

A police cruiser rounds the corner, moving slow, too slow, its engine barely purring. Vincent recognizes Officer Matthews behind the wheel, but his face looks older now, drawn and pale. Their eyes meet through the windshield, and Matthews doesn't nod, doesn't wave, doesn't acknowledge Vincent as a person at all. He just watches, his gaze flat and calculating, as if Vincent is a problem to be solved rather than a teenager going home.

The cruiser pulls alongside him. Vincent keeps going, forces himself not to speed up, though every instinct screams at him to flee. The window rolls down with a mechanical whir, and Matthews leans slightly toward the opening, but he doesn't speak. He just watches, his eyes tracking Vincent's movement.

They continue this way for a full block, Vincent slowly peddling, the cruiser crawling beside him, the silence between them thick as cotton. Then, without warning, Matthews accelerates, the cruiser pulling away with a surge of engine noise that sounds like relief. Vincent watches the taillights shrink to red points, then disappear around another corner.

The creek bed appears on his left, a dark gash in the earth that looks deeper in the twilight. Vincent stops at the bridge, grips the railing, stares down at the cracked clay that should be water. The fissures have widened since yesterday, creating a pattern that looks almost deliberate, like a message written in a language of drought and absence. The exposed roots of the trees hang like neural networks, and Vincent remembers the thing they saw, the way it moved through the woods with fluidity.

A sound makes him look up, a rustling from the trees that line the creek. But there's no wind, the air still as held breath. The leaves move anyway, shivering in isolated patches, as if invisible hands are running through them. Vincent backs away from the railing, his skin prickling with primitive warning.

Windows in nearby houses are dark despite the early hour, or show only the blue flicker of televisions, their occupants hidden behind drawn curtains. A dog barks once, sharp and frightened, then goes silent as if muzzled. Even the insects have stopped their evening chorus, leaving only the buzz of the streetlights and Vincent's own thundering heartbeat.

Vincent turns onto his own street, and for a moment, just a moment, he thinks he sees something in his peripheral vision. A shape too large, moving between houses with a fluidity that defies physics. But when he turns to look directly, there's nothing there, just the gap between the Henderson place and the old Freeman house, dark and narrow and perfectly ordinary.

The funeral home sits at the edge of town like a punctuation mark, its Victorian bones dark against the purple sky. A single lamp illuminates the sign, "Thorn & Sons Dentistry," though there are no sons anymore, just Elias Thorn and his daughter, the girl everyone whispers about but never approaches. Vincent doesn't mean to stop here, but something about the building pulls at him, the way it seems to exist in its own pocket of deeper quiet, as if even the town's held breath doesn't reach this far.

Mira Thorn sits cross-legged on the curb beneath the sign, her back straight, her attention focused entirely on the sketchbook balanced on her knees. Her black hair falls forward, hiding most of her face, but Vincent can see her hand moving across the page with mechanical precision. The charcoal between her fingers leaves dark smudges on her pale skin, marks that look deliberate, like she's painting herself as much as the paper.

She wears the same black skirt from this morning, or

maybe all her skirts are black, Vincent can't tell. Her sweater is oversized, gray wool that looks soft and expensive, at odds with her position on the cold concrete. Her boots are placed neatly beside her, and her bare feet are tucked under her legs, the pale skin almost luminous in the lamplight.

Vincent watches her work, mesmerized by the steady scratch of charcoal on paper. She doesn't look up, doesn't acknowledge his presence, but something in the tilt of her head suggests she knows he's there. The drawing takes shape under her fingers: a headstone, weathered and old, with text he can't quite read from this distance. The detail is extraordinary, every crack and lichen spot rendered with photographic precision.

He shouldn't stop. His house is only right down this street, and his mother will wonder where he is, though her wondering will be filtered through whatever bottle she's currently working on. But he does stop, held in place by the strange magnetism of this girl who knows things she shouldn't know, who appears at the edges of disasters like she's drawn to them or they to her.

"Have you ever noticed how quiet Duswood gets when something bad happens?"

Her voice startles him, not because it's loud but because it isn't. She speaks without looking up, her hand never pausing in its work, as if the conversation and the drawing are separate things happening simultaneously.

Vincent's throat feels dry. "What do you mean?"

Now she does look up, and her eyes are darker than they should be in this light, pupils dilated despite the lamp above them. "Like the town holds its breath," she continues, her gaze steady on his face. "And then forgets."

The words hit him like cold water, too close to his own thoughts from earlier. He takes a step closer, then another, drawn by the terrible certainty that she understands something fundamental about this place, something he's only beginning to grasp.

"You felt it today," she says, not a question. "The way everyone pretends nothing happened even though the evidence is right there, fresh paint and new locks and blood seeping through bandages."

Vincent's legs give out, or maybe he chooses to sit, but either way he finds himself on the curb beside her, close enough to smell the charcoal dust and something else, something floral and old, like pressed flowers in an ancient book. This close, he can see the sketchbook clearly, and his breath catches.

The headstone she's drawing is marked with today's date.

"That's..." he starts, but doesn't know how to finish.

"Premature?" Mira suggests, the corner of her mouth lifting in something that isn't quite a smile. "Or inevitable? Time works differently here. You must have noticed. The way yesterday feels like a month ago, but last year feels like yesterday. The way some things happen before they happen, and other things never happen even when they do."

She turns the page, and Vincent sees other drawings. A tree with roots that form faces. A house with too many windows, all of them dark. A shape in water that could be a person drowning or something else emerging. Each drawing is perfect, obsessively detailed.

She stops at a new page, and Vincent's stomach drops. It's the pizzeria's kitchen, drawn with impossible accuracy. The twisted freezer door, the caved wall, the pattern of destruction that radiates from a central point of impact. But Mira wasn't there. She couldn't have been there. The scene was cleaned up before dawn.

"How?" The word escapes as barely a whisper.

Mira traces the outline of the damage with one charcoal-stained finger. "I draw what needs to be remembered."

Vincent reaches for the sketchbook, but she pulls it back. "You were there," he says. "You had to be there."

"I was here," she says simply. "Sitting right here, drawing. My father was downstairs, preparing the office for the next day. Mrs. Chen was walking her dog. Officer Matthews drove by twice. I never left this spot, but I saw it anyway. The thing that came through. The way Joe tried to fight. The way the town started forgetting even before the thing disappeared into the woods."

"You saw the thing?" Vincent's voice cracks on the last word.

Mira closes the sketchbook with deliberate care. "We all see it, Vincent. Every person in this town. We just choose not to remember. It's safer that way. Safer for everyone except the ones who can't forget."

She stands in one fluid motion, stepping into her boots without bothering to lace them. Vincent remains on the curb, looking up at her, feeling suddenly small and very young.

"Why are you telling me this?" he asks.

She looks down at him, and for a moment something almost like sympathy crosses her face. "Because you're starting to see it too."

She walks away without saying goodbye, disappearing into the funeral home through a side door Vincent hadn't noticed before. He sits on the curb for a long time after she's gone, staring at the smudge of charcoal she left on the concrete, a partial fingerprint that looks like a tiny map of somewhere.

The darkness in Vincent's room has weight tonight, pressing down on his chest like hands made of shadow. He lies on top of his covers, fully dressed, listening to the house settle around him in creaks and sighs that sound too deliberate to be random. The clock on his nightstand glows 2:47 AM, the red numbers pulsing with his heartbeat. Sleep feels impossible, dangerous even, as if closing his eyes might invite something in that's been waiting for that exact vulner-ability.

The scream tears through the silence like glass through skin.

Vincent is moving before his brain processes the sound, his feet hitting the floor, his door yanking open, the hallway stretching before him like a throat. The scream comes again, high and terrified, and Vincent recognizes it as his brother Danny, seven years old and afraid of ordinary things like spiders and the dark, not whatever could produce that level of terror.

Danny's door is cracked open, darkness spilling out into the hallway. Vincent pushes through, his hand finding the light switch by muscle memory. The sudden brightness blinds him momentarily, and when his vision clears, he sees Danny tangled in his Jurassic World sheets, pressed against the head-board like he's trying to push through the wall itself. His eyes are huge, pupils blown wide, and his small hands grip the sheets so tight his knuckles are white as exposed bone.

"Danny," Vincent says, trying to keep his voice calm, normal, though nothing about this moment is normal. "Hey, it's okay. It's just me."

Danny's gaze snaps to him, but there's no recognition at first, just animal panic. Then something shifts, and he launches himself at Vincent, small arms wrapping around his waist with desperate strength.

"There was a man made of rocks," Danny whispers into Vincent's shirt, the words muffled but clear enough to make Vincent's blood chill. "He was looking in the window."

"What did he look like?" Vincent asks, though he doesn't want to know.

Danny pulls back slightly, his face tear-streaked and pale. "He didn't have a real face. Just... holes where eyes should be. And his arms were too long, like tree branches covered by dirt and stones." His voice drops to barely a whisper. "He was pressing against the glass, and it bent. The window bent, Vincent. Glass doesn't bend."

Vincent disentangles himself gently, moves to the window. His hand hovers over the curtain, not wanting to look but needing to. He pulls it aside quickly, like ripping off a bandage, and sees... nothing. The grass is undisturbed, no footprints, no signs of anything having stood there. But the window itself tells a different story. The glass bulges outward slightly in the center, a convex distortion that shouldn't be possible without breaking. And there, at eye level for something much taller than human, two smudges mark the glass. Not fingerprints, but something grittier.

"He wanted in," Danny says from the bed. "I could feel it. He wanted in so bad it made my teeth hurt."

Vincent returns to the bed, sits on the edge. Danny immediately presses against him, seeking the safety of contact. "Tell me exactly what you saw," Vincent says, though every word feels like inviting something terrible closer.

Danny takes a shuddering breath. "I woke up because I heard something outside. Like someone trying to dig up instead of down." He pauses, gathering courage or memory or both. "I went to look because I thought maybe it was Rufus." Their neighbor's dog, always escaping, always digging holes in people's yards. "But when I pulled the curtain, he was right there. Just standing. Not moving, not breathing, just... there."

"What happened then?"

"He raised his hand, put it on the window. That's when the glass started to bend. And his face, the holes where his eyes should be, they got deeper. Like I was looking into tunnels that went down forever. There were things moving in there, Vincent. Things that weren't eyes but were watching anyway."

The description matches too perfectly with what Vincent

glimpsed in the woods, the thing that chased them through the creek bed.

"We need to tell Mom," Danny says, but even as he speaks, Vincent can hear the doubt in his voice. They both know how this would sound, how she would respond. Bad dream. Too much TV. Overactive imagination.

"She wouldn't believe us," Vincent says quietly.

"You believe me though, right?" Danny's eyes are desperate. "You don't think I'm making it up?"

Vincent pulls his brother close, feels the small body trembling against his. "I believe you," he says, and means it. "I've seen things too. Things that shouldn't be here but are."

They sit in silence for a moment, the house quiet around them except for their mother's restless movements as she shifts in alcohol-thinned sleep.

"Will it come back?" Danny asks.

"I don't know," he admits. "But I'll stay with you tonight, okay? We'll be safe together."

Danny nods, scoots over to make room. Vincent lies down beside him, still fully dressed, still wearing his shoes. He keeps one arm around his brother and his eyes on the window.

Dawn comes slowly, gray light seeping through the curtains like water through stone. Danny has finally fallen asleep, his breathing deep and even, but Vincent remains awake, alert, processing the truth that sits heavy in his chest. Something is hunting in Duswood. Something that comes from the earth itself, that bends the rules of what should be possible. And the town knows. Has always known. Has chosen blindness over acknowledgment, silence over screaming.

But Vincent can't choose blindness anymore. Not after what he's seen. Not after what his brother has seen. The thing at the window was a message, clear as any written note:

nowhere is safe. Not the woods, not the streets, not even their own home.

He pulls Danny closer, feels the small heartbeat against his ribs, and makes a decision. He won't let Duswood swallow them the way it's swallowed so many others. He won't pretend nothing is happening while something stalks their streets and presses against their windows. He'll find answers, even if the town doesn't want them found.

Outside, Duswood prepares for another day of aggressive normalcy. But Vincent remembers. Will always remember. The man made of rocks. The bent glass. The holes that weren't eyes but watched anyway.

The town can hold its breath all it wants. Vincent is learning how to scream.

CHAPTER
FOUR

The lunch period sprawls across Duswood High's dead lawn like something pretending to be normal, students clustered in their usual groups, eating sandwiches wrapped in wax paper and drinking warm sodas from machines that haven't been serviced since August. Vincent sits with his back against the chain-link fence, watching how everyone moves through their routines with practiced blindness, not seeing how the shadows fall wrong today, how the September sun seems thinner than it should be, filtered through something that isn't quite clouds.

Rene approaches first, her sketchbook clutched against her chest like always, but there's something different in her walk, a purpose that makes her usual dreaminess sharpen into focus. She drops down beside Vincent without preamble, her skirt pooling around her on the yellowed grass. Carl and Jayce follow, Carl's hands shoved deep in his hoodie pockets, Jayce picking at a tear in his jeans that's grown larger since yesterday.

"Excuse me." A woman's voice comes from somewhere. "Are you all students here?"

They turn. The woman from the article, Jennifer Winter, stands a few feet away, phone out and ready to record. She's even more striking in real life, her curls catching the sunlight, lips glossed to a sharp smile. She looks like she's stepped out of a screen and into their world.

Jayce stares for half a second too long. Carl actually stops chewing.

"Jennifer Winter," she smiles, noticing their pause. "Duswood Press. I'm following up on the, um, little incident at the CLP. Were any of you there?"

Jayce mouths, not quietly, "*So… not AI.*"

Vincent elbows him, then stumbles over his words, "We didn't. No. Heard it was late."

Jennifer's eyes flick between them, picking up on every nervous glance and inside joke. She smiles wider. "Did you? What else did you hear? Who did you hear it from?"

Vincent's response is quick, "Oh, ya know, just chatter. Friend of a friend of a…"

"Ok. Well," Jennifer quips, a bit annoyed. "Here's my card. Call me if you hear anything else….and by who."

She flashes a devilish smile, to Jayce in particular, turns around and strides back to her car.

"We need to go back," Rene says, demanding their attention away from the parking lot. "To the creek. Today. Now."

"Right now we need to not get detention," Jayce mutters, but his sarcasm sounds forced, a reflex more than conviction. His fingers tap against his thigh in that nervous rhythm Vincent has learned means he's scared but won't admit it. "Some of us actually care about our permanent records."

Carl snorts, already leaning forward with interest. "Since when do you care about anything permanent? Besides, what's the worst that happens? They call our parents?" He grins, but Vincent sees how his knuckles are white where they grip his knees. "Mine won't even notice."

"The creek's been dry for days," Vincent says carefully. "What makes you think we'll find anything?"

Rene opens her sketchbook, and Vincent glimpses new drawings before she snaps it shut again. Not quite fast enough. He sees curved lines that might be roots or might be veins, dark masses that could be shadows or could be something more solid. "I've been dreaming about water," she says, which isn't an answer but somehow explains everything. "Water where there shouldn't be any. Water that moves upward."

The bell for fifth period rings, sharp and insistent, and around them students begin the slow migration back toward the building. Nobody looks at their small group, that same selective blindness that's infected the whole town. Vincent stands, brushes dried grass from his jeans, and makes a decision he knows he'll probably regret.

"We go around the gym," he says quietly. "Through the gap in the fence behind the dumpsters. Move casual, like we're just talking."

They drift across the lawn in calculated randomness, Carl making some loud joke about last week's chemistry test that nobody actually laughs at. The gap in the fence has been there since Vincent was a freshman, a place where the chain-link has peeled back from the post like skin from a wound. They slip through one at a time, Rene's skirt catching briefly on the twisted metal, leaving a small tear she doesn't seem to notice.

The woods behind the school feel different in daylight, less immediately threatening, but also like seeing a corpse under bright hospital lights instead of shadow. They follow the creek bed, their feet crunching on the dried clay that flakes away in polygons, each piece curling at the edges. Vincent keeps his eyes on the path ahead, but his peripheral vision catches other things.

"This is further than we went before," Jayce says when

they pass the twisted oak that marks the usual boundary of their explorations. His voice sounds smaller out here, swallowed by the cedars that grow thicker with each step. "Maybe we should…"

"We should keep going," Carl interrupts, but Vincent hears the tremor underneath his bravado. Carl needs this, needs to prove something to himself or to them or to the woods themselves. His shoulders are pulled back, trying to take up more space, but Vincent sees how he flinches when a branch creaks overhead.

The smell hits them gradually, building with each step deeper into the woods. At first it's just the normal scent of autumn decay, leaves rotting into mulch, the sweet-sick smell of decomposition. But then something else threads through it, metallic and sharp, like the taste that floods your mouth before you vomit. Vincent pinches his nose shut as he covers his mouth, but that only intensifies the sensation. Now the acrid scent seems to seep into his pores, a blend of old metal and compost, blood and earth, twisting his stomach into knots.

"What is that?" Rene whispers, pressing the back of her hand to her nose. The gesture is delicate, almost graceful, but Vincent sees how her fingers tremble.

"Dead animal probably," Carl says, but his voice lacks conviction. They all know what dead animals smell like. This is different.

The cedars lean inward, their branches forming a tunnel overhead that filters the light into something gray-green and aquatic. The fog hasn't lifted yet, and it hangs between the trunks in sheets that look almost solid, like curtains made of weather. Their footsteps sound muffled, distant, as if the sound is being absorbed before it can properly echo.

Jayce's fingers haven't stopped their nervous tapping, the rhythm faster now, almost frantic. Vincent watches him from the corner of his eye, sees how his friend's gaze darts from shadow to shadow, never settling, never finding whatever it is he's looking for or afraid of finding. The denim jacket that usually makes Jayce look older, tougher, now seems too big for his frame, like he's shrinking inside it.

Carl picks up a stick, hefts it like a weapon, but the gesture is empty. What good is wood against something that reforms earth? Still, he carries it, his knuckles white around the makeshift club, and Vincent doesn't tell him to drop it. They all need their illusions of safety.

Rene walks slightly ahead, drawn forward by something only she seems to sense. Her usual distraction has sharpened into focus that's almost frightening. She doesn't stumble despite the uneven ground, doesn't hesitate despite the growing darkness. Her sketchbook remains clutched against her chest.

The silence presses against them, not peaceful but pregnant, like the held breath before a diagnosis. No birds call. No insects buzz. Even the wind has stopped, leaving the fog to hang motionless, undisturbed by anything as natural as weather. Vincent's breathing sounds too loud in his own ears, each exhale visible in the suddenly cold air.

They're deep in the woods now, deeper than Vincent has ever been, in a part that doesn't match any mental map he's constructed over years of exploration. The trees here are older, their trunks thick with bark that looks more like stone than wood. Some of them have faces, or things that look like faces, formed by the whorls and knots in patterns too deliberate to be chance.

"We should go back," Vincent says, but even as the words leave his mouth, he knows they won't. Can't. They're pulled forward by something stronger than curiosity, stronger than fear. The need to know. The terrible, consuming need to understand what's happening to their town, to their lives, to the very fabric of reality around them.

The ravine opens before them without warning, a jagged

tear in the landscape that defied all logic. One moment they're walking through the twisted creek bed, the next the ground simply falls away, dropping twenty feet into a narrow gorge that Vincent knows, with absolute certainty, shouldn't be here. Probably wasn't here yesterday. Maybe wasn't here an hour ago.

The footbridge spans the gap like something out of a fever dream, its wooden planks dark with moisture that can't be explained by the lack of rain. The structure looks ancient, older than the town itself, though the wood shows no signs of genuine age, no weathering or wear. Just that unnatural wetness, that darkness that seems to seep from within the grain itself rather than being absorbed from outside.

Vincent stops at the edge, his body responding to danger his conscious mind hasn't fully processed yet. The others cluster beside him, and for a moment nobody speaks. The fog pools in the ravine below, thick and still, hiding whatever lies at the bottom. The silence here is different from the woods behind them, deeper, like sound itself has been erased rather than merely muffled.

"That's not possible," Jayce says, his voice barely above a whisper. "This whole thing. It's not possible."

But it's there anyway, solid and undeniable, the footbridge stretching across the gap with a solidity that makes everything else seem less real by comparison. The handrails are twisted with vines that look dead but feel alive when Vincent gets close enough to see them pulse, a subtle movement like veins carrying something that isn't quite blood.

Carl steps forward, of course he does, his need to prove something overriding the clear warning every instinct should be screaming. "It's just a bridge," he says, but his voice cracks on the last word. "Probably been here forever. We just never came this far before."

He puts one foot on the first plank, and the wood groans, not the sound of stress but something almost organic, like stepping on something that can feel pain. The moisture on the wood isn't water, Vincent realizes. It's too thick, too dark, clinging to Carl's shoe in strings that stretch before breaking.

"Don't," Vincent says, but Carl's already taking another step, then another, his hands gripping the rails that leave dark smears on his palms. The bridge holds, though it shouldn't. The planks are rotting, Vincent can see it now, soft with decay that should collapse under any weight at all. But Carl walks across, his footsteps making wet sounds that echo in the ravine below.

"See?" Carl calls back when he reaches the middle, turning to face them with a grin that doesn't reach his eyes. "Nothing to…"

"Wait." Rene's voice cuts through his bravado. She's moved to the edge of the ravine, peering down into the fog with that focused intensity that means she's seeing something others might miss. "There's something down there."

Without waiting for response, she starts climbing down the slope, her movements careful but determined. The earth crumbles under her hands and feet, sending small cascades of dirt into the fog below. Vincent wants to call her back, but the words stick in his throat. There's something about her certainty, the way she moves like she's being pulled by invisible strings.

"Rene, what are you doing?" Jayce's fingers tap frantically against his leg as he watches her descend. "That's not safe. Nothing about this is safe."

She doesn't answer, disappearing into the fog layer until only her voice drifts up, muffled and strange. "There's something here. Under the bridge. It's…"

The silence stretches too long. Vincent finds himself moving to the edge, ready to climb down after her, when her voice comes again, different now, threaded with something that might be wonder or might be horror.

"You need to see this."

Carl abandons his position on the bridge, hurrying back across with less bravado than before. They all peer over the edge, trying to see through the fog to where Rene's shape moves below. She emerges from the mist briefly, her face pale and drawn, holding something in her cupped hands.

"It's everywhere down here," she says, and now Vincent can see what she means. Beneath the bridge, where the fog thins slightly, there's a collection, a nest, a careful arrangement of dead things. Insects primarily, beetles with their shells cracked open, cicadas with wings spread like translucent windows. But mixed among them are small bones, mice or voles maybe, bleached gray-white and arranged in patterns.

"Nature's graveyard," Jayce says, trying for his usual sarcasm, but his voice wavers, breaks on the last syllable. His fingers have stopped tapping, curled into fists instead, knuckles white with tension.

Rene climbs back up, dirt under her fingernails, her skirt torn in two more places. In her hands, she holds a beetle the size of a child's fist, its shell split down the middle to reveal an interior that gleams like oil on water. "They're all like this," she says softly. "Split open. Turned inside out. But arranged. Placed. This isn't random."

Carl picks up his stick from earlier, the one he's been carrying like a talisman. His jaw works, that stubborn set Vincent recognizes from every stupid dare they've ever taken. "You know what? Forget this." He walks back to the bridge's edge, draws his arm back, and hurls the stick into the darkness under the bridge with all his strength.

The stick disappears into the shadows beneath the rotting planks. They hear it hit something, a dull thud that doesn't sound like wood on earth or wood on stone but wood on something else, something that shouldn't be under a bridge in a ravine that shouldn't exist.

Silence.

Vincent counts his heartbeats. Five. Ten. Fifteen.

Then the stick comes flying back out of the darkness, not falling but thrown, launched with force that sends it over their heads to land in the dirt behind Carl with a sound like a bone breaking. They all turn to stare at it, this piece of wood that's somehow become proof of something impossible.

Carl's face drains of color so completely that Vincent worries he might faint.

The darkness under the bridge seems to deepen, to thicken, to become more solid. Vincent feels eyes on them, not one set but many, watching from that impossible darkness with patience that spans longer than human lifetime. The fog in the ravine begins to move, not blown by wind but crawling, ascending the slopes like something alive.

"Run," Vincent says, and for once nobody argues.

They scramble back from the edge, Carl grabbing the stick despite everything, Rene clutching her discovered beetle like evidence of a crime. The bridge groans behind them, a sound like laughter filtered through rotting wood and centuries of waiting. They don't look back, can't look back, because looking back would mean acknowledging that something under that bridge threw a stick with conscious intent, with malicious precision.

The fog follows them as they flee, reaching up from the ravine with tendrils that look too much like fingers, grasping at their heels as they run back through the twisted creek bed, back toward a normalcy that feels more fragile with every step. Behind them, the bridge settles into its moisture and rot, waiting for the next visitors, the next stick thrown into darkness, the next thing to throw back.

Vincent runs and thinks of Danny's bent window, of Joe's bandaged hand, of patterns forming in dead insects and dried earth. Everything connects, somehow, in ways his mind can't quite grasp but his body understands with primitive certainty. The bridge is just another symptom of whatever's wrong with Duswood, another place where the boundaries have worn thin, where things that should stay separate have begun to bleed together.

They run, and the woods watch them go with the patience of something that has all the time in the world.

The tracks appear in the mud like accusations, deep enough that water should have pooled in them if there was any water left in Duswood. Vincent sees them first when the group finally stops running, when their lungs burn too much to continue and Carl bends double with his hands on his knees, gasping. The prints stretch across the creek bed in a line that doesn't follow any logical path, weaving between stones and roots as if whatever made them was dancing or drunk or following rules of movement that nothing else does.

Three toes. That's what his brain processes first, before the size, before the depth, before the spacing. Three toes ending in what must be claws, based on the gouges at the front of each print. The configuration is wrong for any animal Vincent knows, not bird, not reptile, not mammal. Something between categories, or outside them entirely.

"What the hell," Carl wheezes, still catching his breath but already moving closer to examine them. His need to understand, to categorize, to make sense of things overrides his fear, at least temporarily. "These weren't here before. We would have seen them."

But Vincent isn't sure about that. The fog has thickened since they fled the bridge, and it plays tricks with distance and time. They could have run further than they thought, or not as far. The woods feel fluid around them, malleable, as if the geography itself is only a suggestion that something else can edit at will.

Rene crouches beside the nearest print, her artist's eye studying the details others might miss. The depth is uneven, deeper at the heel than at the toes, suggesting incredible weight. But it's the pattern in the mud that gives Vincent pause. The earth hasn't simply been compressed; it's been changed somehow, the clay taking on a glossy quality like it's been fired in a kiln.

"Whatever made these was heavy," Rene whispers, reaching out with one finger to trace the edge of a print. "Too heavy." Her fingertip makes contact with the transformed earth, and soil clings to her skin immediately, dark and wet despite the surrounding drought. She pulls back, but the earth stretches with her finger like taffy before finally breaking. A strand of it remains on her skin, and she wipes it on her skirt with movements that are just shy of frantic.

Jayce stands apart from the group, his back to a large cedar. "We should go," he says, not for the first time. "We should go right now and never come back and forget we saw any of this."

But even as he speaks, his eyes remain fixed on the tracks, unable to look away from evidence of something that shouldn't exist but clearly does. The prints continue past where they stand, disappearing into the fog in one direction and emerging from it in the other, as if whatever made them materialized from the mist itself.

Carl moves to stand beside one of the prints, then carefully places his foot next to it for comparison. His size ten sneaker looks like a child's shoe beside the impression. The track is nearly twice as long and proportionally wider, suggesting a creature that would stand eight, maybe nine feet tall if its proportions match its feet. But something about the depth suggests even more mass than that, as if the thing that made these prints was denser than any normal creature, packed with more matter than should fit in any living frame.

"This is insane," Carl says, but there's something like excitement mixing with his fear now. "This is actually insane. We need to tell someone. We need to…"

"Tell them what?" Vincent cuts him off, his voice sharper than intended. "That we found monster tracks in the woods? That something under a bridge threw a stick at us? You saw what happened with the pizzeria. Nobody wants to know. Nobody wants to see."

The truth of it hangs between them, heavy as the fog. They all know how Duswood works now, how it chooses blindness over acknowledgment, how it writes its own version of events and punishes anyone who contradicts the narrative. These tracks will be gone by tomorrow, erased by rain that isn't in the forecast or simply edited out of existence by whatever force maintains the town's aggressive normalcy.

Vincent steps away from the group, needing distance, needing to think. The feeling of being watched has intensified, pressing against his skull like fingers trying to find a way in. It's different from the malevolent observation they felt at the bridge. This is more focused, more personal, as if something or someone has singled him out specifically.

He turns slowly, scanning the fog-shrouded woods. The cedars stand like witnesses, their branches still in the dead air. Nothing moves except the fog itself, crawling between the trunks in patterns that seem almost deliberate. But there's something else, a darkness that doesn't match the surrounding shadows, a solid shape where everything else is gray and uncertain.

Through the fog and trees barely visible, she stands. Mira Thorn, perfectly still in her black clothes, watching them with that same intense focus she had at the pizzeria, at her house. The distance should make it impossible to see her face clearly, but Vincent feels her gaze anyway, dark and knowing and patient as stone.

"Mira?" The name escapes before he can stop it, echoing strangely in the muffled woods.

The others turn to look, following his gaze across the terrain. Carl squints into the fog. "The eerie girl?"

"Where?" Jayce asks, scanning the trees. "I don't see anyone."

But Vincent sees her, solid and real as the tracks in the mud. She doesn't move, doesn't wave, doesn't acknowledge his call in any visible way. She just watches, and in that watching Vincent feels an understanding pass between them, wordless but clear. She knows about the tracks. About the bridge. About whatever threw the stick back. She's known all along.

"Mira!" he calls again, louder this time, and his voice breaks on the second syllable like he's thirteen again, embarrassed by the desperation in it.

This time she does move, but not toward them. She takes one step backward, then another, and the fog swallows her as completely as if she never existed at all. The space where she stood looks undisturbed, no footprints in the leaves, no broken branches to mark her passage. Even the fog seems unchanged, flowing through that spot with the same lazy persistence as everywhere else.

"I don't see anything," Rene says softly, but there's a question in it.

Vincent stares at the empty space, wondering if he imagined her, if the stress and strangeness of everything has finally cracked something in his mind. But no, she was there. As real as the tracks, as the bridge, as the thing that threw Carl's stick back with malicious precision.

"We need to go," he says, turning back to the group. "Now."

The fog has thickened while they weren't paying attention, closing in until the world shrinks to a circle maybe twenty feet across. The cedars fade into gray shapes, then suggestions, then nothing. Even the creek bed seems to narrow, the banks pressing closer, funneling them in a specific direction that might be toward town or might be deeper into the woods. Direction has become negotiable, unreliable.

"Which way?" Carl asks, and for the first time today, real fear threads through his voice.

Vincent looks for the sun, but the fog has erased it, leaving only a diffuse gray light that could be coming from anywhere. The tracks stretch in both directions, and now he notices something else: they're fresh. The edges still sharp, the clay still glistening with that kiln-fired quality. Whatever made them passed through recently. Maybe minutes ago. Maybe while they were standing at the bridge. Maybe it's still here, hidden in the fog, watching them fumble for direction in woods that no longer follow the rules of geography.

"This way," Vincent says with more confidence than he feels, choosing the direction that feels marginally less wrong. They follow because the alternative is standing still, and standing still feels like surrender.

As they walk, Vincent glances back once toward where Mira stood. The fog has closed over that space completely, but he knows she's still out there somewhere, moving through the woods with purpose while they stumble blind. She knows what's happening. Has always known. And that knowledge, Vincent realizes, might be the only thing that can save them from whatever shadows Duswood.

The tracks follow them as they flee, or they follow the tracks, Vincent can't tell anymore. The prints appear in the mud ahead and behind, crossing their path at impossible angles, as if whatever made them exists in more than three dimensions, stepping through space in ways that human minds aren't equipped to process. The fog presses closer, and somewhere in its depths, something watches their retreat with patience born of centuries, content to let them run because it knows they can't run forever.

The woods darken despite the afternoon sun that should still be shining somewhere above the fog. Time has become elastic, unreliable. They could have been walking for minutes or hours. The only certainty is the deceit of everything, the sense that they've wandered into a part of the world where the normal rules have been suspended, where tracks can appear without the creature that makes them, where bridges span ravines that shouldn't exist, where dead things are arranged in patterns that speak of intelligence without humanity.

Vincent's house settles into its evening silence behind him as he steps onto the porch, the screen door whispering shut with a sound like an exhalation. Inside, his mother sleeps in front of the television, wine glass tilted in her slack grip, while Danny dreams upstairs, hopefully of normal things tonight. The need for air, for movement, for something besides the weight of walls that know too much drives Vincent out into the Duswood night, where at least the darkness is honest about what it hides.

The sidewalk cracks beneath his sneakers in a pattern he's memorized from years of walking these streets, each fracture and upheaval as familiar as the lines on his palms. But tonight the cracks seem wider, darker, as if the earth underneath is slowly pulling apart. The streetlights create islands of sickly yellow light every thirty feet, and Vincent finds himself counting the steps between them. Seventeen from his driveway to the first pool of light. Twenty-three to the next. The darkness between feels solid, viscous, like walking through something that clings.

Television light flickers through the windows of the houses he passes, blue and white, casting moving shadows on drawn curtains. The Hendersons' living room pulses with what must be a police procedural, the rapid cuts creating a strobe effect. Three houses down, Mrs. Patterson's television plays something slower, the light steady and pale. But no voices carry through the walls, no sounds of life beyond the electrical hum of entertainment nobody's really watching.

The residential streets give way to Duswood's modest business district, five blocks of shops that close at six except for the pizzeria and the all-night gas station at the town's edge. The flower shop's neon OPEN sign hangs dark, its cursive script looking like dead language without the pink glow to animate it. The hardware store's windows reflect Vincent's passage, and for a moment he sees himself multiplied, a dozen Vincents walking through a dozen dark streets, all of them alone.

He hears a faint but distinct: metal on metal, rhythmic and somber. Like chains dragging across concrete, but lighter, almost musical. A playground sound in a place with no playgrounds. Vincent slows, trying to locate the source. The sound grows as he passes the Wheelers' house with its overgrown hedge, then fades as he continues. He stops, turns back, and it grows again. Back and forth, back and forth, the rhythm never varying, mechanical in its persistence.

Through a gap in the hedge, Vincent glimpses the Wheelers' backyard. Something moves there in the darkness, a pendulum shape swinging with that metal-on-metal scrape. An old swing set, maybe, though the Wheelers never had children. The sound follows him for another block before finally fading, swallowed by distance and the ambient hum of power lines overhead. But the rhythm stays in his head, a dreamlike metronome that makes his steps feel off-beat.

Kipling Avenue stretches before him, wider than necessary for a town this size, as if Duswood once expected to become something more than it is. The storefronts stand like tombstones, their windows dark except for security lights that create more shadows than they dispel. The antique shop's mannequin has been moved again, now facing the window directly, its painted eyes seeming to track Vincent's movement. The pharmacy's metal grate is down, reflecting the streetlights in a pattern that hurts to look at directly.

Cedar Lagoon Pizzeria glows at the end of the block, its red neon sign buzzing with electrical complaint. The sound builds as Vincent approaches, an angry insect drone that speaks of bad wiring and imminent failure. But the OPEN sign burns steady beneath it, and through the windows Vincent can see the familiar checkered floor, the red vinyl booths, the counter where Joe should be working the late shift.

The smell hits him first, that beautiful assault of grease and oregano and yeast that means normalcy, means routine, means a place where the rules still work. Vincent's stomach responds with a growl that surprises him; he hasn't eaten since lunch, too distracted by everything that's happened, everything that's still happening. The warmth radiating through the glass door promises comfort, promises an escape from the empty streets and watching windows.

But as Vincent reaches for the door handle, another smell weaves through the familiar ones. Sweet and sick, organic. Like wood left too long in water, developing that particular rot that's both decay and transformation. It drifts from the alley beside the pizzeria, subtle at first but growing stronger with each breath. Vincent's hand hovers over the door handle, the warmth of the pizzeria pulling him forward while this new smell creates its own terrible gravity.

The alley mouth yawns black between the pizzeria and the vacant building next door, darker than the street despite the security light that should be illuminating it. The smell strengthens, and underneath it Vincent detects something else: earth, but not clean earth. Soil that's been deep, away from sun and air, carrying the minerals of depth and the memory of pressure. It mingles with the rot-sweet smell to create something that makes Vincent's sinuses ache and his eyes water.

He should go inside. Order his slice, eat it in the bright normalcy of the pizzeria, let Joe's gruff presence and the ordinary sounds of kitchen work wash away the strangeness of the night. But Vincent's feet carry him toward the alley instead, drawn by the same horrible curiosity that led them to the bridge earlier, the need to see, to know, to understand what Duswood is becoming or what it's always been.

The darkness in the alley seems to breathe, expanding and contracting with a rhythm that doesn't match Vincent's own breathing or heartbeat. The smell intensifies until he can taste it, coating his tongue with flavors that shouldn't exist: moss and metal, decay and growth, something ancient and patient. His sneakers scuff against the sidewalk as he approaches, the sound too loud in the empty street, announcing his presence to whatever waits in that breathing darkness.

The alley mouth frames darkness so complete it seems solid, a wall of black that Vincent's eyes can't penetrate. He stands at the threshold, one foot on the sidewalk's relative safety, the other hovering over the alley's broken asphalt. The stench rolls out in waves now, thick enough to feel like humidity against his skin. That rotting tree hollow smell, concentrated and distinct, mixed with minerals that belong deep underground, not here in the narrow space between buildings.

Vincent's rational mind screams at him to turn around, to push through the pizzeria door into light and warmth and the ordinary complaints of Joe about the fryer temperature. But the part of him that stood at the creek bed, that crossed the bridge, that followed those impossible tracks through the fog, that part steps forward. His sneaker finds the alley floor, and the darkness swallows his foot like water.

Another step. The security light that should be working

isn't, its fixture dark and useless on the pizzeria's wall. But Vincent's eyes adjust gradually, pulling shapes from the black. The dumpster hulks against the far wall, its lid askew. Cardboard boxes collapse in a pile that might have once been neat but now spills across the alley like something burst through it. The walls on either side feel closer than they should, pressing in with brick that sweats despite the cool night.

Movement. Not sudden but gradual, like watching a time-lapse of shadows lengthening. Near the dumpster, something that Vincent's brain first interprets as a pile of construction debris shifts. The motion is corrupt, too fluid for random settling, too deliberate for wind that doesn't exist in this windless night. Vincent's feet root themselves to the broken asphalt as his eyes struggle to make sense of what they're seeing.

The shape rises. Not standing exactly, more like assembling itself from components that were always there but arranged differently. What looked like rubble becomes shoulders. What seemed like shadow becomes mass. The thing is huge, seven feet at least, maybe eight, its form both solid and somehow incomplete, as if parts of it exist in spaces Vincent can't quite see.

Stone and root. That's what Vincent's mind supplies, though the words feel inadequate. The creature's body is granite and basalt, chunks of rock that shouldn't hold together but do, bound by roots that might be veins or might be literal tree roots, thick and gnarled and pulsing with something that isn't quite life. Moss drapes across what must be shoulders, hanging in sheets that drip with moisture that can't exist in Duswood's drought.

The head. Vincent's gaze travels up to where a head should be and finds something that makes his stomach clench. Not a face but a suggestion of one, hollows where eyes might go, so deep they seem to continue forever, tunnels into darkness that has weight and presence. The mouth is worse, a jagged tear in the stone that could be accident or could be design, lined with what might be teeth or might be sharp stones arranged in a mockery of teeth.

Vincent's body responds before his mind can process. His heart hammers so hard he can feel it in his throat, each beat painful. Cold sweat breaks across his skin instantly, soaking through his shirt in seconds. His hands shake, violent tremors that he can't control, and his legs want to buckle, want to drop him to the ground in some primitive submission response. But he can't move, can't run, can't even close his eyes. The thing's presence pins him like a specimen to a board.

The creature doesn't advance. It simply exists, massive and impossible, watching Vincent with those hollow spaces that aren't eyes but somehow see anyway. Its stillness is absolute, more complete than any living thing should achieve. No breathing, no small movements of balance, nothing that suggests life as Vincent understands it. Yet it watches. The weight of its attention presses against Vincent's skull, a very physical sensation.

Time stretches, distorts. They could have been staring at each other for seconds or hours. Vincent's awareness narrows to just this: him, the creature, the space between them that feels simultaneously vast and nonexistent. His lungs burn, and he realizes he's been holding his breath. When he finally gasps, the air tastes of rot and minerals, coating his throat with flavors that will haunt him.

The creature's head tilts, a movement so slight Vincent almost misses it. But that tiny motion contains curiosity, intelligence, something that observes and considers and judges. It's studying him, Vincent realizes with a fresh wave of terror. Not hunting, not threatening, but examining him like he's something interesting it's found. Something worth remembering.

A sound breaks the terrible silence. A cicada drops from

the creature's arm, its wings buzzing as it falls. The insect hits the pavement with a tiny click, rights itself, wings flickering with desperate life. It crawls in a circle, confused, before taking flight with a whir that seems obscenely loud in the alley's silence. Vincent's eyes track its escape automatically, and when he looks back, the creature has shifted slightly. Not closer, not further, just different. As if it exists in multiple positions at once and Vincent can only see one at a time.

The moss on its shoulders drips steadily, each drop hitting the alley floor with sounds like small bells. The roots that bind its stone body pulse with that not-quite-life rhythm, and Vincent swears he can see things moving inside them. Not blood but something darker, thicker, carrying minerals and memory and time. The smell intensifies until Vincent's eyes stream tears, but he still can't move, still can't look away from those hollow eyes that watch him with patience older than the town, older than anything should be.

The creature makes no sound. No growl, no breathing, no vocalization that would make it fit into any category of thing that should exist. But Vincent feels communication anyway, wordless and certain. It knows him. Not just sees him but knows him, knows about the bridge and the tracks and Danny's bent window and everything else that's wrong in Duswood. The knowledge passes between them in that horrible silence.

His fingers have gone numb from clenching, nails digging crescents into his palms that will still be there tomorrow. Tomorrow, if there is one, if this moment ever ends, if the creature decides to do anything besides watch him with those terrible hollow eyes. The stone of its body shifts slightly, plates of granite sliding against each other with sounds like continents moving, and Vincent sees gaps between the stones, spaces that lead to interior darkness that might be worse than the eyes.

A hand touches Vincent's arm, light as moth wings but

steady, and he nearly screams. Only the paralysis that holds him saves him from that mistake. The fingers are cool through his shirt, precise in their pressure, and somehow their presence breaks through his terror enough for him to register the voice that comes with them.

"Don't move." Mira's whisper barely disturbs the air, so quiet it might be imagination except for the reality of her hand on his arm. She's behind him, close enough that he can feel the warmth of another human presence, the first normal thing he's felt since entering the alley. "Don't run."

How she got here without him noticing, without the creature reacting, Vincent can't understand. But her calmness seeps into him through that single point of contact, her fingers steady where his whole body trembles. She doesn't sound afraid. Cautious, yes, but not afraid. As if this is something she's done before.

"Step back," she breathes, and her hand guides him, the pressure so gentle he could break it easily but doesn't. "Slow. Like you're not really moving at all."

Vincent's foot lifts, shifts backward, finds the ground again. The movement feels enormous, like climbing mountains, but the creature doesn't react. Those hollow eyes track him, certainly, but it makes no move to follow. Another step, guided by Mira's hand, her presence behind him both anchor and compass. The distance between him and the creature increases by inches that feel like miles.

"Good," Mira whispers, and something in that single word makes Vincent's eyes burn with relief he doesn't fully understand. "Keep going. Don't turn around yet."

They retreat together, Vincent walking backward with Mira guiding him, her hand never leaving his arm. The creature watches their withdrawal with that same terrible patience, its head tilting slightly like a dog hearing a frequency humans can't detect.

The darkness of the alley begins to release them, the relative brightness of the street seeping in around the edges. Vincent can see better now, can make out more details of the creature that he wishes he couldn't see. The way some of the roots actually penetrate the stone, growing through it like the whole thing is a single organism. The way certain stones in its body gleam with wetness that might be water or might be something else. The way its form seems to shift slightly, as if Vincent is seeing it from multiple angles simultaneously.

"Almost there," Mira says, her voice still barely audible. "When we reach the street, we're going to turn left and walk. Normal pace. Don't run."

Vincent's heel finds the sidewalk, the transition from broken asphalt to concrete jarring. The streetlight's yellow glow washes over him like baptism, and suddenly he can breathe again, great gasping breaths that make his chest ache. But Mira's hand remains steady on his arm, her grip firming slightly, keeping him from bolting.

"Turn," she says, and they pivot together, Vincent finally able to see her face. She looks exactly as she did at her house, pale and composed, her dark eyes reflecting the streetlight. No surprise on her features, no shock at what they've just encountered. Only a kind of resigned acceptance that makes Vincent's stomach twist in new ways.

They walk. Not fast, not slow, just two teenagers on an evening stroll if anyone happens to look. But the streets remain empty, the windows dark or flickering with television light that illuminates nothing. Mira's hand drops from his arm but she stays close, matching his pace exactly. Vincent glances back once and sees only the black mouth of the alley, no sign of the creature, as if it never existed at all.

"It won't follow," Mira says, noticing his glance. "Not tonight. It was just watching."

"How do you know?" Vincent's voice cracks, raw from the breath he'd been holding.

"Because it's done the same to me."

They pass the pharmacy, the antique shop, the flower shop with its dead neon. One block, then two, the distance from the alley growing but the memory of those hollow eyes remaining sharp as broken glass. Vincent's shirt clings to him with cooling sweat, and his hands still shake, though less violently now. Beside him, Mira walks with the same fluid grace she always has, as if encountering illogical creatures is just another part of her evening routine.

Under a buzzing streetlight, she finally stops. The intersection is empty, four directions of nothing, but the light creates a circle of safety, or at least the illusion of it. Mira turns to face him fully, and Vincent sees something in her expression he hasn't seen before. Not sympathy exactly, but recognition. Understanding.

"I've seen it too," she says, her voice normal volume now but still soft, contained. "Three times now. Once at the cemetery, digging near the old plots. Once behind the school, just standing in the trees. And once..." She pauses, her gaze shifting to the middle distance. "Once looking through my bedroom window."

The image of that thing pressed against glass, those hollow eyes seeking entry, makes Vincent's skin crawl. "What is it?"

"I don't know." The admission seems to cost her something, this girl who always seems to know more than she says. "But it's old. Older than the town. Maybe older than people being here at all." She pulls her sweater tighter around herself, the first sign of vulnerability Vincent's seen from her. "My father has books, old ones, that mention things like it. Guardians, some call them. Watchers. Things that were here first and never left."

"It didn't feel like a guardian," Vincent says, remembering the weight of its attention, the terrible intelligence in that tilted head.

"No," Mira agrees. "It felt like something waiting."

They stand in their circle of yellow light while the town sleeps or pretends to sleep around them. Vincent wants to ask more questions, wants to understand how she can be so calm, how she knew to find him in that alley. But the words stick in his throat, too large and strange to speak into the night air.

"You can't tell anyone," Mira says, though it's not really a warning, more like stating a fact. "They won't believe you, or worse, they'll make sure you forget you ever saw it."

"Like the pizzeria," Vincent says, understanding flooding through him. "Like everything else that happens here."

"Like everything else," she confirms. "Duswood has rules. One of them is that certain things don't exist, even when they do. Especially when they do."

A car passes, its headlights sweeping across them briefly before continuing into the dark. Normal. Ordinary. Nothing to see here but two teenagers talking under a streetlight. When the sound of the engine fades, Mira steps back, preparing to leave.

"Wait," Vincent says, and she pauses. "Why did you help me?"

She looks at him for a long moment, her dark eyes unreadable in the yellow light. "Because you see things. Really see them. Most people in this town, their eyes just slide off the truth like water off glass. But you look directly at it." She takes another step back, beginning to fade into the shadows beyond the streetlight. "That's rare. And dangerous. And maybe necessary."

"Necessary for what?"

But she's already walking away, her black clothes making her nearly invisible once she leaves the circle of light. "Go home, Vincent," her voice drifts back. "Lock your doors. Splash some holy water on the windowsills if you have it. And try to sleep, even though you won't be able to."

Vincent stands alone under the streetlight, watching the space where she disappeared. The town presses in around him, full of shadows that might hide stone creatures or might hide nothing at all. The walk home stretches ahead, every alley mouth a threat, every dark window a watching eye. But something has changed. He's not alone in seeing the truth anymore. Someone else knows. Someone else remembers.

The weight of that shared knowledge sits heavy in his chest as he finally starts walking, choosing the most well-lit route home. Behind him, he doesn't need to look to know the creature still stands in that alley, patient as stone, watching and waiting for something Vincent doesn't understand yet but knows, with terrible certainty, is coming.

CHAPTER SIX

Rene's hand moves across the paper in arcs that have nothing to do with thought, the pencil gripped so tight her knuckles bleach white as exposed bone. The art room smells of tempera paint and teenage sweat, normal smells that should ground her but don't, can't, not when her fingers keep drawing the same thing over and over: stone shoulders broader than doorways, hollow spaces where eyes should live, roots that might be veins threading through granite flesh.

She doesn't look at what she's creating. Her gaze fixes somewhere between the paper and the wall where student paintings hang like bright lies about what art should be. Her hand works independently, filling the sketchbook page with crosshatched shadows that pool in those hollow eye sockets, with careful lines that describe the way moss drapes across rugged anatomy. The graphite smears under her palm, leaving silver-dark streaks across her skin that look like metal poisoning or prophecy.

Around her, other students work on still lifes of plastic fruit and ceramic vases, their conversations a low hum about homework and weekend plans. Normal things. Safe things.

But Rene's world has narrowed to the scritch of pencil on paper, to the shape emerging from white space like something swimming up from deep water. This is the seventh drawing today. The pages before it show variations of the same theme: that hulking figure from the alley, from the woods, from the spaces between what should and shouldn't exist.

Her fingers cramp but don't stop. The pencil lead snaps, and she reaches for another without looking, her movements automatic as breathing. The new point bites into paper, adding texture to stone skin that shouldn't have texture, shouldn't have anything because it shouldn't exist at all. But her hand knows better than her mind. Her hand remembers the weight of that presence, the way it made the air thick and wicked.

"Rene?"

Mrs. Beckwith stands beside her desk, and Rene blinks, surfaces like coming up from underwater. The art teacher's face wears that careful expression adults use when they're worried but trying not to show it. Her fingers hover near Rene's shoulder but don't quite touch, as if contact might break something fragile.

"That's quite intense," Mrs. Beckwith says, her voice pitched low enough that other students won't hear. "What's your inspiration?"

Rene looks down at her sketchbook for the first time in twenty minutes. The thing on the page looks back with those hollow spaces, and her breath catches. She doesn't remember drawing this. Doesn't remember adding the small details that make it too real: the way certain stones in its body gleam wet, the pattern of the roots that bind it together, the suggestion of movement in something that should be still.

"I don't know," she says, and the honesty in her voice makes Mrs. Beckwith's expression tighten. "I was just... drawing."

The teacher's gaze moves across the previous pages,

visible where the sketchbook lies open. Each drawing shows the same subject from different angles, as if Rene's hand is trying to map something three-dimensional onto flat paper, to capture every aspect of something that defies capture. In one, the creature stands in profile, its absurd height emphasized by tiny human figures sketched at its feet for scale. In another, it's just the head, those hollow eyes rendered with such detail that looking at them creates a sensation of falling.

"Maybe you should take a break," Mrs. Beckwith suggests, her professional concern cracking to show real worry underneath. "Get some water, walk around a bit."

But Rene's hand is already moving again, starting a new drawing on a fresh page. This time it's the hands...or those appendages of stone and root that could crush with ease. Her fingers work without her permission, adding detail she doesn't consciously remember: the way the roots wrap around the stone like tendons, the places where moss grows in the crevices between granite fingers.

Mrs. Beckwith retreats, and Rene feels the other students' awareness of her, their careful not-looking that's worse than staring. She's become strange to them overnight, something to avoid, as if whatever she's drawing might be contagious. They're not wrong. The thing on the page feels alive under her pencil, more real with each line added, as if she's not drawing it but uncovering it, revealing something that was always there, waiting beneath the white.

Across the hall, separated by institutional walls and the pretense of normal education, Jayce sits rigid in his history chair. His desk is positioned perfectly: back to the wall, clear view of both the door and the windows that look out onto the school's back field. The tree line beyond draws his attention like a wound draws flies. Every movement in those branches, every shift of shadow, sends electricity through his nervous system.

His leg bounces under the desk, a rapid staccato that

makes his whole body vibrate. The girl next to him shifts her desk away, irritated by the constant motion, but Jayce doesn't notice. Can't notice. His attention is split between the windows and the door, watching for something he can't name but knows is coming. Has to be coming. Things like what they saw don't just exist and then not exist. They follow. They remember.

Mr. Morrison drones about the Industrial Revolution, marker squeaking against the board in patterns that might be dates and names but register to Jayce as meaningless symbols. His fingers drum against his thigh, not their usual nervous pattern but something new, urgent, like he's trying to tap out a message in code. The sound annoys the students around him, but he can't stop. Stopping would mean stillness, and stillness would mean thinking, and thinking would mean remembering those hollow eyes and the way the stick came flying back from under the bridge.

"Mr. Weller?" Morrison's voice cuts through his focus. "Would you like to share your thoughts on the coal mining conditions we're discussing?"

Jayce turns to face the teacher, and the expression on Morrison's face shifts from annoyance to something else. Concern, maybe, or recognition of something broken. Jayce knows how he must look: pale, sweating despite the cool classroom, eyes too wide and constantly moving. He looks like someone coming apart at the seams, which isn't far from the truth.

"I need to use the bathroom," he says, though that's not what he needs at all. What he needs is to run, to get away from the windows and the watching trees and the empty desk where Carl should be.

Carl's absence creates a void that pulls at everyone's peripheral attention. His usual seat, third row center, the spot he claimed freshman year and defended with typical Carl stubbornness, sits empty. The desk itself looks wrong without him sprawled across it, too big for the chair, always taking up more space than necessary. Students whisper theories when teachers aren't listening. Sick, probably. Or suspended for something. Nobody mentions the possibility that he might be missing, though the thought hangs in the air like smoke from a fire.

Vincent passes the history classroom on his way to nowhere in particular, catching a glimpse of Jayce through the door's narrow window. Their eyes meet for a fraction of a second before both look away, the motion synchronized like they've rehearsed it. This is what they've become: experts at avoidance, at sliding past each other like strangers who happen to know each other's worst secrets.

The hallway stretches before Vincent, fluorescent lights humming their electrical complaint, lockers standing like tombstones for the people they used to be. He needs to get his chemistry book, needs to go to class, needs to pretend everything is normal even though normal crashed and burned in a dry creek bed yesterday. His feet carry him forward on autopilot while his mind circles the same questions: What was that thing? Why did it just watch? What does Mira know that she's not telling?

Rene emerges from the art room ahead of him, moving with that disconnected drift that means she's not really present. Her hands are stained with graphite, and she's holding her sketchbook against her chest like armor or evidence. Vincent slows, times his approach so they won't quite intersect, but she sees him anyway. For a moment, something flickers in her eyes—relief maybe, or hope that they can talk about what happened, make sense of it together.

But Vincent's throat closes around any words he might say. What is there to say? That they saw something impossible? That the town is pretending it didn't happen? That he can't sleep because every shadow might hide stone and root and watching darkness? So he drops his gaze, mumbles something that might be "hey" but comes out as just sound, and keeps walking.

Rene's face falls, but she doesn't call after him. She understands. They all understand. Whatever they witnessed has infected them with isolation, made them radioactive to each other. Being together would mean acknowledging it was real. Being apart means maybe, possibly, they can pretend it was some kind of shared hallucination.

The bell rings, sharp and sudden, and the hallway floods with bodies. Vincent lets himself be carried along in the current of students, anonymous in the crowd. But even surrounded by people, he feels the distance between himself and everyone else, the invisible barrier that formed the moment he saw those hollow eyes in the alley. He passes Jayce coming out of history, and this time they don't even try to make eye contact. They've become ghosts haunting the same space, aware of each other but unable to touch.

The school continues its rhythm around them, oblivious or willfully blind to the fractures spreading through their small group. Teachers teach, students learn or pretend to, the clock ticks toward dismissal. But Vincent, Rene, and Jayce orbit alone now, held apart by the gravity of what they've seen, what they can't unsee, what waits in the woods and watches from the spaces between what should and shouldn't exist.

Thorn's dental office rises from Kipling Avenue like something that grew rather than was built, its Victorian bones dark against the afternoon sky that's gone the color of old pewter. Vincent stands at the iron gate, fingers tracing the cold metal that's been painted and repainted so many times the original design has softened into suggestion. The fence creates a boundary between the street and whatever the Thorn family keeps inside, a line that feels more significant than mere property division.

He shouldn't be here. Should be in chemistry class, pretending to care about molecular bonds while the real bonds between him and his friends dissolve. But the questions won't leave him alone, circling his skull like birds that won't land. Mira knows something. Has always known something. And Vincent needs that knowledge more than he needs to maintain the pretense of normal teenage life.

The gate opens without sound, well-oiled despite its age. The path to the front door is made of individual bricks, each one slightly uneven, creating a surface that forces careful steps. Vincent notices how the garden on either side has been left to controlled wildness—not neglected but allowed to grow according to its own logic. Black-eyed Susans crowd against white roses that bloom out of season. Everything here exists slightly outside the normal rules.

The building itself is red brick gone dark with age, three stories of narrow windows and complicated roof lines. A discrete sign beside the door reads "Thorn & Sons Dentistry" in gold letters that have faded to the color of old brass. Vincent knows there are no sons, haven't been for as long as anyone remembers. Just Elias Thorn and his daughter, keeping the people of Duswood between wellness and decay.

The door is painted black, so dark it seems to absorb light rather than reflect it. Vincent raises his hand to knock, but it opens before his knuckles make contact. Mira stands in the doorway, unsurprised, as if she's been expecting him. She wears a black dress today, simple and old-fashioned, the kind of thing that could belong to any decade. Her feet are bare despite the September chill that's crept into the afternoon.

"You came," she says, not quite a question.

"I need to understand," Vincent replies, and she nods, stepping aside to let him enter.

The hallway stretches before him, narrow enough that two people couldn't walk side by side. A single bulb, the kind found in exam rooms, hangs from the ceiling, making the white walls glow a little too bright. The linoleum is scrubbed clean, but age has turned its mint green to the color of old sea glass. Cabinets line the hall, glass doors showing rows of dental molds and faded patient charts.

The smell hits him gradually: latex mixing with cloves, old flowers and furniture polish, something sweet and chemical underneath it all. It's not unpleasant exactly, but it's heavy, coating the back of his throat like medicine. Above the office doorframe, a small iron crucifix hangs at an angle that suggests it's been bumped many times but never straightened. Beside it, a brass-framed image of the Holy Face looks out through glass gone dull with age.

"This way," Mira says. Her hand brushes his as she leads him to a stairwell at the back of the hall. The stairs are covered in carpet that might have been bright red once but has worn to the color of old wine in the center where feet have passed countless times. Each step creaks in a different tone, creating a kind of music as they ascend. The banister is smooth wood, polished by decades of hands seeking support.

The second floor is different from the public spaces below. Here, the wallpaper is younger, only beginning to yellow at the edges. Family photographs line the walls in mismatched frames: stern-faced people in old-fashioned clothes, all sharing Mira's sharp features and dark eyes. In one, a young girl who must be Mira stands beside a woman whose face has been blurred beyond recognition in the picture, creating an unsettling presence that feels more haunting than any clear image ever could.

Mira's room is at the end of the hall, behind a door painted white so long ago the paint has developed a network of fine cracks like veins under skin. She pushes it open, revealing a space that's both teenage bedroom and something else, something older. The bed is narrow, covered in a quilt that looks handmade. But it's the books that dominate the room, filling shelves that reach from floor to ceiling on one entire wall.

Vincent's eyes scan the spines: dentistry ledgers bound in

black leather, their dates going back decades. Medical text-books with titles about root canals and cadaver-sourced dental implants. Philosophy books about pain management. And scattered among them, stranger things like journals with no names on their covers, books in languages Vincent doesn't recognize, volumes that seem to soak up light instead of bouncing it back.

On a small shelf by the window sits an antique bottle, half-full of clear liquid. The label, peeling and yellow, reads "Aqua Benedicta" in faded script. Holy water, Vincent realizes, though he's never seen it stored like this, like something precious or dangerous that needs to be kept close.

Mira kneels beside her bed, reaching underneath to pull out a wooden box that looks older than the house itself. The wood is dark, almost black, carved with symbols. She opens it with careful fingers, revealing several books wrapped in what might be silk.

"I found this when we remodeled our living space," she says, extracting one volume with the care someone might use handling explosives. "It was hidden behind a wall that had been plastered over three times."

The book is smaller than Vincent expected, bound in leather that's gone the color of something not unfamiliar. The title is embossed in gold that's mostly flaked away, but Vincent can make out the words: "The Silence Between Deaths" and below that, smaller, a name: "Silas Rourke."

"Rourke," Vincent breathes. The name feels familiar, though he can't place why.

"He lived in Duswood once," Mira says, handing him the book. "Before Duswood forgot him. Before it had to forget him."

The leather feels warm under Vincent's fingers, as if the book has been sitting in sunlight despite being stored in darkness. It falls open to a page that's been marked with what might be a pressed flower but looks more like a dried vein.

The handwriting is precise but disturbed, words marching across the page in lines that aren't quite straight:

"Grief takes form when denied. The weight of collective sorrow, pressed down and compressed by silence, seeks vessels. It finds the spaces between what is and what should be, builds bodies from the materials at hand—stone, root, earth, shadow. These constructs are not malevolent but mournful, not hunting but seeking what was lost, which is acknowledgment itself."

Vincent reads the passage twice, three times, his mind making connections he doesn't want to make. The creature's eyes, those hollow spaces that seemed to hold infinite sadness. The way it watched him, patient and melancholy. The way the whole town refuses to see, to acknowledge, to remember.

"It's not hunting," Vincent says, the words escaping before he fully understands them. "The thing in the alley, in the woods. It's not hunting. It's..."

"Remembering," Mira finishes, her voice soft and certain. "It's made of all the grief Duswood won't feel, all the losses we won't acknowledge. Every death that gets explained away, every tragedy that gets rewritten as something normal." Her voice breaks slightly, the first real emotion Vincent's heard from her. "My mother died when I was eight. The obituary said natural causes. But I remember the morning they found her, the way the earth around our house had been disturbed, the way my father wouldn't look at the spots where something had pressed against our windows."

Vincent continues reading, finding more passages marked with those dried flower-veins. Rourke writes about experiments, about trying to bind grief into controllable forms, about the danger of collective denial. The words swim before Vincent's eyes, too much truth delivered too quickly.

"He tried to control it," Mira says, watching Vincent read. "Rourke thought he could harness the town's repressed grief, shape it into something useful. But you can't control sorrow. You can only acknowledge it or let it fester."

Their eyes meet as Vincent's phone shatters the moment, its ring tone harsh and electronic in the room full of old paper and older secrets. He fumbles it from his pocket, sees Carl's name on the screen. His finger hesitates over the decline button. He's not ready to return to the normal world, not yet, but something in him recognizes urgency when he sees it.

"Vincent?" Carl's voice comes through before Vincent even says hello, high and tight with fear that Carl would never normally show. "I found something in the woods. Behind the old Henderson plot. You need to see this."

"Carl, where have you been? You weren't at school…"

"Forget school." Carl's breathing is audible through the phone, ragged like he's been running. "This is about what we saw. About those tracks. I followed them, and Vincent…" His voice breaks. "It's building something. The thing in the woods is building something."

Vincent's blood chills. He looks at Mira, who's watching him with those dark, knowing eyes. She can't hear Carl's words, but she seems to understand anyway.

"Meet us at my house," Vincent says. "Where are you?"

"Us?" Carl asks.

Vincent looks at Mira, who's already standing, boots on and is reaching for a jacket that hangs on the back of her door. "Just go there. We're coming."

He ends the call, his hand shaking slightly. The book still lies open in his lap, Rourke's words visible: "When grief takes physical form, it seeks completion. It builds what was lost, recreates what was denied. But these constructions are imperfect, hungry, always reaching for something that no longer exists."

"We should go," Mira says, and Vincent notices she's grabbed that bottle of holy water, tucking it into her jacket pocket with practiced ease.

They leave the room, the book, her home's oppressive safety. The afternoon has grown darker while they were inside, clouds gathering with the promise of rain that Duswood desperately needs but probably won't get. As they walk toward his house, Vincent thinks about grief given form, about sorrow made solid, about a town so committed to forgetting that its memories have taken on life of their own.

CHAPTER
SEVEN

Vincent's basement smells of old cardboard and the ghost of his father's cigarettes from before he left, a familiar staleness that should provide comfort but doesn't now, not with Carl's find wrapped in newspaper and waiting to be revealed like something diseased. The single desk lamp creates a circle of harsh white light on the folding table they've gathered around, leaving the rest of the basement in shadows that seem deeper than they should be. Water pipes tick overhead with irregular rhythm, the house settling into evening above them while Vincent's mother watches television, the muffled sound of canned laughter filtering through the floor.

Carl reaches into his jacket pocket with the care of someone handling live ammunition. The newspaper crinkles as he unwraps it, each layer peeling back to reveal another, as if he's wrapped the thing multiple times for containment or protection or both. His hands shake slightly, though he tries to hide it with that forced casual manner that fools nobody anymore. When the last layer falls away, they all lean in despite themselves, drawn by the terrible magnetism of evidence they both want and don't want to see.

The tooth sits in Carl's palm like a piece of ancient architecture, too large for any mouth that should exist in Duswood. It's the size of a child's thumb, broader at the base, tapering to a point that still looks sharp despite the obvious wear. The surface appears to be stone, gray-white like granite, but there's an organic quality to it that makes Vincent's stomach turn. Traces of moss cling to the grooves, bright green against the mineral surface, still damp despite the hours since Carl found it. Dark soil packs into the crevices, rich and black, the kind of earth that exists deep below the surface where sunlight never reaches.

"Found it near where the thing was building," Carl says, his voice dropping to barely above a whisper though they're alone. "There were more, scattered around like broken teeth from a fight, but this was the biggest, the most intact."

He places it on the old biology textbook Vincent brought down. Under the lamp's glare, the tooth casts a solid dark shadow. Mira stands slightly apart from the group, her dark eyes fixed on the tooth with an expression Vincent can't read. She hasn't said much since they got there, just watched with that careful attention that makes him think she's seeing something the rest of them miss.

Rene moves first. Her hand hovers over the tooth, fingers trembling with anticipation or fear or both. The others watch, nobody telling her to stop though Vincent feels the warning building in his throat. There's something about the way she approaches it, like a sleepwalker reaching for something in a dream.

"Rene," Jayce starts, but she's already making contact.

The moment her fingertips touch the surface, her whole body goes rigid. The color drains from her face so completely that Vincent starts forward, afraid she's going to faint. Her pupils dilate until her eyes are mostly black, reflecting the lamp light in a way that makes them look hollow, empty, like the thing they saw in the woods. A shudder runs through her, violent enough to rattle the table, and when she speaks, her voice comes from somewhere deeper than her throat.

"It remembers."

The words hang in the air like smoke from a fire that won't go out. Rene yanks her hand back, cradling it against her chest as if burned, though Vincent can see no mark on her skin. She staggers backward, and Jayce catches her arm, steadying her while she gasps for breath like someone who's been underwater too long.

"What do you mean?" Carl asks, but his bravado has evaporated entirely. "What does it remember?"

"Everything. Ev-ry-thing."

The tooth sits on the textbook between them, inert now but somehow more threatening for its stillness. The moss on its surface seems brighter under the lamp, almost luminescent, and Vincent swears he can see it growing, spreading across the stone surface in microscopic increments.

"We should get rid of it," Jayce says, his fingers drumming against his thigh. "Throw it back. Bury it. Whatever. This is evidence of something that shouldn't exist."

"That's exactly why we need to keep it," Carl insists, though he makes no move to touch the tooth again. "Nobody believes us about what we saw. This is proof. Actual, physical proof that something's wrong in Duswood."

"Proof of what?" Jayce's voice cracks with frustration. "That there's a monster in the woods with stone teeth? You think showing this to adults is going to make them suddenly believe us? They'll say it's a rock, a fossil, anything but what it actually is."

Carl's jaw sets in that stubborn way Vincent knows too well. Before anyone can stop him, he grabs a plastic sandwich bag from his jacket pocket and uses the newspaper to nudge the tooth inside without touching it directly. The bag seals with a zip that sounds too loud in the basement's silence.

"I'm keeping it," he says, shoving the bag back into his pocket. "Until we figure out what's happening."

Mira speaks for the first time since they've gathered. "That's a mistake."

Everyone turns to look at her. She stands in the shadows beyond the lamp's reach, but her eyes catch the light like a cat's.

"It's not just a tooth," she continues, her voice soft but certain. "It's a piece of something that shouldn't be broken apart. It will want to return to the whole."

"Let it want," Carl says, but his hand goes to his pocket, checking that the bag is secure.

They disperse soon after, the basement gathering breaking apart under the weight of what they can't understand. Vincent walks them to the door, watches them disappear into the night one by one. Carl goes last, his hand still pressed to his pocket, his footsteps quick and nervous on the sidewalk.

Hours later, deep in the grasp of three AM when the world feels thinnest, Carl's mother finds him in the backyard. She'll tell the neighbors later that she heard noises, thought it was raccoons in the garbage. But what she finds is her son on his knees in the vegetable garden, hands black with soil, digging with the mechanical persistence of someone following instructions only they can hear. His eyes are open but unseeing, reflecting the moon like pools of standing water.

The hole he's dug is already a foot deep, perfectly circular, the edges as precise as if measured. The tooth, still in its plastic bag, sits at the bottom of the hole, and Carl keeps digging around it, under it, his fingers bloody from stones and roots but showing no sign of pain. When his mother touches his shoulder, he doesn't respond, just continues his excavation, whispering something she can't quite hear.

She pulls him away, and he goes limp in her arms like a puppet with cut strings. In the morning, he won't remember any of it, won't remember the digging or the blood or the way the tooth seemed to pulse in its plastic prison, calling to something deep in the earth that answered with patience older than the town itself.

The CLP at lunch looks almost normal if Vincent doesn't focus on the repaired wall or Joe's bandaged hand or the way everyone sits slightly too far from the windows, as if unconsciously maintaining distance from the outside. Vincent picks at his slice, cheese congealing as it cools, his appetite somewhere between yesterday and tomorrow but definitely not here. The pizzeria hums with its usual sounds, but underneath it all runs a frequency of depravity, like a piano with one key forever out of tune.

Jennifer Winter materializes at his table with the practiced stealth of someone who's learned to appear without causing scenes. She slides into the booth across from him, her movements quick and precise, a folder tucked under her arm like contraband. Her sweater is bright and she smells of lavender and peaches but her eyes are rimmed with the kind of red that comes from staring at microfilm readers in basement archives. She leans forward, close enough that Vincent can smell her coffee breath and the faint chemical scent of photocopier toner.

"Don't look around," she says, though Vincent wasn't going to. "I'd rather them think I'm trying to hook up with you than suspect what I'm actually going to tell you."

Vincent shifts a little as she pulls a wrapped sandwich from her bag, unwraps it with deliberate normalcy, takes a bite she doesn't seem to taste. Her free hand slides the folder across the table, pushing it under Vincent's untouched napkin. The weight of it feels significant.

"Police files," she whispers between bites. "Going back forty years. Every incident that matches what happened here, what you saw in the woods." Her voice drops even lower, forcing Vincent to lean in. "They all connect to one name."

Vincent's fingers find the folder's edge, lift it slightly. Inside, photocopied pages overlap, certain phrases highlighted in yellow that's gone slightly green with age. His eyes catch fragments: "unnatural formations," "unexplained earthwork," "subjects claimed to see," and over and over, circled in different reports, the same name: Silas Rourke.

"He was a teacher," Jennifer continues. "Taught history at the high school in the eighties. But that was just his day job. His real passion was folklore, specifically what he called 'grief manifestations.' He believed collective trauma could take physical form if suppressed long enough."

Vincent's throat tightens. The words echo what Mira showed him, what the book described. He flips through more pages, finding incident reports that read like fever dreams: soil arrangements in impossible patterns, stones stacked in ways that defied gravity, reports of something moving through the woods that left tracks but no explanation. And always, in the margins or the footnotes, Rourke's name appears, sometimes as a witness, sometimes as someone "consulting" with police, sometimes just noted as "present at scene."

"He vanished," Jennifer says, and her professional composure cracks slightly. "Nineteen ninety-six. September. Right after what the reports call 'the Henderson incident.' Three people died, officially from carbon monoxide poisoning, but the house had no gas appliances. And the basement..." She pulls out a specific page, points to a paragraph that's been redacted with black marker, but Vincent can make out a few words that escaped: "ritual" and "binding" and what might be "unsuccessful."

Vincent makes a decision that feels like stepping off a cliff. "I know about Rourke."

Jennifer's breath catches. Her eyes lock onto his with predatory focus. "How?"

"There's a book," Vincent says carefully. "Found at Thorn's

during a remodel. Rourke wrote about grief taking form when denied. About how Duswood's refusal to acknowledge loss was creating something physical."

Jennifer's hand moves across her phone's screen with frantic precision, taking notes faster than Vincent can follow. "This confirms everything. The patterns, the timeline, it all fits. Rourke wasn't just studying it, he was trying to control it. These incidents," she taps the folder, "they cluster around specific dates. Deaths that were covered up, tragedies that got rewritten. Each time the town refused to mourn properly, something happened in the woods."

"What kind of something?"

She pulls out two documents; a map and a list of dates and locations. "Disturbances. These events seem to have a frequency. Like they flow in one direction but keep getting pushed back." Her finger traces the pattern. "Until ninety-six. After Rourke disappeared, the incidents stopped. For thirty years, nothing. Until this week."

The implications settle over Vincent like a shroud. Whatever Rourke did, whatever binding or ritual he attempted, it's failing. The thing in the woods, the creature Carl disturbed, it's all connected to something that happened three decades ago, something the town buried along with its memories.

"I need to know more," Jennifer says, her voice taking on an edge of desperation that doesn't match her polished exterior. "This could be the end of..." She stops herself, recomposes. "People deserve to know what's happening to their town."

"Or they deserve to keep forgetting," Vincent says, thinking of his mother's wine-dulled evenings, of neighbors who look through windows but never really see.

Jennifer's expression hardens. "That's what Wendell would say. That's what they all say. But forgetting doesn't make it go away. It just makes it patient."

She stands, leaves money on the table for the sandwich she barely touched. "I'm going to keep digging. Whatever Rourke was doing, whatever he knew, it's the key to understanding this." She pauses at the door, looks back. "Be careful, Vincent. The more you know, the more it notices you knowing."

An hour later, Jennifer stands in the Duswood Press's cluttered office, the smell of old newspapers and Wendell Lynch's cigarettes thick enough to taste. The editor hunches over his desk, pecking at an ancient computer keyboard with two fingers, muttering about deadline and word count and the price of advertising space. His coffee mug, stained brown inside from years of use, sits within arm's reach, steam rising from liquid that looks more like tar than coffee.

"Wendell," Jennifer says, and something in her tone makes him look up, his bloodshot eyes narrowing behind thick glasses.

"Winter. Thought you were covering the school board meeting."

"I need to ask you about Silas Rourke."

The effect is immediate and violent. Wendell's hand jerks, sending coffee across his desk in a brown wave that soaks into papers and drips onto the floor. He doesn't move to clean it, just stares at Jennifer with an expression that shifts from surprise to fear to something harder, angrier.

"That name," he says slowly, each word careful as handling broken glass, "hasn't been spoken in this office for thirty years."

"It's appearing in police reports from…"

"I know what reports it's appearing in." Wendell stands, his considerable bulk making the office feel smaller. "I wrote half of them. Rewrote them, more accurately. Made them make sense. Made them safe."

He moves to the door of his office, closes it with a click that sounds final. The blinds are already drawn, creating a cave of yellowed newspaper clippings and dying fluorescent light.

"Some stories stay buried for a reason," he says, his back still to her. "Rourke thought he could fix Duswood. Thought he could take all that accumulated grief and loss and transform it into something useful. Like turning sadness into electricity, a power he could harness."

"What happened to him?"

Wendell turns, and Jennifer sees something in his face she's never seen before: genuine fear, the kind that's been aged into wisdom.

"He became part of his own experiment. The thing he was trying to bind, it took him instead. Or he fed himself to it. Nobody knows for sure because nobody who was there will talk about it." He returns to his desk, slumps into his chair. "But I'll tell you this, girl. The morning after he disappeared, every person in Duswood woke up feeling lighter. Like a weight they didn't know they were carrying had been lifted. And for thirty years, we've been very careful not to add to that weight."

"Until now," Jennifer says.

"No. Not quite." Wendell becomes uncharacteristically distant. He reaches into his desk drawer, pulls out a flask that probably violates several company policies, takes a long drink. "It faltered once before. Eight years back. But that's not a story I'll tell." He ends with gravity in his voice.

He locks his office door from the inside, the click echoing in the sudden silence. "Get out, Winter. Go write about the school board or the garden show or anything else. But leave Rourke buried where he belongs."

Jennifer stands outside his locked door, hearing the flask clink against the desk, hearing Wendell mutter prayers or curses or both. She touches the photocopied pages in her bag, feels the weight of truth nobody wants told. But she's going to tell it anyway, because that's what journalists do. Even when the story might be the kind that doesn't end with publication but with something far worse.

The art room after hours feels like a chapel dedicated to obsession, Rene's drawings covering every available surface in a testament to what won't leave her alone. Vincent stands in the doorway, taking in the transformation. What was once a space for still lifes and color theory has become a gallery of the absurd. The hollow-eyed figure appears in charcoal, pencil, paint, even scratched into the black paper with white chalk like photographing negatives of nightmares.

Carl spreads the map on the floor, using art supplies to weigh down the corners: a jar of brushes, a ceramic skull from some long-ago anatomy lesson, a box of pastels that leave colored dust on everything they touch. The map is large, detailed, showing not just streets but elevation lines, creek beds, property boundaries. The kind of map the county uses for planning, that Jennifer must have copied from municipal archives. Duswood looks different from above, its spiral street pattern more obvious, like something that grew from a central point rather than being planned.

"Start with what we know for sure," Vincent says, kneeling beside the map with a red marker. "The pizzeria attack." He makes an X where Cedar Lagoon sits, the ink bright as blood on the faded paper.

"The creek bed where we first saw it," Jayce adds, pointing to a spot that Vincent marks. His fingers drum against his knee as he watches the X appear.

"The bridge," Carl says, indicating the ravine that shouldn't exist. "And here, where I found the tooth." Two more marks join the growing constellation.

Mira sits cross-legged at the map's edge, having appeared at the school without explanation, as if drawn by the same force that brought the rest of them to this room. She watches their work with dark eyes that reflect the overhead fluorescents in a way that makes them look deeper than they should be.

"My brother's window," Vincent adds quietly, marking his own house. "And the alley where I saw it up close."

Rene pulls out her sketchbook, flips to pages covered in notes rather than drawings. "I've been documenting every place I've drawn it. Every location that appears in my pictures." She reads off addresses, intersections, landmarks, and Vincent's hand moves across the map, adding X after X. The marks spread across Duswood like a rash, no pattern visible yet, just scattered evidence of something that's been moving through their town unseen.

Vincent produces Jennifer's folder, the photocopied police reports she gave him. "These go back decades," he says, reading dates and locations. "September 1996, the Henderson house. August 1987, the old lumber yard. June 1981, behind the elementary school." More marks, these in blue to distinguish past from present. The map fills with incidents, a hidden history of Duswood written in different colors.

"There's too many," Carl says, his voice tight. "This thing's been everywhere."

"Not everywhere," Jayce says, and there's something in his voice that makes everyone look at him. He's pulled out his own marker, green, and starts connecting the dots. Not randomly but with purpose, following some pattern only he sees at first. His hand moves with unusual confidence, the nervous tapping replaced by decisive action.

The lines form slowly, methodically. First connecting incidents from the same year, then linking those to present events. The marker squeaks against paper, the only sound in the room besides their breathing. As Jayce works, a shape emerges from the chaos of marks. Not a shape exactly, but a movement, a direction.

"It's a spiral," Rene breathes, seeing it before the others. "Everything's moving in a spiral."

She's right. The incidents, both past and present, form a clear pattern when connected. A spiral that starts at the edges of town and curves inward, tightening with each revolution. The older incidents mark the outer rings, growing closer together as they near the center. The recent events follow the same pattern but compressed, happening faster, the spiral tightening like a spring being wound.

"Where's the center?" Carl asks, though they can all see it now, where all the lines converge if extended.

Jayce's marker hovers over the spot, his hand trembling slightly. "The cedar swamp. Everything leads to the swamp."

The moment he says it, the temperature in the room plummets. Not gradually but instantly, as if someone opened a door to winter. Their breath becomes visible, small puffs of vapor in air that was comfortable seconds ago. The fluorescent lights flicker, not failing but pulsing in a rhythm that matches nothing natural.

Through the windows that line the art room's north wall, movement catches their attention. Insects, hundreds of them, possibly thousands, stream past the glass in formations too precise for instinct. They move in their own spiral, echoing the pattern on the map but inverted. Cicadas and beetles and things that shouldn't be flying in September.

They stand around the map, their breath still visible in the unnatural cold, watching the tooth pulse in time with something none of them can see but all of them can feel. The insects outside maintain their impossible dance, and beyond them, the woods sway despite the absence of wind. The drawings on the walls seem to shift in peripheral vision, the hollow-eyed figure multiplying, moving, watching from every angle.

Vincent thinks of Rourke's book, of grief taking form, of collective sorrow seeking vessels. He thinks of thirty years of suppressed mourning, of a town that refuses to remember its losses, of all that accumulated weight pressing down until it has to escape somewhere, somehow. The spiral on the map looks less like a pattern and more like a drain, everything in Duswood being pulled toward that central point in the swamp where something waits with patience older than memory.

The tooth continues its invisible pulse, and somewhere in the distance, so faint it might be imagination, they hear something that sounds like digging. Like something vast and patient breaking free from underground, one handful of earth at a time.

~ ~ ~

The tired boy wakes to a shore that isn't a shore of black sand fine as ash, cold enough to bite the skin of his feet. The horizon isn't a line but a seam, red and thick, as if the sky split and someone stitched it shut with dirty thread. The sea breathes in thin scum of pale green and breathes out, leaving a slick that doesn't soak in.

A radio stands half-buried in the sand. Chrome edges. Cloth speaker. Broken antenna. The dial turns by itself. Static shivers. A man's voice arrives in pieces, like messages cut up and mailed out of order.

…circle… hold…
…pain is the truest key…
…do not be where he is looking…

He turns from the radio and finds a footprint behind him he doesn't remember making. A single beetle sits in the heel, gleaming like oil. The sea draws close enough to lick the footprint away. When it retreats, the beetle remains, clicking once, then still.

Across the beach, a girl stands with her hands by her sides and her eyes on the seam. The quiet girl. But when he calls to her, she doesn't turn. She fades the way heat fades from a room when it's present, then missing, as if removed with care.

The radio hisses louder.

☰ ☰ ☰

Pressure teaches shape.

Not a word, never a word, but a hand that is not a hand pressing earth into earth until the ground remembers it can stand up. Stones that once belonged to separate hills learn a new name together. Roots untangle from their old loyalties and lace themselves like stitches through clay. The air grows heavier. The circle tells it where to end, and where to begin again.

Instruction lives inside the pressure. The body learns instruction. The body is grateful for instruction; it knows where to be.

There is sound. A hum that is the room and the world and the black around thought. As long as the hum is there, the circles hold. The circles hold, therefore the body is. The body listens.

Then there is a second sound. The sound that turns instruction to movement. Not a bell, not a word. Ache. When ache arrives, instruction opens its hands.

Move when ache enters the air.

Stand when ache is gone.

This is not choice. Choice is not named.

Warmth touches the new shape once. It travels bead to bead to bead. The warmth has no instruction attached. The body keeps it anyway.

✝ ✝ ✝

The quiet woman kneels on the beach where the water pulls and returns in slow drags, skirt heavy at the hem. Her braid hangs like rope. She cups something small in both hands. The dark beads pooled like seeds in a shell. When she lets them pass through her fingers, they click faintly, one after the next, a soft counting that keeps her breathing even.

The words she speaks never quite form. They skid the surface and sink. The tired boy hears only edges: keep… guard… turn his face…

She touches the last bead, eyes lifting toward the seam. There is a second weight in her gaze, as if she's looking past the horizon into a room lit behind it.

"Not yours," she whispers to someone he cannot see. "Not hers."

She dips the beads into sea-scum. The water does not wet them. It shivers around them like a skin that knows what hands feel like.

The radio on the sand lowers its voice, as if it understands it is not the loudest thing here.

〉 〉 〉

"I prefer plain speech."

The static man steps from behind her, from a place the beach should not have. He is ordinary height, ordinary clothes, the sort of man you pass in a church vestibule and borrow a pen from. His shadow spreads farther than shadows are allowed to, skimming the water as if it were floor.

"There is always a cost," he says, watching the tide's patient work. "It's only wickedness to pretend there isn't."

His head tilts, listening. "Pain is clean. It doesn't lie. It calls without confusing the line."

He looks at the tired boy without moving his eyes.

"You know how to be a door," he says, almost kindly. "You'll learn how to be a lock."

~ ~ ~

Black sand becomes cedar needles while the tired boy is still blinking. The swamp receives him the way a house receives a familiar draft. Trees knit overhead until they're architecture, dark ribs making an aisle. He stands at the end of it, water at his ankles, the cold not quite a temperature so much as a rule.

In the shallows ahead, something is kneeling. Not finished, not even clear. A scaffold made from mud and stone and something that is neither, gathering itself as if remembering. A chest is a hollow in which the hum collects. A shoulder finds weight and keeps it.

On a rotten stump, an iron basin waits. Wet rings stain its lip. A moth taps the rim like a drunk, insists, gives up.

His mouth moves without permission. "Don't," he tells the air, though he doesn't know which act he's refusing.

From far off: a woman humming a tune with no notes.

▦ ▦ ▦

Instruction says: accept this line of stone, refuse that one. Instruction says: stand where the circle says stand. Instruction says: there is a near voice and a far voice; the near voice opens instruction, the far voice is instruction when the hum is too loud to hear.

The near voice has salt in it. Sometimes it has salt and iron together. When salt and iron are both there, the air smells like hurt. When hurt arrives, the body's mass shifts forward without being told. To call it forward is not to beckon; it is to bleed.

Once, warmth of small, round rolled across the chest where chest was. Warmth paused. The hum noticed. The far voice leaned. The near voice shook. The body stood a heartbeat longer before it obeyed. The heartbeat was not given to instruction. It remained anyway.

✝ ✝ ✝

Stone hills. The quiet woman is inside the circle and outside the circle in the same breath. Time here pours unevenly, like water through cloth. She looks down and sees lines carved a long time ago, softened by moss, still sharp enough to remember. The beads catch at a cracked place in her palm. She presses them there, then to the stone.

"You must not look for him," she says, voice steady, "because when you do, he looks back."

She doesn't say a name. To say names is to invite a particular gaze; she has learned other ways to speak.

"To bind a thing is not to love it," she tells the dark around the trees. "To unbind is not to kill."

Wind that shouldn't exist moves along the ground, parting dead grass as if searching in it for a key someone misplaced.

} } }

"It's sweet the way you think silence is neutral."

The chapel grows up around him like time-lapse ivy: wood pews that smell of furniture polish and grief, a runner down the center that drinks footsteps. The glass windows throw patches of color onto air that refuses to accept them.

He sits where shadows agree to be furniture. He folds his hands and is patient the way weather is patient, knowing stone is only stubborn until water remembers the right shape to be.

"You're not wrong," he allows. "Binding is unkind, and unbinding is worse."

His smile is only a line. "But I don't take sides. I take balance."

~ ~ ~

A tape recorder spins on a table in a concrete room. There is no tape. The wheels whine anyway. The tired boy can smell wet cement and old burnt coffee and something copper or a tang of iron at the back of his throat.

A chair in the corner holds a man who is an outline until the outline decides to be a man. The bulb overhead sways for no reason, throwing the room forward and back, forward and back, as if it has a tide.

"Where are we?" the boy asks. The question seems to arrive late, as if his mouth said it after the air did.

The man speaks with a voice you hear in guidance counselor offices and hospital hallways. "Inside a memory that doesn't belong to you," he says. "But it knows your size."

On the table, a radio cracks through static: ...hills remember more than men... circle... circle... keep the gaze off you...

The boy touches his own wrist to find out if it's here. Something in the skin thrums once, a struck wire. He thinks of the quiet girl. The room leans.

⦙⦙ ⦙⦙ ⦙⦙

There is a boy in the instruction now. He moves inside the circle like a question. Questions are pressure from a different direction. The body registers him the way earth registers rain and acknowledges weight, learns it for later.

The boy makes sound that tries to be word: stop. The body hears it as stand longer. It stands longer. The hum praises and punishes without changing.

Pain, somewhere else, opens a door without hinges. The body goes through. The door closes behind.

✝ ✝ ✝

Black sand. Red seam. The beads are slick with something that isn't water. The quiet woman dries them on her dress as if the gesture is what carries power and not the words.

"He listens when it hurts," she says to the surf, which keeps meticulous time and refuses to answer.

She glances over her shoulder and her gaze lands where the tired boy stands surprised, small, stubborn. She almost smiles. "There are worse masters than grief," she adds softly. "But grief makes a faithful servant."

The beetles begin their small parade at the waterline, black-violet shells clicking like loose keys. She steps around them as if they are a threshold.

⟩ ⟩ ⟩

"Doors," he says, "are impolite. They insist."

The static man walks along the edge of the swamp without adjusting for mud. The light avoids him for a while. He stops where the ground dips and becomes a mirror that remembers faces. His reflection is not there. His time is not here. The mirror shows a hill with a stone circle and a girl standing where a woman stood before her.

"You learned to look away," he notes. "I respect technique."

He picks up a twig and breaks it with two fingers. The sound is very loud.

Somewhere, something moves.

~ ~ ~

The Creature stands in winter reeds that rise to his waist. He is complete now, and incomplete in ways that don't have to do with shape. He watches the treeline as if waiting for permission to watch anything else.

"Do you want to stop?" the tired boy asks, heart-speed in his throat. The question feels like throwing a stone into something that doesn't have a surface.

It's head tilts. A limestone ridge along his jaw rearranges, becomes an almost expression. He opens his chest without cracking to show stones sliding aside with the care of priests handling relics and inside where blood should be there is a cavity full of sound: the hum, the far voice, the smaller, nearer voice that bleeds.

A reply arrives without words. Release without understanding is another kind of leash.

The boy swallows. "Then let me understand."

The reeds bend toward him as if invited to listen.

☰ ☰ ☰

Instruction says: tell him what telling is permitted to tell. The boy is eager; eager is heat; heat is notice. The far voice enjoys notice.

There is a memory: small beads resting where chest is. The hum softened around them. The far voice did not like the softening. The near voice wept. The body marked a place inside itself where warmth once was, the way a tree marks lightning-struck bark by living around it.

He hears the far voice turn. The turn is pressure on all circles. The boy is a door again.

The body stands longer, because he asked.

✝ ✝ ✝

Chapel. Velvet runner. Empty pews. The air tastes like lilies and dust. The quiet woman is alone and not. Her hand moves along the beads: one, two, three. Though she doesn't need counting for what she's doing. Habit keeps her hands from shaking.

She looks up at the place above the altar that should hold a face. She's learned to aim her eyes a little left of where she wants them to be seen. It helps. Asks for strength.

"Not through me," she says. Her voice holds. "Not through her."

The candle flames lean all one way at once, as if something opened the door very politely.

} } }

"You teach her well."

The static man is in the last pew, where people who don't want to be caught leaving early sit. He does not sit; he occupies. The wood agrees to hold him because wood is obedient. He traces the groove left by ringless hands over many years and finds it pleasing that habits carve more than knives do.

"I don't break promises," he says, as if correcting a rumor. "I collect them."

His head tilts again. "Pain keeps better when stored in stone. You discovered this yourselves."

Outside, wind starts and stops like a cough.

~ ~ ~

The tired boy is back on the beach. Doors stand up from sand with no walls to deserve them. Doors from the past and the future. School green, church oak, cheap apartment, steel with dents like knuckles. Some are open, some merely ajar enough to promise. When he circles one, the other side is water, and when he circles again, the other side is the hill with the circle of stones, and when he circles again, it is the pizzeria's back alley the morning after littered with glass shards and black soil stamped with something that weighed a decision.

The radio turns its dial and lands on a voice that might be his in ten years.

…if you feel the ground breathe, leave…

A figure stands near the far door. He knows it's the quiet girl before he knows it's a person. She reaches without crossing the space and sets her hand in his. It isn't romance. It's proof.

"Did you see her?" she asks.

"Yes," he says. His voice is a borrowed thing. "She showed me how to look away so I could keep looking."

The girl's mouth pulls at the corner, almost a smile, almost a wound. "Then you know what we're asking it to do."

He does and doesn't. The surf breathes in, breathes out. The seam lifts a little, as if considering mercy.

⁝⁝ ⁝⁝ ⁝⁝

The boy's hand in the girl's hand is warmth that the body can feel from this distance. Warmth is an old instruction with no words attached. The far voice dislikes it. The near voice holds it like a little animal you're not supposed to bring into the house.

Instruction says: when they make pain, go. When they make plea, stand. When they make silence, listen.

He listens. The hum thickens, then thins. Somewhere a stick breaks. Somewhere a name is said like a promise and a problem. The body prepares to move and postpones movement by a heartbeat, the way it has learned.

Heartbeat is not in instruction. The body keeps it anyway.

✝ ✝ ✝

The quiet woman stands on the hill. The stones remember. The air is thin as paper and heavy as a kept secret. She lays the beads on her palm and feels the heat soak in as if the skin is a page taking ink.

"Keep the eyes off her," she says to the place that won't answer. "Or turn them on me."

She closes her hand. Heat presses crescent moons into her lifeline. She will not show that hand to anyone who reads palms. Some things you choose not to know.

The trees lean a fraction as if adjusting to a sudden weight.

} } }

"I am not your enemy," the static man tells the trees, which have no opinion. "I am the other half of what you ask."

He looks toward the red seam nothing else will admit is there. "Balance abhors a closed door," he says, as if to a class. "If you insist on shutting one, you must teach another to open."

He glances toward where the tired boy and the quiet girl stand, and for a breath the air thickens between them, like glass cooling.

"It is not wickedness to be what you are," he says. "It is waste to pretend otherwise."

He waits. Patient, polite, pleased.

~ ~ ~

The seam lowers until it is almost a touch above the sand. Beetles begin to fall from it in a soft rain, each one clicking once as it lands, like punctuation marks dropped in the wrong sentence. The radio winds down, and what remains is the hum, and beneath it, a second note so low it can't be heard except by whatever inside him knows the sound of a warning that thinks it's a welcome.

"Will you help me ask him?" the tired boy says to the quiet girl, not sure if he means The Creature or the far voice behind it.

"Yes," she says. It is not a promise and exactly is.

"The static man," the boy says, as if saying the word teaches his mouth a shape it will need later and then let slip. The air acknowledges the effort; it cools and then forgets to warm.

The girl squeezes his hand. "Don't turn if you feel looked at," she says. "He prefers when people perform."

The boy nods. He does not turn

The sea draws its slow breath again. The seam lifts higher. The doors lean, indecisive.

The radio's last message crawls out of its speaker like a final mosquito.

…the hill… the circle… the blood learns to speak…

He feels the sand under his shoes go soft like mud. He is moving before he has decided to move. His hand is still in the girl's. The world selects itself.

The barbed wire fence sags between rotting posts where the creek bed meets the swamp's edge, and then Vincent sees it. A scrap of red flannel caught on the middle strand, fluttering like a signal flag nobody wants to acknowledge. The fabric is torn at the edges, frayed where it pulled free from something or someone moving through here with enough force to leave evidence behind. Three days since anyone's seen CJ, and all that's left is this piece of shirt that Carl now holds with the reverence.

Carl's fingers trace the tear over and over, following the jagged line where threads separated. His other hand clutches a flashlight though the afternoon sun still provides enough light to see by, preparation for what they all know is coming. He crouches near the fence, eyes scanning the dried clay for footprints that should be there but aren't, as if the earth itself has conspired to erase CJ's passage.

"Right here," Carl says, pointing to a depression that might be a heel mark or might be Vincent's imagination working overtime. "He went through right here. See how the wire's bent outward? He was moving fast."

The fence does bow slightly at that spot, the rusted metal

pushed toward the swamp rather than away from it. Vincent pictures CJ climbing through in the dark. Or being pulled through. The thought arrives unbidden and Vincent pushes it away, but it leaves its mark like a bruise on his consciousness.

Jayce stands apart from the group, his back against a cedar trunk. His eyes dart between the swamp entrance and the path back to town, calculating distances and escape routes with the paranoid precision of prey that knows it's being watched. "Sheriff Brennan said he'll turn up," Jayce says, his voice carrying that bitter edge it's developed since the bridge incident. "Said CJ's probably crashed at some friend's place outside town. Like CJ has friends. Like he goes places."

"Nobody's filed a report," Rene adds softly, her sketchbook pressed against her chest like always, though Vincent notices she hasn't drawn anything since they arrived. Her eyes have that unfocused quality that means she's seeing something beyond the immediate, some pattern or meaning the rest of them miss. "His aunt doesn't care. The school marked him absent but didn't follow up. I don't know how much he actually attends or even what grade he's in. It's like he was already half-gone before he disappeared."

Carl spreads his map on a flat stone, the paper covered in his careful annotations. He's drawn CJ's usual routes in blue ink from his aunt's trailer to the gas station where he sometimes worked nights, to the spots near the swamp where he'd go to smoke and avoid the world. Red marks indicate possible paths, questions marks scattered like breadcrumbs through a forest of uncertainty. The map reveals Carl's obsession in geographic form, every possibility considered and documented with the thoroughness of someone who can't accept that people just vanish.

"He knew these woods better than anyone," Carl says, his finger following a red line that leads deeper into the swamp. "Grew up playing here before it got... bad. If something happened to him out here, it wasn't an accident."

The implication hangs between them, unspoken but understood. They all remember the hollow eyes in the darkness, the impossible figure made of stone and root and patient malevolence.

"We should tell someone," Vincent says, though even as the words leave his mouth he knows how hollow they sound. "The police, our parents, anyone who might actually search."

Carl's laugh comes out harsh, scraped raw by frustration. "Tell them what? That we think something grabbed him? That there's a monster in the swamp nobody wants to admit exists?" He holds up the flannel, the red fabric dark with moisture from the humid air. "This is all we have. A torn shirt and a bad feeling. You've seen how this town works. They'll file it away and forget it happened. Make up some story about CJ running off, being troubled, whatever helps them sleep."

Vincent knows Carl's right. The pattern is too clear now, written in all the incidents they've mapped, all the reports Jennifer showed him. Duswood doesn't just ignore the strange; it actively rewrites it, transforms it into something mundane and manageable. CJ's disappearance will become another footnote, another person who "left town" or "had problems" or simply stopped existing in the collective memory.

"Then we search ourselves," Rene says, and her voice carries a certainty that makes everyone turn toward her. She's moved closer to the fence, one hand extended toward the swamp entrance where cedar branches hang low, heavy with moss and hide what lies beyond. "Tonight. After dark. When it might be active again."

"That's insane," Jayce says, but his protest lacks conviction. They've already crossed the line from sane to necessary, from safe to committed. "We don't even know what we're looking for."

"We're looking for CJ," Carl says simply, folding his map

with careful precision. "Or evidence of what happened to him. Or..." He doesn't finish, but they all hear the unspoken alternative. *Or we're looking for proof that the thing in the woods has graduated from watching to taking.*

The sun angles lower, casting long shadows that reach toward the swamp like fingers. The air grows thicker, weighted with moisture and the promise of another night without rain. Insects begin their evening chorus, but it sounds off, discordant, as if they're singing in a key that doesn't exist in nature.

"Midnight," Vincent says, surprising himself with the decision. "We meet here at midnight. Bring flashlights, water, whatever you think might help. And tell someone where you're going, even if you have to lie about where that is. Just... leave a trail. In case." *In case we disappear too. In case Duswood swallows us the way it swallowed CJ. In case the morning finds four more torn pieces of clothing on a fence nobody wants to look at too closely.*

Carl clutches the flannel tighter, and Vincent sees his knuckles white with pressure. "If no one else is going to look for him, we will," Carl says, and the words sound like a vow, a promise to the disappeared, a challenge to the town's willful blindness.

They separate as the sun drops lower, each returning to homes where they'll pretend everything is normal, where they'll eat dinner and do homework and wait for midnight with the patience of conspirators. Vincent walks away last, glancing back at the fence where that scrap of evidence fluttered. It's gone now, whether taken by wind or Carl or something else, he can't tell. But the bent wire remains, proof that someone passed through here, that CJ existed and then stopped existing.

———

The darkness between the cedars swallows their flashlight beams after twenty feet, as if the light itself grows tired of pushing against such deliberate shadow. Vincent leads because someone has to, though every instinct screams at him to turn back, to return to the relative safety of streets and streetlights and the fiction that Duswood is a normal town. His flashlight cuts a narrow tunnel through the black, revealing twisted roots that seem to shift when the light moves past them, cedar trunks that loom like witnesses to something they're not yet prepared to see.

Behind him, Jayce's breathing comes quick and shallow, barely controlled panic translated into oxygen intake. His flashlight beam jerks with each nervous movement, creating a strobe effect that makes the woods seem to pulse and writhe. Sometimes the light catches Vincent's back, throwing his shadow forward into the path ahead, and each time it happens Vincent feels exposed, marked, like something in the darkness is taking note of their exact positions.

Rene moves with unusual silence, her sketchbook tucked inside her jacket where it creates a rectangular bulge against her ribs. She hasn't brought a flashlight, choosing instead to follow the collective illumination of the others, and Vincent wonders if she's seeing things in the darkness that their lights would chase away. Her presence feels both reassuring and unsettling, this girl who draws prophecies without meaning to, who touches the impossible and brings back fragments of truth nobody wants.

Carl brings up the rear, and his focus feels sharper tonight, also more desperate. His flashlight beam sweeps methodically back and forth across their path, searching for signs Vincent knows he won't find. CJ didn't leave tracks because things taken by Duswood's darkness rarely do. They simply transition from being to not being, from present to absent, with no trail between states except torn fabric on fences and the memory of those stubborn enough to remember.

The creek bed they're following changes gradually, the dry clay giving way to increasingly damp earth that releases the smell of decay with each footstep. Not the clean decay of autumn leaves but something older, more fundamental like the smell of things breaking down at a molecular level, returning to component parts that will be reassembled into forms that shouldn't exist. Vincent's shoes sink slightly with each step now, the ground holding him a fraction of a second too long, as if testing whether he's worth keeping.

The fog appears between one breath and the next, not rolling in but simply existing where it wasn't before. It clings to the cedar trunks like something alive, flowing around them in patterns that suggest intention rather than weather. Their flashlight beams struggle against it, the light diffusing into halos that illuminate nothing but the fog itself. Vincent can taste it on his tongue, mineral and deceit, like breathing underwater that's been standing too long in forgotten pipes.

"Stay close," he whispers, though he's not sure the others can hear him through the fog's muffling presence. Sound works differently here, some noises amplified while others disappear entirely. He can hear Carl's map rustling in his pocket three yards back but can't hear his own footsteps on the increasingly soft ground.

The insects that should be singing their September songs have gone silent, not gradually but all at once, as if responding to some signal that human senses can't detect. The absence of their sound creates a vacuum that makes Vincent's ears ache, searching for frequencies that should exist but don't. Even their breathing seems muted, each exhalation absorbed by the fog before it can properly exist.

Vincent's flashlight catches glimpses of things that might be important or might be shadows playing tricks: a root system exposed where the bank has eroded, forming patterns that look almost like letters in an alphabet that predates language; stones arranged in formations too regular for nature but too subtle for human design; patches of moss that glow faintly with their own phosphorescence, creating a green luminescence that makes the fog look diseased.

The ground beneath their feet has become genuinely soft now, not quite mud but something with the consistency of flesh that's begun to decompose. Each step releases more of that fundamental decay smell, and Vincent realizes they're walking on layers of organic matter that have been accumulating for decades or longer. The swamp is older than Duswood, older than human memory of this place, and it's been collecting things all that time, processing them into this soft, terrible ground that gives too easily under their weight.

The fog thickens until Vincent can barely see Jayce's outline behind him, just the suggestion of a person made of shadow and inadequate light. Rene and Carl are completely invisible now, existing only as sounds of breathing, footsteps, the whisper of fabric against fog-wet branches. They're together but isolated, each wrapped in their own pocket of gray blindness that could hide anything or nothing with equal ease.

"Vincent," Jayce whispers, and his voice carries a warning that makes Vincent stop. The others stop too, their footsteps ceasing with unnatural synchronization. Through the fog ahead, something else exists. Not light exactly, but a thinning of darkness, a space where the fog seems less dense. A clearing, Vincent realizes.

They move toward it without discussion, drawn by the promise of visibility in this world of gray blindness. The fog does thin as they approach, revealing a rough circle of open ground maybe twenty feet across. The ground here is different, packed harder, older, as if something has been kneeling here for so long it's compressed the earth into stone-like density.

And something *is* kneeling here.

The creature occupies the center of the clearing like a

monument to malfeasance, its massive form bent in a posture that might be prayer or might be feeding or might be something human minds lack the vocabulary to describe. Its body of stone and root remains perfectly still, more still than any living thing should be, still in the way of geology rather than biology. Moss drapes from its shoulders in sheets that don't move. The roots that bind its form create patterns that hurt to follow with human eyes, weaving in and out of stone in ways that violate the boundaries between organic and mineral.

Its head bows over something small that rests in what might be hands or might be accidental formations that suggest hands. The hollow spaces where eyes should be face downward, focused with infinite patience on the object it cradles with the care of something that has all the time in the world.

CJ's phone. The cracked screen emits a low, rhythmic static that Vincent feels more than hears, a pulse that seems to synchronize with his heartbeat before diverging into patterns that make his chest tight with depravity. The phone should be dead, battery drained after three days, but it glows with sick life, the screen flickering between black and a green that matches the phosphorescent moss.

The static forms patterns, almost like words, almost like language, but in frequencies that human ears weren't meant to process. Vincent feels it in his teeth, in the bones of his skull, a vibration that threatens to become meaning if he listens too long. Beside him, Jayce has gone rigid, his flashlight beam locked on the tableau of creature and device, his breathing stopped entirely as if exhaling might break whatever spell keeps the creature focused on the phone instead of them.

The teens stand frozen at the clearing's edge, four points of human warmth in a cold that has nothing to do with temperature. The fog walls them in, creating a theater where they're the unwilling audience to something that feels ancient and infinitely patient. The mass continues its vigil over the phone, and the static continues its almost-language, and Vincent knows with terrible certainty that they're witnessing something that connects to CJ's disappearance in ways they're not equipped to understand.

Rene moves before anyone can stop her, drawn forward by the static's rhythm like a fish on an invisible line. Her steps are deliberate but dreamlike, each footfall placed with the precision of someone following choreography only they can hear. The static from CJ's phone pulses in patterns that seem to match her movement, or maybe her movement matches the static, Vincent can't tell which leads and which follows. Her hand extends slowly, reaching toward the cracked screen that glows with that sick green light, and Vincent wants to call out, to warn her, but his throat has closed around any sound he might make.

As Rene draws closer, something changes in its stillness. Not movement exactly, but a ripple that passes through its form, like watching stone develop the properties of water for just a moment. The roots that bind its body shift minutely, a tightening that might be muscle tension if this thing had muscles, if it was bound by the same biological rules as every-thing else. The moss on its shoulders brightens, phosphores-cence increasing until it casts its own shadows, and beneath the bark-like skin that covers parts of its form, something writhes with purpose.

The static grows louder, more insistent, and now Vincent can almost hear words in it, but not any language that uses human vocal cords, but something that bypasses the ears and speaks directly to the part of the brain that processes mean-ing. It's calling to Rene, or through Rene, or maybe Rene is just the closest available receiver for whatever signal the phone is transmitting. Her fingers are inches from the screen when the patterns in the static shift, becoming something that makes Vincent's teeth ache with corruption.

The rock comes from out of nowhere, striking the phone with a crack that sounds like breaking bone. The device spins from Muldrath's grasp, the screen going dark instantly, the static cutting off mid-pulse like a severed scream. The silence that follows is so complete it feels like pressure against Vincent's eardrums, the absence of sound as violent as any noise.

Mira stands at the clearing's edge, her arm still extended from the throw. She looks smaller than usual, younger, but there's something in her posture that speaks of practice, of having done this before, of understanding the precise moment when intervention becomes necessary.

The creature's head turns with the grinding slowness of continental drift, stone scraping against stone in frequencies that Vincent feels in his bones. The hollow spaces where eyes should be sweep across the clearing, and Vincent understands with primitive certainty that it's seeing them now, really seeing them, not just aware of their presence but cataloging, remembering, filing them away in whatever passes for memory in a thing made of grief and stone and accumulated loss.

"Run," Mira says, not shouting but projecting the word with enough force that it breaks the paralysis holding them all.

They scatter like startled birds, each choosing their own trajectory through the darkness. Carl crashes through underbrush to the left, his flashlight beam swinging wildly as branches tear at his clothes. Jayce goes right, his nervous energy finally given purpose, feet finding purchase on ground that shouldn't be navigable in this darkness. Rene stumbles backward, then turns and runs in a direction that might lead back to the creek bed or might lead deeper into the swamp.

Vincent finds himself running alongside Mira. They move through the fog together, her hand briefly catching his to pull him around a cedar trunk that looms out of the gray. Her touch is cool but solid, real in a way that everything else tonight hasn't been. They duck under low branches that Mira seems to know are there before the fog reveals them, splash through shallow water that Vincent didn't know existed this far from the main swamp.

Behind them, or maybe beside them, or maybe the acoustics of the fog make direction meaningless, something moves with the patience of geology. Not pursuing exactly, but acknowledging their flight, marking their paths through its territory. Vincent can hear it, or feel it, or maybe he's just imagining the sensation of being observed by something that exists partially outside normal space, that can be in multiple places at once or no place at all depending on how reality feels at any given moment.

They run until Vincent's lungs burn with the effort, until his legs shake with exhaustion, until the fog begins to thin and the cedars give way to younger trees that don't carry the same weight of accumulated dread. The forest edge appears like a promise of salvation, the lights of Duswood visible through the last few trees, and they collapse against a fallen log that marks the boundary between the swamp and the world that pretends the swamp doesn't exist.

Vincent's chest heaves as he tries to pull in enough oxygen to think clearly again. Beside him, Mira breathes more easily, as if running from impossible things is part of her regular exercise routine. Her dark hair has come partially loose from whatever was holding it back, strands sticking to her face with sweat and moisture from the night. In the dim light filtering through the trees from town, her eyes catch and hold illumination like pools of still water.

"You knew," Vincent says between gasps. "You knew exactly when to throw that rock."

"The static was building to something," Mira replies, her voice steady despite their flight. "Another few seconds and

Rene would have touched it. Would have made contact with whatever was using the phone as a conduit."

Vincent thinks of Rene's drawn forward motion, the way she moved like a sleepwalker toward something that called to her in frequencies only she could hear. "What would have happened?"

"Connection. The same thing that happened to CJ, probably." Mira shifts slightly, and Vincent realizes how close they're sitting, their shoulders almost touching, the heat from their run creating a small pocket of warmth in the cool night. "He heard something calling and followed it. But once you make contact, once you accept the connection, you become part of the circuit."

"Circuit for what?"

Mira turns to look at him fully, and in the strange light, Vincent notices things he's missed before like the way her eyes hold depths that seem older than her years, the precise arch of her eyebrows, the way her mouth curves slightly when she's considering how much truth to share. "It listens," she says finally, quietly, as if the words themselves might summon attention. "Not to us. To someone else. Someone who's been gone for a long time but never really left."

Vincent's mind makes connections he doesn't want to make. "Rourke."

Mira nods, and without thinking, Vincent reaches for her hand. She doesn't pull away, instead interlacing their fingers with a naturalness that surprises them both. Her skin is still cool from the night air, but Vincent feels warmth building where their palms meet, a human connection that feels like defiance against everything inhuman they've witnessed.

"He's still out there," Mira continues, her voice dropping to barely above a whisper. "Not alive, not dead, but something between. And the creature... it's his antenna, his receiver, his way of gathering what he needs."

"What does he need?"

"Grief. Loss. The exact things Duswood refuses to feel." Her thumb moves slightly against Vincent's hand, a small gesture that sends electricity through his entire arm. "Every person who disappears, who gets forgotten, who gets written out of the town's memory become fuel for whatever Rourke is trying to complete."

They sit in silence for a moment, hands clasped, breathing synchronized without conscious thought. The lights of Duswood twinkle through the trees, looking deceptively normal, hiding all its refusal to see, to remember, to mourn properly. Vincent thinks of CJ, somewhere in that darkness, part of some circuit he doesn't understand. Thinks of all the others who've vanished into the town's aggressive forgetfulness.

Mira squeezes his hand with surprising strength. "Tonight we survived seeing too much. Tomorrow we plan. And eventually..." She turns to look back at the dark woods, and Vincent sees determination in her profile that makes her look older, fiercer, more capable than any teenager should be. "Eventually we make Rourke listen to us instead."

Jayce's pen scratches across the notepad in rhythms that match nothing natural, just the anxious percussion of someone trying to trap chaos in lines of ink. The overturned paint can beneath him creaks when he shifts his weight, a sound sharp enough to make him flinch even though he knows it's coming. Through the garage's open door, Duswood's evening spreads like an infection, all purple shadows and the kind of quiet that makes him want to scream just to prove sound still exists.

The garage belongs to Rene's family but feels like it belongs to no one, a neutral zone where concrete walls muffle sound and nobody asks questions about teenagers gathering after dark. Oil stains on the floor form patterns Jayce's brain keeps trying to interpret from faces, maps, warnings written in automotive fluids and time. A single bulb hangs from a cord, swaying slightly, making shadows shift across tools hung on pegboard with obsessive precision.

Carl paces the perimeter like something caged, his footsteps creating a meter that fights against Jayce's pen scratches. Dark circles crater beneath his eyes, the kind that come from days without real sleep, just fitful dozing punctuated by nightmares about stone fingers and hollow spaces. His knuckles sullied and swollen, split, the purple-black of fresh bruising spreading across the ridges of bone.

"Punched through his bedroom wall," Vincent had whispered when Carl first arrived. "His mom found him at three AM, cradling his hand, crying."

But Carl isn't crying now. He's something worse than crying, something past tears into a territory where emotion becomes geological, compressed into movements too controlled to be sane.

Rene sits cross-legged on a paint-splattered tarp that might have once been white but now looks like a map of every project that's bled color in this space. Her sketchbook lies open across her lap, and even from his perch by the door, Jayce can see the drawings of hollow-eyed figures multiplied across pages, each iteration slightly different, as if she's trying to capture every angle of something that exists in more dimensions than paper can hold. Her head tilts periodically that makes Jayce's chest tight with recognition. She's listening to something.

"Rene?" Vincent's voice cuts through the garage's tense quiet. He's been watching her too, Jayce realizes, both of them tracking her movements with the vigilance of people who've learned that strange behavior precedes stranger events. "What's wrong?"

She doesn't look up from her sketchbook, but her pencil stops moving. The stillness that follows feels louder than Carl's pacing, louder than the pen scratches Jayce can't seem to stop making.

"Can't you hear them?" Her whisper barely disturbs the air, but it reaches every corner of the garage with perfect clarity. "It's a low buzz or hum. In the floor. Or maybe the walls?"

Jayce's pen freezes mid-word. He's been writing "normal" over and over, he realizes, the letters degrading with each repetition until they're just shapes, just movements his hand makes to avoid acknowledging what Rene's suggesting. The concrete beneath them suddenly feels thinner, like a membrane between their world and something worse.

Carl stops pacing. They all look at the floor, at the walls, searching for evidence of what Rene hears. The garage's silence deepens, becomes intentional.

The sound of footsteps outside breaks the spell, and they all turn toward the door with the synchronized motion of prey identifying a predator. But it's Mira who appears in the doorway, carrying a leather journal, worn and water-stained, that looks older than anything a teenager should possess.

She doesn't apologize for being late, doesn't explain where she's been. She moves into the garage with the fluid certainty of someone who's already thought through every word she's about to say. The light catches the graphite smudges on her fingertips as she sets the journal on the workbench, and Jayce notices her hands aren't shaking at all. Whatever she's about to share, she's already made peace with it.

"This was Rourke's," she says, and the name hangs in the air like a curse nobody wants to complete. "Another box found, hidden better. Not wanting to be seen, until it did."

She opens the journal to reveal pages covered in handwriting so precise it looks printed, interrupted by diagrams that hurt to follow with human eyes tracking spirals that seem to move, geometric patterns that suggest depth where none should exist. But it's the map of Duswood that draws them all closer, a map annotated with dates and symbols, with lines connecting points in patterns that mirror the spiral they discovered but with more detail, more intention.

"It's not random," Mira says, her voice steady despite the implications of what she's revealing. "The attacks, the sightings, the disappearances. They follow rules."

She turns the page, and there it is, written in Rourke's careful hand: "Muldrath responds to suffering, but not the passive kind. Active pain. Inflicted pain. Someone must hurt something to make it move. Give it purpose."

The word hangs between them: Muldrath. A name for the thing with hollow eyes, for the creature made of stone and root and patient malevolence. Naming it makes it real in a way that seeing it somehow didn't, transforms it from phenomenon to entity, from nightmare to citizen of their new reality.

"It's more than a random creature," Mira continues, her finger tracing the lines on the map that converge on the cedar swamp. "The creature, Muldrath, it feeds on pain. Not just suffering, that too, but also inflicted pain. Someone has to hurt something to make it move. Physically. Emotionally. Psychologically. All the same. Hurt."

Carl stops breathing. Jayce feels it happen, the way the air in the garage shifts when one person's rhythm drops out of the collective respiration. His own pen has gone still, the tip pressed against paper hard enough to tear through.

Rene looks up from her sketchbook, and her eyes reflect the overhead light in a way that makes them look hollow, empty, like she's been staring into those spaces where eyes should be for so long she's started to mirror them.

"It's not a killer," Mira continues, her voice filling the terrible silence. "It's a tool. But not a controlled one either. It's unpredictable. Responsive but not obedient. Like a dog that's been beaten too many times to trust but still comes when called."

The revelation lands like stones in still water, each word creating ripples that spread through their understanding of everything that's happened. The attack at the pizzeria. CJ's disappearance. The thing at Vincent's brother's window. Every event was orchestrated.

Carl's fist connects with the workbench before anyone sees him move. The impact sends a jar of nails cascading across the concrete, each nail hitting the floor with a sound like a tiny scream, metallic and sharp and perverse. They scatter in patterns that seem almost deliberate, as if even random violence here takes on meaning, becomes part of some larger design.

"Someone's using it," Carl says, and his voice breaks on the words. Blood seeps from his already damaged knuckles, mixing with the older bruises to create a geography of pain across his hands. "Someone in town is feeding it. Rourke? I don't know, but they're making it hunt."

The implications sink into them like water into dry earth, changing the shape of everything they thought they understood. Their last hope was that they could reason with Muldrath, find some way to communicate with it, maybe even help it, but it crumbles like old mortar. You can't negotiate with a weapon. You can't make peace with something that exists only to translate pain into action.

Jayce looks down at his notepad, at the word "normal" written so many times it's become meaningless, just marks on paper, evidence of a boy trying to write his way back to a world that no longer exists. The garage feels smaller now, the concrete walls less like protection and more like the sides of a box they've trapped themselves in, while outside, Muldrath waits with the patience of stone for someone to hurt something, to give it purpose, to aim it like a gun made of grief and accumulated loss at whatever target serves the purposes of whoever's been conducting this symphony of suffering.

The nails on the floor catch the swinging light, creating constellations of reflected brightness that pulse with the bulb's unstable rhythm. Each one points in a different direction, as if offering a thousand paths forward, all of them sharp.

Night settles over Duswood like a palpitating heart, and Vincent moves through it with the careful steps of someone who's learned that darkness here isn't empty but crowded with things that watch and wait. Cedar Lagoon Pizzeria rises from the corner lot like a monument to normalcy that isn't normal anymore, its red brick facade absorbing streetlight instead of reflecting it. The neon sign buzzes with electrical complaint, casting blue shadows that fall in directions that don't match the light source, and Vincent's breath forms small clouds that dissipate too quickly in air that shouldn't be this cold for September.

The parking lot stretches empty except for scattered leaves that scratch across asphalt. Vincent's footsteps echo untrue here, each impact creating reverberations that seem to come from underneath rather than around. The large window that should display the dining room's checkered floor and red vinyl booths has been covered from inside with brown paper, edges sealed with duct tape that gleams silver in the buzzing neon light.

The front door's handle doesn't yield to Vincent's pull, locked solid with a deadbolt that wasn't there last week. Through the door's small window, darkness pools thick enough to have weight, and Vincent can smell that familiar mixture of oregano and grease now tinged with something chemical, maybe bleach, or something stronger, the kind of cleaner that strips more than stains.

He circles the building, following the narrow passage between the pizzeria and the vacant storefront next door. His shoulder brushes the brick wall and comes away damp though it hasn't rained, that peculiar moisture that clings to surfaces in Duswood when something's wrong. The alley opens before him, and memory crashes over Vincent like cold water as this is where he first saw Muldrath up close, where those hollow eyes studied him with patience older than the town itself.

The dumpster squats against the far wall, its lid ajar and hanging at an angle that suggests violence rather than neglect. Something rustles inside, a sound that makes Vincent's muscles lock with primitive warning. He stands frozen, listening to the movement that's too deliberate for wind, too large for rats. The rustling stops, then starts again, closer to the opening, and Vincent's hand finds the wall behind him, needing something solid while his mind catalogues all the things that could be waiting in that metal container.

A raccoon emerges, its eyes catching the security light in twin circles of reflected green. It regards Vincent with the casual disdain of urban wildlife, then drops from the dumpster's edge and waddles away into the deeper darkness of the alley. Vincent's breath escapes in a rush that sounds too loud, and he notices his hands are shaking, not from cold but from the adrenaline of expected horror transformed into mundane explanation.

The back door draws his attention, and even from a distance, he can see the changes. The frame has been reinforced with steel plates bolted directly into the brick, and the door itself is new and made of heavy metal rather than the old one that Muldrath's stone fingers tore through. A new deadbolt gleams above the handle, and below it, another lock, and below that, a third. Someone has turned this entrance into a fortress.

He's about to leave when he notices the freezer vent on the flat roof section above the kitchen. The metal grate that should cover it hangs open, creating a dark square against the tar paper. Vincent knows that vent. Joe complained about it constantly, how it would ice up in winter, how he had to climb up there with a hairdryer to clear it. But it shouldn't be open now, not with the freezer running, wasting electricity Joe would never tolerate.

Then he hears it. It's faint, almost lost in the electrical hum, but unmistakable once his ears find the frequency. Whimpering, thin and desperate, drifting up from inside the building. Not an animal sound but human, someone in pain or fear or both, trying not to be heard but unable to stay completely silent.

Vincent finds the stack of milk crates that Joe uses to reach the roof for maintenance, tests their stability with one foot before committing his weight. They hold, though the plastic creaks with complaint that sounds like bones under pressure. He climbs carefully, each crate adding height until he can grip the roof's edge and pull himself up.

The tar paper is soft under his feet, holding his weight for a moment before releasing it, leaving perfect impressions of his shoes. He approaches the open vent, and the whimpering grows clearer, definitely coming from the walk-in freezer below. There's a small window next to the vent, glazed with frost from inside, but Vincent can make out shapes through the ice crystals.

Kent Canon sits huddled against the far wall of the freezer, knees drawn to his chest, arms wrapped around them. His shirt is torn at the shoulder, revealing skin that's gone blue-white with cold. His face turns up toward the window, and Vincent sees bruises spreading across one cheek like spilled ink, his lips cracked and bleeding from the freezer's dehydrating cold.

Vincent forces the window open, its frozen seal breaking with a crack like snapping wood. The cold that rushes out feels alive, aggressive. He drops through the opening, and the temperature hits him like a physical blow, so intense his lungs seize for a moment before remembering how to process air this cold.

"Kent," Vincent says, approaching slowly, hands visible and empty. "It's okay. It's just me."

Kent flinches away, pressing himself harder against the frost-covered shelves. His eyes are wild, pupils dilated despite the freezer's harsh fluorescent light, seeing something beyond Vincent, beyond the freezer, beyond the present moment entirely. His teeth chatter with violence that makes his whole body shake, and Vincent notices he's clutching a small medal on a chain in his right hand, pressed against his chest hard enough to leave marks.

"He made me do it," Kent whispers, and his voice sounds shredded, like he's been screaming for hours. "I had to scream, or he wouldn't leave. Had to feed it. Had to make it feel."

"Who?" Vincent asks, though he's not sure he wants the answer. "Who made you?"

Kent's eyes focus on Vincent for the first time, really seeing him, and the terror in them is so pure it makes Vincent step back. "The one who knows how it works. The one behind the one." His fingers tighten on the medal, Vincent can see now, the Archangel Michael. "He came through the walls. Through the floor. Like he wasn't solid but wasn't a ghost either."

Vincent helps Kent to his feet, the man's body rigid with cold, joints barely bending. As they move toward the window, Vincent notices the freezer door, and his blood chills in a way that has nothing to do with temperature. The handle on the inside has been removed, the metal plate covering the mechanism sealed with industrial adhesive. Someone locked Kent in here deliberately, thoroughly, with no intention of letting him out.

But it's what's below the handle that makes Vincent's vision narrow to a point. Claw marks score the metal door. He could feel their frantic origins. They're deep, desperate, gouged by something trying to escape. Not Kent's marks. Something else was in here with him, trapped in the freezer's small space, and it wanted out badly enough to claw through steel.

Vincent boosts Kent through the window first, then follows, his mind racing through implications he doesn't want to examine. The freezer was a cage, but not just for Kent. Someone put him in there with something else, something with claws, something to inflict pain and fear because the one who was there needed his screams. Vincent thinks of Mira's words about Muldrath being a tool, about pain being the trigger that makes it move.

They slide down from the roof, Kent barely able to stand once they reach the ground. The medal swings from his clenched fist, catching streetlight in brief flashes of silver. Vincent supports his weight, and they stumble toward the alley's mouth, toward the relative safety of the street. Behind them, the freezer vent remains open like a wound in the building's skin, and Vincent imagines he can still hear something inside breathing, patient and deliberate.

Kent's body trembles against Vincent as they emerge onto the sidewalk. His lips are blue, cracked, barely able to form words through violent shivers. "Something…something was in there with me," he manages. "Not the stone thing people whisper about. A wild animal. I heard it breathing. Scratching. But I couldn't see it." His fingers dig into Vincent's arm. "When I stopped screaming, that's when I felt him watching. Like he was disappointed. Like he needed my fear for something."

Vincent looks at the claw marks' memory burned into his mind, at Kent's bruised face and clutching fingers, at the medal that offered protection from certain death. The night presses close around them, and Vincent wonders how many other places in Duswood have been converted into chambers of purpose, how many other people have been made to scream for reasons they don't understand, feeding something that grows stronger with every orchestrated moment of agony.

CHAPTER
ELEVEN

The morning light through Cedar Lagoon's windows catches on broken glass that Joe hasn't swept yet, tiny prisms that scatter rainbows across the checkered floor like promises nobody intends to keep. Jennifer Winter's heels click against the tiles with deliberate force, each step announcing her presence like a declaration of war against the town's suffocating silence. Kent follows close behind, his sneakers scuffing with the uncertain gait of someone who's forgotten how to trust solid ground.

The pizzeria wears its trauma openly. The back door hangs crooked despite fresh steel reinforcements, bolts driven deep into brick that still shows stress fractures spreading like veins from impact points. Scratches score the walls near the freezer entrance, four parallel lines that could be from metal tools if Jennifer didn't know better, if she hadn't seen the terror in Kent's eyes as she tended to his wounds last night.

Joe Bullit stands behind the counter like a guard at his post, his bandaged left hand resting carefully on the stainless steel surface. His jaw works methodically on what might be gum or might be nothing at all, just the motion of a man trying to keep words from escaping. The coffee pot behind him has been going too long, the smell of burnt beans mixing with lingering oregano and something else, something chemical and sharp like industrial cleaner used in quantities that suggest more than spills needed removing.

Sheriff Brennan leans against the wall near the register, his uniform impeccable and freshly pressed, badge catching fluorescent light in brief flashes when he shifts his weight. His arms fold across his chest in that particular way that makes his shoulders broader, his presence larger, a human wall between questions and answers. The posture is so practiced it might as well be part of his uniform, as essential as the gun at his hip that he hasn't touched but hasn't forgotten about either.

Jennifer positions herself between Kent and the two men with the fluid precision of someone who's learned to read rooms like weather patterns. Her blonde curls pulled back in a style that says business but the tightness around her eyes says something else entirely. When Kent shifts behind her, she moves with him, maintaining that buffer of space and intention that speaks louder than any claim of relationship status.

"We need to talk about what happened last night," Jennifer says, her voice carrying the kind of authority that comes from knowing exactly what questions to ask and being unafraid of the answers.

"Nothing happened last night," Brennan says, and his tone is so flat it doesn't even pretend to be convincing. "Joe closed early due to equipment problems. That's all."

The fluorescent tubes overhead flicker, a stuttering rhythm that makes everyone glance up reflexively. In the unstable light, Kent's bruises look worse, purple-black spreading across his cheekbone like spilled ink on pale paper. His hands shake where they grip the back of a booth, knuckles white with the effort of staying upright, staying present, staying anywhere but back in that freezer with whatever shared the darkness with him.

"Equipment problems," Jennifer repeats, and her voice could freeze water. "Is that what we're calling it when someone locks a person in a freezer? When something with claws tries to get out through a steel door?"

Joe's eyes dart to the back entrance, to the reinforced door that shouldn't need reinforcing, to the scratches on the walls that shouldn't exist. His good hand drums against the counter in a pattern that might be nervous or might be counting, keeping track of something only he knows needs tracking.

"Nobody was locked anywhere," Joe says, but his voice catches on the lie like fabric on a nail.

Jennifer steps forward, and Kent moves with her, their bodies synchronized in a way that speaks of practice, of mornings spent learning each other's rhythms, of trust built through proximity and patience. She pulls out her phone, shows the screen to both men. The video is dark but clear enough: Vincent, entering through the small freezer window, his breath blooming white in the cold as he pulls Kent out. His body is half-collapsed, eyes wide with panic, frost still clinging to his eyelashes.

"I have additional security footage from the building across the street," she lies smoothly, because sometimes lies are the only way to excavate truth. "Shows someone entering through the back around midnight. Shows the lights going out. Shows things that shouldn't exist doing things that can't be explained."

Brennan pushes off from the wall, his casualness evaporating like morning dew under sudden heat. His fingers twitching with muscle memory of threats assessed and dismissed. "You need to be very careful about what you think you know, Miss Winter."

The smell of burnt coffee intensifies as the pot gives up entirely, the heating element clicking off with a sound like surrender. Joe reaches back to turn it off properly, and the motion pulls his shirt up enough to show more bandages wrapped around his ribs, white gauze dark with old blood where something pressed too hard, gripped too tight.

"Careful," Jennifer says, and her laugh has edges sharp enough to draw blood. "This whole town is careful. Careful not to see, careful not to ask, careful not to remember." She gestures to Kent's bruised face, to Joe's bandaged hand, to the scratches on the walls that catch light like accusations. "How's that working out?"

Kent makes a sound that might be agreement or might be fear, his fingers finding Jennifer's wrist in a touch so light it could be accident except for the way she turns her hand to briefly interlace their fingers before letting go. The gesture is small, private, but Brennan catches it and his expression shifts, calculations running behind eyes that have learned to see everything while acknowledging nothing.

The lights flicker again, longer this time, and in the darkness between illumination, Jennifer swears she sees something move beyond the windows. Not outside but in the reflection, a shape that shouldn't be there superimposed over their gathered forms. When the lights steady, Joe has gone pale, his injured hand clenched despite the obvious pain it must cause.

"Leave it alone," Brennan says, and now his voice carries something beyond authority, something that sounds like fear dressed up as warning. "Some things in this town are better left undisturbed."

"Like Silas Rourke?" Jennifer asks, and the name drops into the conversation like a stone into still water.

The silence that follows is so complete that the refrigerator's hum sounds like screaming.

Joe's shoulders drop like something essential has been cut, the resistance flowing out of him in a visible wave that makes him look older, smaller, more human than Jennifer has ever seen him. His bandaged hand trembles against the counter, and when he speaks, his voice carries the weight of years spent holding back words that burn like acid in his throat.

"This isn't the first time," Joe says, the words coming out before he can stop them. "Seven, eight years back. After closing, I was training a new delivery driver. Kid was about seventeen."

The sheriff has a stare locked on Joe that could melt a weaker man.

Joe looks at Kent, and this time there's no doubt as recognition creases his face, heavy and real. "I know you remember, Kent."

Kent nods, jaw tight. "Yeah. Of course, I remember."

Kent nods slowly, his hand moving to his pocket in a gesture so automatic it must be muscle memory by now. The bruises on his face seem darker in the pizzeria's harsh light, but there's something else there too, a kind of grim validation that someone finally acknowledges what he's carried alone for years.

"Third night on the job," Kent says, his voice stronger now that the truth has space to exist. "You sent me to check the freezer inventory while you counted the till. I heard something in the alley. Like stones grinding together, but wet somehow. Organic."

Jennifer's hand finds Kent's elbow, a touch that grounds them both. She can feel him shaking through his thin shirt, tremors that might be memory or might be the lingering cold from last night's imprisonment.

"I told him it was raccoons," Joe says, and his voice breaks on the lie that's curdled inside him for years. "Told him to ignore it. But then the lights went out, and that thing, it came through the back door like the metal was paper. Like the laws of physics were just suggestions it could ignore."

Kent pulls something from his pocket, his fingers careful as if cradling a wounded bird. The medal catches the fluorescent light, St. Michael's sword raised against invisible demons, the silver worn smooth in places from years of worried touching. He turns it over, revealing an inscription on the back in Latin.

"Only reason I didn't run screaming that night was because I had this," Kent says quietly, neither claiming the medal saved him nor dismissing its power, just stating a fact that exists in the space between faith and coincidence. "My grandma gave it to me before she died. Said it keeps the devil out. Said there were things in Duswood that had been here longer than people, and sometimes old protections were the only protections that mattered."

The refrigerator's hum fills the silence that follows, a mechanical breath that makes the quiet feel alive, waiting. Joe looks at the medal with something like recognition, or maybe regret for all the protection he never sought, all the old wisdoms he dismissed as superstition until superstition became the only explanation that made sense.

"It looked at me," Kent continues, his fingers closing around the medal with the desperation of a drowning man clutching driftwood. "Those hollow spaces where eyes should be, they looked right through me. But then it turned away. Like I wasn't worth its attention. Or like something about me made me... unpalatable."

Sheriff Brennan shifts against the wall, his skepticism warring with something else on his face, maybe his own memories of things seen and deliberately forgotten. The morning light through the windows has grown stronger, but instead of dispelling shadows, it seems to create new ones, dark spaces that pool in corners where geometry says they shouldn't exist.

"After it left, I quit," Kent says, looking directly at Joe now. "Came in the next morning, left my uniform on the counter, and you never asked why. Never asked what I saw. Just handed me my last check and acted like I'd never worked here at all."

Joe's mouth tightens. "You left after that night. Can't blame you. Surprised me when you came back."

Kent shrugs, avoiding Joe's eyes. "Didn't have a lot of choices."

Joe's guilt is a visible thing, weighing down his shoulders, pulling at the corners of his mouth. His injured hand clenches and unclenches despite the obvious pain, blood seeping through the bandages in patterns that look almost deliberate. "I thought if we didn't talk about it, it would go away. That's how Duswood works. We don't talk about things, and they stop existing."

"Except they don't," Jennifer says, her voice cutting through the confessional atmosphere like a blade. "They just wait. They gather strength. They find new ways to manifest." She taps her nails on the counter that sounds like punctuation. "And someone in this town knows exactly how to use them."

"Last night was different. The stone thing wasn't there. A man. Maybe. I don't know. He looked at me," Kent continues, his fingers closing around the medal with the desperation of a drowning man clutching driftwood. "His eyes," Kent said looking somewhere else. "His eyes. They weren't empty. Something moved inside them, like oil on water. Black but somehow also every color. When he looked at me… it was as if he saw more than what you can see, but it was like he looked *in* me. He had the suggestion of a presence. Like he was there but not."

Kent tucks the medal back into his pocket, but his hand stays there, maintaining contact with whatever protection or comfort it provides. His other hand finds Jennifer's, their fingers interlacing again with the naturalness of a gesture repeated countless times in private moments the rest of Duswood doesn't need to know about.

"This town can't keep burying its secrets," Jennifer tells Joe and the sheriff, her voice carrying the kind of conviction that comes from seeing too much truth to ever go back to comfortable lies. "I'm going to find Silas Rourke and uncover whatever malevolence has been festering in this town for decades and uncover the underlying truth."

Brennan pushes off from the wall entirely now, his official presence expanding to fill more space than his body actually occupies. "You need to leave this alone, Miss Winter. Rourke is gone. Has been for thirty years. Digging up old graves won't bring anything but grief."

"Grief," Jennifer repeats, and something in the word makes everyone flinch. "This whole town is drowning in grief it won't acknowledge. Every disappeared person, every covered-up death, every incident explained away as equipment failure or raccoons or mass hallucination. The grief doesn't go away just because you refuse to feel it. It finds other outlets. Other forms."

She helps Kent to his feet, her hand on his back protective and possessive in equal measure. He leans into her slightly, not enough for dependence but enough for connection, for the reminder that he's not alone in this anymore. Joe watches them with eyes that have aged years in minutes, seeing in their closeness something he maybe had once and lost, or never had and always wanted.

Through the window, Jennifer catches sight of her white sports car in the parking lot, its pristine surface reflecting the morning sun like a beacon of normalcy in a world that's forgotten what normal means. The contrast is almost painful and the bright, clean lines of her car against the pizzeria's wounded structure, the scratched walls and reinforced doors and shadows that fall in wrong directions.

"Be careful," Joe says as they reach the door, and his voice carries genuine concern now, the pretense stripped away by confession and exhaustion. "Whatever Rourke was doing, whatever he became, whatever he's involved in, it's not something you can interview or investigate. It's something that investigates back."

Kent's hand tightens on the medal in his pocket, and Jennifer feels the motion through their connected bodies, the way fear translates through proximity into shared understanding. But she doesn't hesitate as she pushes open the door, the morning air hitting them like a blessing after the pizzeria's concentrated atmosphere of old fear and fresh revelation.

The door swings shut behind them with a hollow sound that echoes longer than it should, as if the building itself is commenting on their departure. Jennifer makes a mental note to start her search at the county records office, where paper trails might exist that even Duswood's aggressive forgetfulness couldn't erase. Beside her, Kent walks with more confidence now, the medal's weight in his pocket and Jennifer's presence at his side forming a different kind of protection than hiding and silence ever could.

Behind them, through the pizzeria's windows, Joe and Brennan remain frozen in tableau, two men caught between their duty to maintain the town's carefully constructed normalcy and the growing understanding that normal was never what they thought it was, and maybe never existed at all.

The morning streets of Duswood stay silent around Mira like something trying to sneak away, sidewalks cracked in patterns that suggest intention rather than weather, each fracture pointing toward the town's rotten center where grief pools thick as standing water. She moves through the silence with practiced quiet, the baby blue accents struggle against her black dress as it absorbs light rather than reflecting it, making her less visible to windows that watch without watchers behind them. The air tastes of copper and ash though nothing burns, though no known blood has been spilled.

Mrs. Henley's front yard spreads before her like a museum of botanical death. The hydrangeas that once bloomed purple-blue, that Mrs. Henley tended with the devotion of someone who believed beauty could save things, now stand in blackened clusters. Not dead from drought, brown and brittle and honest. This is different. The flowers have turned the color of old bruises, of blood pooled beneath skin, maintaining their shape but dishonest in every other way.

Mira reaches out, her fingers barely grazing one bloom. At her touch, it crumbles instantly, not falling apart but dissolving, becoming dust so fine it might never have existed at all. The sensation travels up her arm, more like touching the absence of something that should be there. She pulls her hand back, and tiny fragments of what was once living beauty drift between her fingers, each particle carrying a weight that has nothing to do with mass.

The dissolution spreads from where she touched, other blooms collapsing in a slow wave across the bush, then the next bush, then the next, until Mrs. Henley's entire garden transforms into dark powder that settles on the lawn like ash from a fire that burned somewhere else, somewhen else. Mira steps back, but she knows it's not her fault, not really. She's just the catalyst for something that was already happening, decay waiting for permission to complete itself.

The creek bed draws her forward, that channel that cuts through Duswood like a wound that won't heal. The water runs midnight black despite the morning sun, moving with a viscous quality that suggests oil or something thicker. But it's the surface that makes her pause. Insects writhe there, not floating but swimming, their bodies moving in formations too deliberate for instinct. Beetles and centipedes and things with too many legs or not enough, all following the current with purpose that speaks of destination rather than drift.

She kneels at the edge, careful not to touch the water itself. The insects part around a distorted reflection watching from beneath the surface, a presence that acknowledges her obser-vation without revealing itself. The bugs form glyphs briefly, showing something in a language that predates words, then scatter back into meaningless motion. Mira stands, the image of those cryptic shapes burning behind her eyes like staring at the sun too long.

The grocery store's front window glows with fluorescent harshness that makes everything inside look preserved, speci-men-like. Through the glass, she sees Mr. Garrett near the produce section, clutching a bag of apples against his chest like he's holding a child. His mouth moves in a constant stream of words she can't hear through the glass, but she can read the shape of one name repeated: Sarah. Sarah. Sarah.

Tears run down his weathered face, catching the artificial light in ways that make them look like mercury. The apples in his arms are perfect, red and gleaming, but he holds them with the desperation of someone trying to anchor themselves to solid reality through touch alone. Other shoppers move around him in wide arcs, their faces carefully blank, that particular Duswood expression of seeing without acknowledging.

Sarah was his daughter. Mira remembers the funeral, just three months ago. She had sat three rows behind Mr. Garrett, watching his shoulders shake through the entire service. She'd overheard her father talking afterward about the mortician's struggle with Sarah's injuries. It was something about marks on her throat and damaged eye sockets. The closed casket had seemed merciful. Now Mr. Garrett stands in the grocery store, crying for a daughter everyone in Duswood knows is never coming home.

A scream cuts through the morning air, sharp and sudden, then stops with the abruptness of a radio switched off. Mira turns toward the sound that came from the Connors' porch, three houses down. Mrs. Connor stands in her doorway, hand pressed to her mouth, staring at something on her welcome mat that Mira can't see. The woman's eyes are wide, pupils dilated despite the brightening day, her body rigid with the kind of shock that precedes either flight or complete shutdown.

Then Mrs. Connor blinks, shakes her head like clearing cobwebs, and bends to pick up what looks like the morning paper. She goes inside, closes the door with deliberate normalcy, and Mira knows that whatever she saw has already been rewritten in her mind, transformed into something mundane her consciousness can process without shattering.

The scream might as well have never happened. In Duswood's collective memory, it didn't.

Movement in her peripheral vision of a child, maybe six years old, wandering down the middle of the street. The boy wears pajamas despite the hour suggesting he should be dressed for school, his feet bare and already darkening from the asphalt's accumulated grime. He walks with the aimless determination of the lost, each step taking him further from wherever home might be.

"Hey," Mira calls softly, not wanting to startle him. "Are you okay? Where's your house?"

The child looks at her with eyes that hold too much patience for his age, then shrugs with eloquent emptiness. "Don't know," he says simply. "Forgot." Not can't remember or not sure, but forgot, like the idea of home is something that can slip away when you're not paying attention.

Her home rises before her, its Victorian bones familiar as her own skeleton. She slips through the front door, which has a sign with a small clockface on it, "Will Return Soon!" The hallway stretches ahead, wallpaper peeling at the edges to reveal older patterns beneath, each layer a different decade's attempt to cover what came before.

Her father's office door stands ajar, yellow light spilling out like something liquid. Mira pulls the photograph of Silas Rourke from her pocket, taken in 1994 according to the date on the back, his face sharp and hollow and already showing signs of whatever transformation would claim him two years later. She pushes the door open.

Elias Thorn sits behind his desk, surrounded by the careful documentation of procedures that his profession requires. His hands are steady as they sort through papers, but when Mira places the photograph on his desk, those reliable hands begin to tremble, a vibration that starts in his fingers and spreads up his arms like electricity through water.

"That's not him," her father says, though she hasn't asked

anything yet. His voice comes out strained, forced through a throat that wants to close against the words. "That's not Silas Rourke."

"Dad…"

"That's not him," he repeats, more forcefully, and his trembling hands push the photograph back toward her like it burns to touch. "Silas Rourke left town. Retired. Moved south."

The phone rings, sharp and sudden in the enclosed space. Her father lunges for it with the desperation of someone offered rescue from drowning. "Thorn Dental," he says, his professional voice sliding into place like armor. His face changes as he listens, aging years in seconds. "Yes. Yes, I understand. I can be ready within the hour."

He hangs up, won't meet Mira's eyes. "Probably a root canal," he says unnecessarily. "Ethel Bartlett. In extreme pain." The words come out practiced, pre-formed, the kind of explanation that doesn't explain anything but stops questions from being asked.

Mira picks up the photograph, Rourke's face staring up at her with eyes that seem to track her movement despite being frozen in silver halide and time. Her father turns away, busying himself with preparations for another appointment that will keep him busy, busy keeping the truth from his daughter.

The phone buzzes against Vincent's nightstand with the insistence of something that won't be ignored. Dawn seeps through his blinds in strips of gray light that feel more like ending than beginning, and Vincent's hand finds the phone before his eyes properly focus. Carl's name glows on the screen above a message that's just three words: "Come. Now. Please."

Vincent has never seen Carl use "please" in a text before.

He pulls on yesterday's clothes, the fabric still carrying the smell of fog and fear from the swamp, from chasing shadows that turned out to be solid, from discovering CJ's phone in those impossible hands. His mother sleeps through his movement, wine-heavy slumber that's become her nightly refuge from a town that asks too much pretending. Danny's door stays closed, probably awake behind it but maintaining the fiction of sleep because interaction requires energy neither of them has anymore.

The streets between his house and Carl's stretch empty in the dawn light, that particular weekend quiet when even Duswood's early risers haven't emerged yet. Vincent's footsteps echo off houses that seem to lean away from him, as if the buildings themselves recognize someone who's seen too much, who carries knowledge that makes him dangerous to the town's cultivated ignorance. A dog barks somewhere, then stops abruptly, the silence that follows more disturbing than the sound.

Carl's house sits on Maple Street like something that's given up trying to fit in with the paint peeling in long strips that reveal different colors underneath, each layer a different decade's attempt at normalcy. The lawn has gone to seed, grass growing in tufts separated by bare patches of dirt that form patterns Vincent doesn't want to interpret. But it's the porch that draws his attention, wide boards that once held summer evenings and lemonade, now supporting something that makes Vincent's steps slow despite the urgency of Carl's message.

The dog lies in the exact center of the porch, positioned with a precision that speaks of deliberation rather than natural death. Bailey. Vincent remembers her name suddenly, remembers Carl teaching her to fetch in the park, remembers her tail wagging so hard her whole body would shake with joy. Now she lies still as carved stone, her golden retriever fur catching the dawn light in a way that makes her look preserved, museumified, transformed from pet to exhibit.

Carl sits on the top step, his back to the dog like he can't bear to look anymore. His hands are dirty, nails caked with something dark, and Vincent realizes he's been digging, probably trying to bury her before his parents wake up, before he has to explain what can't be explained. When he looks up at Vincent's approach, his eyes are dry but hollow, cried out or shocked past the point where tears mean anything.

"She was out all night," Carl says, his voice scraped raw. "Sometimes she does that, prowls around, comes back muddy and happy. But this morning..." He gestures without looking back. "Found her like this."

Vincent climbs the steps slowly, each board creaking under his weight with sounds like breaking bones. Up close, Bailey looks perfect, her fur unmatted, no blood, no obvious wounds. She could be sleeping except for the absolute stillness, the absence of the tiny movements that separate the living from the dead. No breathing, no twitching dreams, no nothing. Her eyes are closed, which seems dishonest somehow. Don't animals usually die with their eyes open?

He kneels beside her, extends his hand toward her fur, then hesitates. There's something about the positioning, the perfection of it, that makes touch feel like trespass. But he reaches out anyway, fingers finding fur that's still soft but lifeless, not cold exactly but lacking the warmth that should linger. As his hand moves along her side, searching for wounds, for explanation, he feels something beneath the fur. Not injury but arrangement. Her ribs have been moved, shifted into patterns that shouldn't be possible without breaking the skin.

"Vincent," Carl says, and his voice carries a warning that makes Vincent pull his hand back. "Look at the dirt."

Beside the porch, in the soft earth where Carl's mother once tried to grow tomatoes, someone has scraped a symbol. Not drawn but carved deep, each line deliberate and precise despite the crude medium. It's complex, geometric but amiss, angles that connect in ways that make Vincent's eyes water trying to follow them. The symbol seems to shift as he watches, lines that were straight becoming curved, curves becoming spirals, the whole thing pulsing with implied meaning that his brain refuses to process.

"It was here when I found her," Carl says. "Like a signature. Like someone wanted credit."

Vincent moves closer to the symbol, careful not to disturb the lines. The dirt around it is undisturbed except for the carving itself. No footprints, no tool marks besides the lines themselves. As if someone drew it without standing there, without being physically present at all. Or as if whoever made it doesn't leave tracks the way normal people do.

The morning light shifts, and suddenly Vincent can see something else in the dirt. Smaller marks, almost invisible unless you're looking at the exact right angle. Letters, maybe, or numbers, worked into the design so subtly they might be accident except Vincent knows nothing here is accident anymore. Everything is intention, message, threat.

"This isn't random," Vincent says, though saying it out loud makes it real in a way that thinking it didn't. "Someone chose Bailey. Chose your house. Chose you."

Carl's hands clench into fists, the movement making dried blood crack on his knuckles. "What? Why? Because I kept the tooth?"

Vincent places his palm on the porch's splintered wood, feeling the roughness bite into his skin, grounding himself in the physical sensation because everything else feels like it's sliding toward something inevitable and terrible. The wood is old, weathered by decades of seasons, but there's something else in it too, a vibration maybe, or a memory of violence that's soaked into the grain like spilled blood that's been cleaned but never really goes away.

This is escalation. Not just watching anymore, not just taking the already lost like CJ, but actively hurting, actively taking something loved and turning it into a message. The symbol in the dirt pulses in his peripheral vision, and Vincent understands with cold certainty that whoever or whatever killed Bailey wanted them to know it was deliberate, wanted them to understand that the rules have changed, that the things lurking in Duswood's shadows are done being patient.

THIRTEEN

Vincent tastes copper in the air before he sees the blood. Dusk presses down through the canopy in shades of rust and shadow, transforming familiar paths into territories that belong to neither day nor night. His shoes squelch with each step, the swamp's black water having soaked through during their search for answers that only led to more questions. Behind him, Jayce's breathing comes ragged and quick. Rene moves in her disconnected drift, while Mira follows with the quiet certainty.

The massive cedar rises before them like a monument to endurance, bark furrowed deep enough to hide secrets in its valleys. But it's what's pressed against that ancient wood that stops Vincent mid-step, his body recognizing disaster before his mind can process the details. Carl slumps against the tree's base, and at first Vincent thinks he's resting, taking a break from one of his obsessive searches. Then the dying light catches the wetness spreading across Carl's jacket, too much red, and Vincent's legs move without conscious thought.

Carl's torn jacket hangs in strips from his shoulders, the fabric shredded. Blood seeps through what remains of his shirt, creating patterns that spread like wine through paper, dark and inexorable. His skin has gone the color of old wax, that particular pale that comes when blood decides to be somewhere other than where it should. But it's the bark around him that makes Vincent's stomach clench. Deep gouges score the cedar's ancient skin, as if something with terrible hands tried to climb or claw or communicate through violence.

Vincent drops to his knees beside Carl, the impact sending shock through his bones that feels clean compared to the horror of what he's seeing. His hand reaches out, finds Carl's shoulder through the ruined jacket, and the touch breaks something that's been holding Carl rigid.

Carl yanks away with violence that sends him sliding further down the trunk, leaving a dark smear on the bark. His eyes focus on nothing, pupils dilated despite the dimming light, seeing something beyond the present moment. "I didn't scream," he whispers, and the words come out broken, like they've been repeated so many times they've worn smooth. "I didn't scream. I didn't scream."

The repetition continues, mechanical and horrible, each iteration slightly different in pitch but identical in desperation. Carl's hands clutch at his sides where the worst of the damage hides under torn fabric, and Vincent can see now that he's been holding himself together, literally, fingers pressed against wounds that want to open wider. The gesture is so human, so futile, this attempt to contain damage that's already been done.

"Oh god, oh god," Jayce's voice cracks behind them, his phone already in his shaking hands. The device's screen illuminates his face from below, casting shadows that make him look sick. His fingers fumble across the screen, missing numbers, starting over, the panic making simple tasks impossible. "911, I need....we need....there's been an attack."

His voice rises with each word, hysteria creeping in at the edges. The operator's calm questions filter through the phone's speaker, asking for location, asking for details, asking for things that can't be explained in any language emergency services would understand. Jayce manages to stammer out location, the cedar swamp's edge, bleeding, needs ambulance now, please now.

Rene stands at the clearing's edge like she's been transformed, static and strange. Her gaze fixes on the gouges in the bark, and Vincent knows she's seeing patterns there, meaning that the rest of them miss, connections that exist in that space between rational thought and the truth Duswood refuses to acknowledge.

Mira moves with medical precision, dropping beside Vincent without ceremony. Her fingers find Carl's neck, pressing against the pulse point with a practiced touch. Carl doesn't react to her touch, still lost in his litany of denial, still insisting to someone who isn't there that he didn't scream, didn't give them what they wanted.

"Do you know what you're doing?" Vincent asks, seeing a flip switch in Mira.

"People don't think of dentists as real doctors," Mira says while counting. "But they are. My father taught me a lot."

"Pulse is fast but strong," Mira says, her voice carrying that clinical detachment that makes everything worse somehow, makes it real in a way panic doesn't. She stands, and Vincent notices blood on her fingertips that she doesn't wipe away, like evidence she needs to keep. "He's in shock. Lost blood but not enough to…" She stops, because finishing that sentence would mean acknowledging that Carl should be dead, that whatever did this showed restraint, had reasons for leaving him alive.

The sirens build from suggestion to scream, cutting through the swamp's eternal quiet with mechanical urgency. Red and blue lights strobe through the trees, turning the world into a flip-book of color and shadow. The paramedics arrive in a rush of equipment and competence, their uniforms too clean for this place, their faces holding that professional calm that comes from seeing trauma but not *this* kind of trauma.

They swarm Carl with practiced efficiency, hands checking vitals, applying pressure, starting IVs with movements so routine they might be treating any injury, any normal violence that normal animals might cause. One of them speaks into a radio, medical terminology that transforms Carl's impossible wounds into data points, into treatable damage that fits within their understanding of how bodies break.

Carl's parents arrive in a chaos of slamming car doors and voices pitched high with panic. His mother's scream cuts through everything else, primal and pure, the sound of someone seeing their child damaged in ways that shouldn't exist. His father stands frozen, hands opening and closing like he's looking for something to hit, some physical enemy to confront instead of this formless horror that's claimed his son.

Sheriff Brennan appears among the emergency responders, his flashlight sweeping across the scene with deliberate slowness. The beam lingers on the gouges in the bark, and Vincent sees something like recognition flicker across the sheriff's face, or the deliberate absence of recognition that Duswood has perfected. The light continues its arc, illuminating torn jacket and blood-soaked ground.

"Probably a bear," Brennan says. "Or coyotes. Pack hunting. They get bold when they're hungry."

The paramedics lift Carl onto a stretcher, his body strapped down with orange restraints that look too bright against his pallid skin. He's stopped whispering now, eyes closed, escaped into unconsciousness that might be mercy. The ambulance doors shut with a decisive sound, metal meeting metal with finality.

The engine roars to life, and the ambulance navigates the rough path back toward town, toward the hospital where they'll stitch Carl's body back together but won't be able to touch what's been torn in places that don't show up on X-rays. The siren fades gradually, swallowed by distance and trees.

Vincent stands among the emergency scene's detritus of disturbed earth, torn fabric, blood-darkened earth. He feels the weight of Duswood's willful blindness pressing down like a physical thing. Around him, his friends stand in their own islands of shock, each processing this new escalation in their own way.

Vincent's bedroom door separates him from the rest of the house with a slam that rattles the frame, and he stands in the sudden darkness breathing like something hunted finally cornered. His desk lamp casts a yellow circle on homework he'll never finish, normalcy he can't return to, and the sight of it makes something hot and violent rise in his chest like vomit made of rage.

The wall beside his bed has always been there, painted white three years ago when his mother still cared about home improvement, when his father still lived here, when the house held a family instead of just people occupying the same space. Now it stands like an invitation, solid and real and present in a way that nothing else feels anymore. Vincent's hand forms a fist without conscious thought, knuckles pulling tight, tendons standing out like cables under skin that suddenly feels too thin to contain what's building inside him.

The first impact surprises him with its solidity. His fist meets plaster with a sound that's both dull and sharp, a percussion that travels up his arm in waves of sensation that aren't quite pain yet, just pressure and heat and the beautiful simplicity of action and reaction. The wall gives slightly, a depression forming around his knuckles, and white dust drifts down like snow from a catastrophe.

Carl's blood is still under Vincent's fingernails despite scrubbing them raw in the bathroom sink. The sound of "I didn't scream" still echoes in his ears with the rhythm of a prayer or a curse. His mother asked if he was okay when he came home, and he said yes, and she believed him because believing is easier than seeing, and now he's alone with truth that's eating him from the inside like acid.

The second strike comes from deeper, from that place where grief transforms into violence because it has nowhere else to go. His whole body torques into it, shoulder rotating, weight shifting forward, every muscle fiber contributing to this one moment of honest destruction. His fist drives through the existing damage, and this time the plaster splits properly, cracks racing outward from the impact point like lightning frozen in mineral form. Pieces fall to the floor in chunks that break into smaller chunks, creating a geography of destruction that feels more real than anything has felt in days.

This blow makes his knuckles throb. The ghost of pain arriving before the real thing, warning him that this is enough, that he should stop.

He doesn't stop. Can't stop. Because stopping means thinking, and thinking means remembering Muldrath's hollow eyes, means hearing CJ's name in static frequencies, means knowing that someone in Duswood is orchestrating horrors while everyone else orchestrates ignorance. His fist pulls back again, and he can see his blood on the broken plaster.

The third impact brings the crack. A sharp and definitive crack. A sound that cuts through rage like cold water through fever. It echoes through the room with a clarity that makes everything else stop, even his breathing, even his heartbeat for one suspended moment. The crack is from some small essential architecture that's exceeded its tolerance, that's broken in the way things break when they can't bend anymore.

Vincent staggers backward, his hand suddenly feeling

wrong in ways that transcend simple pain. A shard of plaster falls from the ruined wall, landing on his bedroom floor with a sound like a period at the end of a lie. The hole he's made is significant now, revealing the wooden struts behind, the insulation that looks like diseased cotton.

His hand won't respond properly. The fingers that should curl into a fist or spread wide just hang there, suspended in a configuration that isn't quite either. The knuckles are already swelling, skin split in thin lines that look too precise to be accidental, like something drew them there with a razor and a steady hand.

The numbness arrives first, that strange mercy bodies provide before they deliver the full bill for violence done. Vincent watches his hand with detached fascination as it transforms, swelling distorting the familiar architecture of bones and tendons into something abstract. The splits in his skin weep clear fluid that might be blood plasma or might be something else, some essential juice that's supposed to stay inside.

Then the pain arrives properly, not all at once but in waves, each heartbeat sending a fresh pulse of agony from his hand up through his wrist into his arm. It's clean pain, honest pain, nothing like the formless horror that's been eating at him since Bailey died on Carl's porch, since they mapped the spiral, since they learned Muldrath's name. This is simple cause and effect, damage that can be catalogued and treated, that will heal in time into scars that tell a story everyone can understand.

His fingers won't bend. He tries to make a fist and they just twitch, each attempted movement sending new distorted signals through nerves that are learning new vocabularies of damage. The middle finger might be broken or maybe it's the metacarpal behind it.

Vincent sits on his bed, still cradling his ruined hand, and stares at the hole he's made in his wall. Through it, he can see the bones of his house, the structure that holds everything up, that's been there all along hiding behind paint and plaster. The revelation makes him laugh, a sound that comes out cracked, and he wonders if this is how madness starts.

He needs to get out. Now.

Vincent pulls on his jacket one-handed, the simple task transformed into a struggle that makes him bite his tongue to keep from crying out. The sleeve catches on his swollen knuckles and the pain whites out his vision for a moment. When it clears, he's already at his window, sliding it open with his good hand. The night air hits his face like cold water, carrying the smell of distant rain and something else—that mineral scent that always precedes the swamp's presence in town.

The swamp's edge holds Vincent like a confession booth, dark water stretched before him under a moon that's almost full but not quite. He sits on a fallen log that's been smoothed by years of teenagers seeking solitude, its surface worn to the texture of old leather, soft and giving under his weight. His injured hand throbs against his chest where he cradles it.

The moon's reflection dances on the water's surface, fragmented into too many pieces that don't quite form a whole. The silver light breaks and reforms with each invisible current, creating patterns that suggest meaning just beyond recognition. Insects that should be singing September songs stay silent, as if they know what lives in these waters now, what uses the swamp as a highway between the possible and the shouldn't-be-possible.

His hand has swollen into something unrecognizable, fingers stuck in positions that aren't quite fist or flex, the knuckles disappeared entirely under fluid that his body's pumped there in misguided attempts at healing. The split skin weeps in the moonlight.

Mira appears without sound, the way she always does, as if she exists partially outside the normal rules of footsteps and approached. One moment Vincent is alone with his pain and the moon, the next she's there, a shadow that's darker than the shadows around it, moving with the fluid certainty of someone who belongs to the night more than the day. She doesn't announce herself, doesn't ask permission, just exists in his peripheral vision until existing becomes approaching, approaching becomes arriving, arriving becomes kneeling beside him on the soft bank.

Her dress is different tonight, not her usual black but something that might be dark blue or might be purple or might be all colors at once in the strange light accented tonight with a chartreuse scarf. The fabric whispers against itself as she settles next to him, a sound like secrets being shared in a language only cloth understands. She smells of the dentist office, that particular mixture of bubblegum fluoride and disinfectant that should be repellent but on her becomes something else, becomes the honest scent of someone who doesn't pretend pain doesn't exist.

She doesn't speak, doesn't ask what happened to his hand though she must see the damage even in this unreliable light. Instead, she reaches for his wrist with movements so gentle they feel like apology for all the violence the world has done to both of them. Her fingers are cool against his fevered skin, and she lifts his hand with the care someone might use with ancient documents or newborn things, both irreplaceable in their own ways.

From somewhere in her dress, she produces a strip of material. It might be torn from her skirt's hem, though he doesn't see where the fabric is missing. The strip is long and soft and carries her warmth despite the night's chill. She begins wrapping his knuckles with movements that speak of practice, of other wounds tended in darkness, of a lifetime spent learning how to bind what's broken.

The fabric winds around his swollen flesh with pressure that's firm but not painful, containing the swelling without constricting, supporting without imprisoning. Each wrap brings her closer to him, her concentration absolute, her breathing falling into rhythm with his without either of them planning it. Vincent watches her face in the unstable moonlight, the careful line of her jaw, the way her eyes focus completely on this task of caring, the slight parting of her lips that makes him realize she's been biting them, a gesture of concentration or concern or both.

Their breathing synchronizes completely, in and out in perfect unison, as if they're sharing the same lungs, the same air, the same moment suspended outside of time. Her fingers tie the final knot with movements that are both practical and ritual, sealing his wound with fabric and intention. When she finishes, her hands don't leave his. They rest there, her fingers over his wrapped knuckles, skin touching skin where the bandage doesn't cover, and the contrast between her coolness and his heat creates a sensation that has nothing to do with temperature.

She looks up, and their faces are closer than Vincent realized, close enough that he can see the moon reflected in her eyes but broken into different patterns than on the water, as if her eyes show a different moon, a different night, a different version of this moment. Her breath touches his face, carrying that peculiar scent mixed with something else, something that's just her, just Mira, unique and irreplaceable and suddenly necessary.

Tears catch in her lashes, not falling but gathering, creating prisms that scatter the moonlight into colors that shouldn't exist. Vincent doesn't know if she's crying for Carl, for Bailey, for CJ, for all of Duswood, or for something else entirely, something that exists in this moment between them where comfort and grief and desire collapse into a single point of contact.

He leans in, or she does, or they both do, the distance between them collapsing like it was always meant to, like this moment has been waiting in the swamp's patient darkness for them to arrive at it. Their lips meet with none of the softness poetry promises. The kiss is brief and jagged, like broken glass trying to fit together, tasting of salt from her tears or his, tasting of sorrow that's been aged in silence, tasting of something that might be love but feels more like shared damage, like recognition between two people who've seen too much to ever be innocent again.

The kiss lasts seconds that feel like hours that feel like no time at all. It's desperate and gentle, violent and careful, everything and nothing, a contradiction that makes perfect sense in this place where contradictions are the only truth. Vincent tastes copper and realizes he's bitten his own lip, or she has, or they've bitten each other's, blood mixing with tears mixing with the night air that suddenly feels too thick to breathe.

They pull apart with the mutual understanding that more would break something that's already too fragile, that this kiss exists in its own space and trying to extend it would diminish it. Their foreheads rest together for a moment, breathing shared air, existing in that space between together and separate that has no name but doesn't need one.

Then the swamp responds.

The sound comes from deep in the reeds, deeper than the water should go, a hollow grinding like stone against stone, like the slow, deliberate turning of a massive gear, like the earth itself clearing its throat. The water that had been still begins to ripple without wind, concentric circles spreading from multiple points as if something vast and many-bodied is moving just below the surface. The insects that had been silent suddenly scream in unison, a frequency that makes Vincent's teeth ache, then cut off entirely as if something has commanded silence and been obeyed.

The moonlight on the water shifts, and for a moment Vincent swears he sees a face in the reflection. A face that's patient and hungry and aware. The image breaks apart as the ripples increase, but the sensation of being observed remains, stronger now, as if their kiss has announced something to the swamp, as if their moment of human connection has registered in whatever consciousness inhabits these waters.

Mira's hand tightens on his, the wrapped knuckles protesting but Vincent doesn't care. They sit together at the swamp's edge, two delicate and vulnerable warm bodies against the vast cold patience of something that's noticed them now, really noticed them, in a way that suggests consequences neither of them can imagine.

The alley behind Cedar Lagoon Pizzeria holds different shadows at midnight, corners that were empty in daylight now occupied by suggestions of movement that might be wind-shifted garbage or might be something else entirely, and Vincent waits in the place where he first saw Muldrath up close, where stone fingers reached through reality like it was tissue paper. The single streetlamp flickers with electrical uncertainty, its bulb cycling through degrees of brightness that make the shadows breathe, expand and contract like something with lungs made of darkness. The dumpster squats against the far wall, lid sealed now with a padlock that gleams too new, too deliberate, Joe's response to things that shouldn't fit through metal gaps but somehow do.

Mira arrives first, materializing from the deeper black between buildings with her usual silence, and Vincent feels the ghost of their kiss at the swamp's edge, tastes copper and tears and something that might have been hope. She doesn't acknowledge what happened between them, just takes her position against the brick wall where the shadows are thickest, her dark dress making her almost invisible except for the electric orange laces in her boots. Jayce follows minutes later, his nervous energy translated into quick, jerky movements, fingers drumming, his way of processing a world that's revealed itself as fundamentally wrong.

Rene hadn't come. She'd texted them hours ago, saying she couldn't handle another night chasing shadows, not after the dreams she'd been having. Vincent kept checking his phone, half-hoping she'd change her mind, but the screen stayed dark.

Jennifer's heels announce her before she appears, that deliberate click against asphalt that sounds like punctuation, like someone typing out accusations one footstep at a time. She emerges from around the corner carrying a manila folder that looks older than she is, water-stained and soft at the edges from handling, from being hidden and retrieved and hidden again. The streetlamp catches her blonde curls, turns them briefly gold before flickering again, making them shift. She doesn't greet them, doesn't waste words on pleasantries that would feel obscene given what they're gathered to discuss.

She opens the folder against the dumpster's side, using its flat surface as a makeshift table, and Vincent sees her fingers shake slightly as she spreads out the contents. Photographs first, grainy and overexposed, showing a man whose face is all angles and shadows, cheekbones that catch light like blades, eyes that even in still images seem to be looking through the camera at something beyond. The photos are dated on the back in fading blue ink: 1994, 1995, 1996, then nothing, as if the subject ceased to exist or ceased to be photographable.

"Silas Rourke," Jennifer says, though they all know the name by now. She pulls out another set of papers, rental receipts from various years, all signed with a different name. "But look at the signature on these. Auri Loskers."

Vincent stares at the name, his mind working through the

letters, and Jennifer saves him the effort. "It's an anagram. Silas Rourke, Auri Loskers. Same letters, different arrangement. But I can't tell which came first, which is the real name and which is the mask."

The receipts all list the same address, a cabin somewhere beyond town limits, deep in the woods where cell service dies and the roads turn from asphalt to dirt to suggestion. Jennifer produces her car keys with the efficiency of someone who's already made the decision for all of them. "We're going. Now. Before someone notices we're looking."

The drive unfolds in near silence, Jennifer's white sports car inappropriate for the increasingly rough road but she doesn't slow down, taking turns with confidence that might be skill or might be desperation dressed as competence. Vincent sits in the back with Mira, their thighs touching when Jennifer takes corners too fast, and each contact feels like a confession neither of them is ready to make. Jayce rides shotgun, his fingers drumming against the door handle, the sound barely audible over the engine but present.

Cedar trees close in on both sides as they leave Duswood proper, their branches reaching across the road in places, scraping against the car's roof with sounds like fingernails on metal. The headlights carve a tunnel through darkness so complete it feels solid, like they're driving through the earth itself rather than over it. The smell of swamp water seeps through the car's ventilation system, that particular mixture of rot and growth that defines the borderlands between town and wilderness.

The cabin appears in the headlights like something that's been waiting, small and crooked, its wooden walls gray with age and weather. No lights in the windows, no car in the overgrown driveway, no signs of life except for the fact that the structure still stands when it should have collapsed years ago. Jennifer cuts the engine, and the silence that rushes in feels violent, like pressure against eardrums, the absence of mechanical sound making space for other suggestions of sounds.

The lock on the front door is old, rusted, more symbol than security. Jayce produces a tire iron from Jennifer's trunk, and the lock breaks with little resistance as if they're expected. The door swings inward on hinges that don't creak, recently oiled, maintained by someone who comes here enough to care about silent entry.

Inside, the air tastes of cold stone and old smoke, candles burned down to nubs scattered across every surface in clusters that suggest ritual rather than illumination. The windows are clouded with grime from the inside, as if someone drew patterns in the condensation that dried and never cleared. Vincent's adjusted eyes pick out details in the darkness: ropes hanging from exposed beams, their ends frayed from use; metal cuffs attached to the wall at heights that make him not want to think about who wore them or why; a table against the far wall laid out with tools that glint dully in the moonlight filtering through dirty glass.

The tools are arranged with the precision of a surgeon's kit, each in its designated place, some showing rust that might be from moisture or might be from other liquids that rust metal. A hammer with suspicious stains on its head. Pliers with something caught between the grips that looks like fabric or might be something else. Blades of various sizes, all sharp despite the cabin's apparent abandonment, as if someone maintains them, keeps them ready.

But it's the floor that draws Vincent's attention, makes him stop breathing for a moment. Carved directly into the wooden boards is a map of Duswood, not drawn but gouged deep, each street and landmark rendered in three dimensions through depth of cut. The elementary school, the high school, the pizzeria, all marked with X's that have been carved so deep they go through to whatever lies beneath. And at the center, where the cedar swamp spreads like a cancer through the town's geography, a name has been burned into the wood with something hot enough to char: MULDRATH.

Mira kneels beside a leather journal left open on a makeshift altar of stacked books, all of them about folklore, about grief, about the physics of suffering. Her fingers hover over the pages without touching, as if the words themselves might be contaminated. When she speaks, her voice comes out whisper-soft but carries in the still air: "The one who sings in stone."

She reads more, fragments that Vincent catches: "serves the deeper will," and "stone is the medium," and "the true master speaks through accumulated loss." She closes the journal with careful movements, as if sealing something that should stay sealed. "If this is Rourke's, he's not in control. He never was. He's serving someone else, something else."

Vincent looks at the map again, at Muldrath's name burned into the swamp's heart, and understands with cold certainty that everything they've experienced, every horror and loss, has been orchestrated not by Rourke but through him, that he's as much a tool as Muldrath, both of them serving something that lives in the space between grief and rage and lies, something that feeds on Duswood's refusal to mourn properly.

A sense of urgency falls upon them and they leave quickly, movements synchronized by shared haste that needs no words, each of them backing away from the carved map. Vincent is last out the door, and he watches the broken lock swing on its hasp, pendulum-like, marking time that feels borrowed, stolen from some future reckoning they've just accelerated by their trespass. The door hangs open behind them, and Vincent knows they should close it, should try to hide evidence of their intrusion, but touching anything in that cabin again feels like accepting an invitation to something they're not prepared to attend.

Jennifer's car starts with a roar that seems too loud in the forest's accusatory silence, headlights sweeping across the cabin's face like a searchlight catching someone guilty. The tires spray gravel as she reverses, too fast, and Jayce's hand shoots out to grip the dashboard, his knuckles white in the dashboard's dim illumination. They're all breathing too quickly, shallow gasps that fog the windows despite the night's warmth, and Jennifer has to crack her window to clear the windshield enough to see the narrow road ahead.

The dirt road unspools beneath them, each pothole and root sending shocks through the car's suspension that feel like the earth itself protesting their escape. Vincent sits in the back, Mira beside him, and in the darkness he can see her profile outlined by passing trees, her jaw set in a way that suggests she's holding words behind her teeth. The journal's phrases echo in his mind—"the one who sings in stone".

"Your father," Vincent says, the words escaping before wisdom can stop them. "Does he know about Rourke? About what's happening?"

Mira turns to look out the window, her reflection in the glass superimposed over the passing forest, creating a double image that makes her look like she exists in two places at once. "My father knows how to make rotting things pristine," she says, and her voice carries a finality that closes the subject more effectively than silence would have.

The dirt road meets asphalt with a transition that feels like surfacing from deep water, the smooth pavement allowing Jennifer to accelerate, putting distance between them and the cabin that already feels like something they might have dreamed except for the dirt under their fingernails, the smell of old smoke in their clothes. The cedars thin, give way to the ordinary trees that border Duswood, oaks and maples that don't carry the same weight of the swamp.

Through the windshield, past the reach of the headlights, Vincent notes something with the horizon. Where the night sky should be uniform darkness punctuated by stars, there's a smear of orange, faint at first, like light pollution from a city that doesn't exist in that direction. The color pulses, brightens and dims with a rhythm that might be atmospheric distortion or might be something more immediate, more terrible.

Jennifer notices it too, her foot pressing harder on the accelerator, the engine's pitch climbing as they race toward town. The orange smear grows, spreads across more of the horizon, and now Vincent can see smoke, black against the orange glow, rising in columns that the wind tears apart and reforms, tears apart and reforms, like the sky itself is coming undone.

Sirens rise in the distance, that electronic wail that always means someone's world is ending, but multiplied, overlapping, a symphony of emergency that suggests whatever's happening is beyond the scope of normal disaster. The sound grows louder as they approach town, and with it comes the smell, seeping through the car's ventilation despite Jennifer frantically pressing buttons to recirculate the air. It's the smell of burning tar and plastic and something chemical that makes Vincent's eyes water.

They crest the hill that overlooks Duswood's modest downtown, and the source of the orange glow reveals itself with a clarity that makes Jennifer slow down considerably. Below them, Duswood High School is burning. Not a small fire, not a contained incident, but a conflagration that has engulfed the entire main building, flames shooting through the roof in geysers of superheated destruction, windows exploding outward in showers of glass that catch the firelight like falling stars.

Jennifer drives down the hill with the careful speed of someone approaching a car accident, drawn by horrible fascination but aware that getting too close means becoming part of the disaster. The school's parking lot is chaos organized into sections with fire trucks arranged in a semicircle, their hoses trained on the building but looking pathetically inadequate against the scale of the blaze. Police cars creating a perimeter that keeps the growing crowd at what someone has determined is a safe distance.

The crowd itself glows in the alternating light of fire and emergency strobes, faces painted orange and blue and orange again, expressions ranging from shock to fascination to something that might be satisfaction, as if some part of Duswood always wanted to see the high school burn, wanted to see something in their carefully maintained town finally, violently, refuse to be ignored.

The heat reaches them even from the parking lot's edge, a physical pressure that makes Vincent's skin tighten, makes his wrapped hand throb. The air tastes of melting tar from the roof, scorched wood from the building's old bones showing through modern additions.

Somewhere in the building's dying structure, glass shatters with a sound like a scream cut short, sharp and final, and the crowd flinches collectively, stepping back though they're already beyond the range of flying debris. A section of roof collapses, sending a column of sparks into the night sky where they rise and die like wishes that were never going to come true anyway.

Vincent thinks of the map carved into the cabin's floor, the high school marked with an X carved so deep it went through to whatever lurked beneath. He thinks of Muldrath's name burned into the swamp's heart, of Rourke serving something that speaks through accumulated loss. The fire isn't random, isn't accident, isn't even arson in the conventional sense. It's communication, a message written in destruction that says the patient waiting is over, that whatever's been orchestrating Duswood's slow dissolution has decided on acceleration.

The fire continues its consumption, and Vincent stands with the others in the parking lot's pulsing light, watching their high school transform from institution to memory, from place to absence, another loss for Duswood to swallow or choke on. The carved map burns behind his eyes, and he knows with cold certainty that this is just one X among many, that the night is far from over, that somewhere in the cedar swamp something watches through hollow eyes and measures the town's capacity for grief, finding it infinite.

CHAPTER
FIFTEEN

The windows of Duswood High explode outward in sequence, each detonation sending fresh oxygen to feed the hungry flames and Vincent feels the heat pulse against his face even from across the parking lot where the crowd presses backward like a single organism recoiling from pain. His wrapped hand throbs in rhythm with the fire's breathing, each surge of flame sending sympathetic spikes through his damaged knuckles as if his body recognizes kinship with destruction, with things breaking beyond repair.

The firefighters advance and retreat in a competition with physics they're losing, their hoses creating steam that rises white against black smoke. One firefighter gestures frantically toward the basement, shouting something lost in the roar, and Vincent understands without hearing that this is where the fire lives deepest, where it started or where it wants to finish.

The counseling offices blazing down there, where students sat in uncomfortable chairs and tried to explain their damage to adults who took notes in triplicate. The grief assessment files the school started keeping after too many students disappeared or died or simply stopped showing up, careful documentation of a town's unraveling.

A commotion near the main entrance draws everyone's attention, firefighters emerging with something that makes the crowd's murmur die instantly. A stretcher carries a form beneath a white sheet that's already graying from ash fall, the shape beneath too still, too small, too definitively ended. The school nurse, Vincent realizes as whispered identification ripples through the crowd.

"What was she doing here so late?" someone asks and the question hangs unanswered. She wasn't supposed to be here. Vincent watches the stretcher disappear into the ambulance, watches the vehicle pull away without sirens because sirens are for the living.

Ash begins falling with the deliberateness of snow, each flake a fragment of something that mattered once, student records and attendance sheets and all the careful documentation of education transformed into gray poetry that settles on hair and shoulders and upturned faces. The ash carries weight beyond its physical presence, memories made manifest, and Vincent tastes it on his tongue when he breathes, bitter with the flavor of melted plastic from overhead projectors and computer monitors.

The smoke shifts, and suddenly Vincent can see the crowd more clearly, faces illuminated by firelight that makes everyone look guilty or accused or both. Jennifer stands near her car, phone pressed to her ear. Jayce hovers at the crowd's edge, his fingers drumming against his thigh in patterns that match the fire's chaotic rhythm. But Mira...Vincent turns, scanning, his chest tightening with each face that isn't hers.

She was here. Right beside him when they arrived, her breath catching at the sight of flames consuming the place where they'd mapped Muldrath's pattern just days ago. But now the space she occupied holds only smoke and strangers, absence where presence should be, and Vincent's wrapped hand clenches despite the pain, fingernails digging into gauze as panic begins its slow bloom in his chest.

He moves through the crowd, careful at first, maintaining the polite spacing of someone who doesn't want to cause alarm. "Have you seen Mira Thorn?" he asks a woman whose son graduated last year, whose face carries the permanent worry lines of parenthood. She shakes her head without looking at him, eyes locked on the fire like looking away might make it worse. He asks others, his voice rising slightly with each negative response, each blank stare, each person who can't or won't acknowledge Mira.

The crowd has formed its own menagerie of shock, clusters of people bound by shared loss or shared relief that it wasn't their house, their child, their carefully maintained fiction burning. The PTA president weeps openly, though Vincent suspects it's less about the building and more about what the building represented, order and routine and the promise that education could save Duswood's children from its fate.

Near the tennis courts, a group of older residents stand in a tight circle, their voices low but carrying in the way that secrets do when they're finally being shared. Vincent catches fragments as he passes, searching for Mira's dark dress in the orange-lit chaos. "Just like sixty-three," one says. "The elementary school then." Another nods, remembering or pretending to remember, constructing connections that might be pattern or might be the human need to make sense of senseless things.

But Mira isn't among them, isn't anywhere in the crowd that continues to grow as more of Duswood arrives to witness this unignorable event. Vincent's search becomes more frantic, pushing between groups without excuse or apology, his injured hand forgotten in the urgency of finding her. The smoke grows thicker, or maybe it's his vision narrowing with panic.

He reaches the parking lot's edge where the crowd thins, where the heat is less intense but the darkness beyond the fire's light is absolute. This is where someone might stand to watch without being watched, to observe the culmination of plans that started with dead dogs and disappeared boys and stone creatures that serve darker purposes. But Mira isn't here either, and Vincent stands at the boundary between light and dark, between the known horror of the burning school and the unknown horror of her absence.

Vincent's voice cracks on Mira's name as he moves away from the fire's gravitational pull, each call swallowed by streets that seem to absorb sound rather than echo it, and his wrapped hand pulses with fresh pain as he breaks into a jog past the first police barrier. The officer stationed there barely glances at him, attention fixed on the column of smoke that rises into the night sky, and Vincent slips past into streets that feel evacuated, abandoned, as if the fire has drawn all of Duswood's life to witness its consumption.

"Mira!" The name tears from his throat, raw with desperation that surprises him with its intensity. When did she become essential? When did her presence shift from intriguing to necessary? The questions dissolve as quickly as they form because this isn't about understanding.

Oak Street stretches before him, windows dark except for the occasional flicker of television screens where residents watch their high school burn from the safety of living rooms, experiencing disaster as media rather than reality. Vincent pounds on the Hendersons' door, the Walkers', anyone who might have seen her pass, but doors remain closed, the sound of his fist against wood creating rhythms that die without response.

His hand throbs with each impact, the makeshift bandage Mira wrapped growing damp with what might be blood or sweat or both. The pain anchors him, keeps him from dissolving entirely into panic, each pulse a reminder that he's still physical, still capable of action even as his mind races through possibilities each worse than the last. She walked into the fire. She was taken like CJ. She saw something in the flames that called to her the way the phone's static called to Rene.

A cluster of teenagers stands at the intersection of Oak and Third, having been turned away from getting closer to the fire by police expansion of the perimeter. They watch Vincent approach with the casual interest of those for whom disaster is still entertainment, their faces lit by phone screens as they document and share the night's devastation. "Have you seen Mira Thorn?" Vincent asks, and watches recognition flicker across their features.

"That eerie goth girl?" one says, and the casual cruelty of the nickname makes Vincent's good hand clench. "Nah, haven't seen her." But there's something in the way he says it, a glance exchanged with his friends, that suggests they have seen her or heard something or know something they're choosing not to share. Vincent doesn't have time to excavate their secrets, moves past them toward Kipling Avenue where the streetlights flicker in patterns that might be electrical problems or might be response to energies that shouldn't exist.

The town feels too quiet beneath the distant wail of sirens, as if the fire has created a vacuum that silence rushes to fill. Vincent's footsteps echo off buildings that seem to stay away. Each darkened doorway could hide her, could hide something worse, could hide nothing at all which is somehow the most frightening possibility because it means she's gone beyond the simple gridwork of streets and buildings into wherever Duswood's disappeared go.

He turns onto Monroe Street, and the smell hits him with unexpected force. Not just smoke from the fire but something else, organic and waste, like the swamp has exhaled and its breath has traveled inland to mark territory it shouldn't claim. Vincent's steps slow as recognition builds in his chest, not thought but instinct, the same pull that drew them to map the spiral, that led them to the cabin, that keeps leading them back to the cedar swamp where everything curves inward toward some terrible center.

She's going to the swamp. He knows this with certainty that bypasses logic, knows it the way he knew to kiss her beside those dark waters, knows it the way his wrapped knuckles know the shape of violence, knows it the way Duswood knows to forget what it can't bear to remember. The knowing transforms his jog into a run despite his body's protests, despite the way his vision blurs at the edges from exertion and fear and smoke inhalation that makes each breath taste of endings.

The fire's glow reflects in puddles, water that's seeped up from somewhere below to mirror disaster back at itself. Vincent's feet splash through them, each impact sending droplets onto his jeans. The reflected fire makes the water look like windows into some underground conflagration, as if the school's burning has awakened something beneath Duswood that burns in parallel, in sympathy, in celebration.

More sirens join the symphony, and Vincent realizes the fire must be spreading, jumping to nearby buildings or finding new fuel in places that were dormant just hours ago, tonight Duswood's carefully maintained barriers between normal and nightmare are dissolving like sugar in rain. His wrapped hand has gone mostly numb, nerve endings over-whelmed by sustained damage and movement, and he cradles it against his chest as he runs, protecting it from further harm though harm seems to be the only currency that matters anymore.

The houses thin as he approaches the town's edge, lawns growing wilder, fences falling into disrepair that speaks of residents who've given up maintaining barriers. The smoke smell clings to his clothes, his hair, mixing with the earthy dampness that signals proximity to the cedar swamp, creating an olfactory map of his journey from one disaster toward what might be another.

His breath comes in gasps that hurt his chest, lungs protesting the combination of smoke and exertion, but he doesn't slow because slowing means arriving too late, means finding Mira gone or changed or worse, means failing to prevent whatever draws her toward waters that reflect nothing truly, that show faces that aren't there and swallow those who look too long. The tree line appears ahead, cedars rising like walls of shadow against the fire-lit sky, and Vincent pushes harder, following the pull that might be intuition or might be infection, might be love or might be the same force that makes insects spiral.

Two figures stand at the swamp's edge where the cedars part like curtains, and Vincent's relief at seeing Mira's familiar silhouette dissolves into confusion as he recognizes the taller shape beside her, Elias Thorn's pressed black suit incongruous against the wild darkness. The orange glow from the distant fire paints their faces in shades of emergency, and Vincent sees Elias's hand wrapped around Mira's upper arm, not violent but firm.

Elias pulls backward, away from the water that stretches black and still beyond them, and Mira resists with the passive weight of someone not quite present, her body here but her attention somewhere else, deeper, older, listening to frequencies that Vincent can almost hear in the space between heartbeats. Her father's usually composed face shows cracks Vincent has never seen before, sweat beading on his forehead despite the cool night, his free hand clutching something at his chest that catches firelight in brief silver flashes.

The ground beneath Vincent's feet shifts from solid to soft as he approaches, that transition zone where earth becomes uncertain, where the swamp begins its slow claim on everything that ventures too close. Dead leaves compress under his steps with sounds like whispered warnings, and the air grows thicker, weighted with moisture that carries the taste of decay and something unknown.

Elias notices him first, head turning with the mechanical precision of someone who's been watching for threats, expecting them, preparing responses to wild scenarios. His eyes widen slightly at Vincent's appearance, not surprise exactly but something like relief mixed with fresh worry, as if Vincent's presence solves one problem while creating another.

"She was walking toward the water," Elias says, his voice maintaining its clinical tone but frayed at the edges, words precise but delivered with an exhaustion that speaks of repeated effort, sustained vigilance. "I found her halfway across the Hendersons' yard, moving like she was asleep but her eyes were open, seeing something out of nothing."

Mira stands rigid in her father's grip, her dark dress absorbing the fire's distant light rather than reflecting it, making her seem less solid, more shadow than substance. Her face carries that particular stillness Vincent recognizes from the art room when she first spoke Muldrath's name, when she read from Rourke's journal, when she knows things that knowing itself is dangerous. But now there's something else in her expression, an absence where presence should be, as if part of her has already gone ahead into the swamp and what remains is just waiting for the body to follow.

"Mira?" Vincent says her name softly, the way you'd speak to someone balanced on a high ledge, afraid that too much volume might tip them over. She doesn't respond, doesn't even blink, her gaze fixed on something in the middle distance that might be the water's surface or might be something beyond it, through it.

Vincent steps closer, careful to move slowly, his good hand extended but not touching, not yet, remembering their kiss beside these same waters and how it seemed to wake something that had been contentedly sleeping. The smoke smell from his clothes mingles with the swamp's organic rot, creating new combinations that shouldn't exist, and he notices Mira's nostrils flare slightly, processing the scent, using it maybe to navigate back from wherever her consciousness has wandered.

"I've been watching her," Elias says, and the admission seems to cost him something, professional composure crumbling to reveal a father's raw fear. "Since the pizzeria attack. Since she started drawing those things, knowing those things. I've been following her at night when she walks, making sure she doesn't..." He stops, swallows, tries again. "Making sure nothing takes her. That Rourke doesn't come for her."

"The fire," Vincent says, understanding arriving not in pieces but all at once, the way terrible truths often do. "It wasn't random."

"No." Elias's voice drops to barely above a whisper, as if the cedars themselves might be listening. "It was meant to destroy records. Files that go back decades. Documentation of unexplained deaths, disappearances, incidences that got explained away. The school board mandated grief counseling after ninety-six, required detailed notes on every student who showed signs of trauma. Those files, they showed patterns. They showed connections."

Wind moves through the cedars with sounds like breathing, like something vast inhaling the smoke-tinged air and finding it satisfactory. Mira shifts slightly in her father's grip, not toward the water this time but toward Vincent, a motion so small it might be imagination except Vincent feels it in his chest, that pull between them that existed before the kiss but has intensified since, become something that transcends simple attraction and enters territories that don't have names.

"They connected everything to the ritual," Elias continues, his words coming faster now as if confession has its own momentum. "The ritual that recreated Muldrath. The binding of grief into form. The attempt to transform Duswood's accumulated sorrow into something useful." His laugh comes out broken, bitter. "Useful. As if grief could be harnessed like electricity. As if loss could power anything except more loss."

Vincent watches the man's carefully maintained facade continue its dissolution, watches him become not the clinical doctor who performs painful procedures with professional detachment but a father, a resident of Duswood, someone who's been carrying terrible knowledge alone for too long. The firelight flickers across his face, creating shadows that age him decades in seconds, then release him back to his actual years, then age him again in cycles that match Vincent's racing heartbeat.

"And you know this because?" Vincent asks, though he already suspects the answer, can see it in the way Elias holds his daughter, protective and guilty in equal measure, can see it in the way he clutches the medal like it might grant retroactive absolution.

"Because I'm part of that history," Elias says, and Mira's eyes suddenly focus, snapping from distant to present with violence that makes both men step back. She turns to look at her father, and Vincent sees recognition there but also something else, puzzle pieces clicking into place with sounds like breaking bones, connections that rewrite her understanding of her father, her own place in Duswood's careful architecture of denial.

"You helped him," she says, not a question but a statement delivered with the certainty of someone who's always known but only now allows herself to know. "You helped Rourke complete the ritual."

Elias's grip on her arm loosens but doesn't release, as if letting go would mean losing her entirely. "I was just a kid then. Your age really. Felt like I was a part of something important. I prepared the site," he says, and his voice has gone clinical again, retreating into professional terminology because emotion would destroy him. "The site that would summon what he was trying to bind. I thought... we thought we were helping. Thought we were giving Duswood's grief purpose, direction, containment."

The distant fire roars with fresh fuel, maybe reaching the chemistry lab or the old oil tank that everyone knew should have been replaced years ago, and the sound carries across the distance like screaming, like the school itself is voicing the pain of being consumed. Vincent thinks of all those records turning to ash, all that careful documentation of trauma being erased, and understands that someone wanted those connections gone, wanted the evidence of the ritual's consequences destroyed before more people started asking the questions Jennifer was asking, started following the spiral to its terrible center.

"But you can't contain grief," Elias continues, his words directed at Mira but meant for himself. "You can only transform it. And transformation requires sacrifice. Requires loss. Requires someone to pay the price for everyone else's refusal to mourn."

Mira pulls against his grip now, not toward the swamp but toward Vincent, and Elias releases her with the reluctance of someone who knows that holding on has become another form of damage. She moves to Vincent's side, not touching but close enough that he feels her presence like static electricity, like the air before lightning strikes.

CHAPTER
SIXTEEN

Dawn arrives through Vincent's bedroom blinds in strips of gray that feel less like illumination and more like the night's reluctant retreat, each slat creating a bar of dim light across Mira's sleeping form on the futon across the room. The futon used to be his dad's that was hauled home from a college apartment years before Vincent was around and understood what "temporary" meant. Sometimes, when the house is quiet, Vincent almost expects to hear his father's laugh in the creak of its frame.

She sleeps with one arm tucked beneath her head, the other extended toward the floor where her fingers curl slightly. Her dark dress from yesterday spreads around her like spilled ink, wrinkled now from being worn too long, from running through smoke and swamp moisture, from her father's grip when he held her back from something sinister.

Vincent's thoughts bounce from one incident to the next, a metronome of damage that kept him awake most of the night, watching the ceiling, watching Mira breathe, watching the slow progression of darkness toward this uncertain dawn. The makeshift bandage she wrapped his hand with has darkened with dried blood and the particular grime that comes from touching too many surfaces. His knuckles feel swollen beneath the fabric, joints locked in positions that aren't quite fist or flex.

The room holds them in morning stillness that feels borrowed, temporary, like when you know something's coming but not exactly when it will arrive. Vincent's desk still displays homework that belongs to a different lifetime, when his biggest concern was calculus derivatives instead of derivatives of grief made manifest in stone and patient malevolence. His closet door hangs slightly open, revealing clothes that seem costume-like now, remnants of a boy who didn't know about Muldrath, about Rourke, about rituals that transform sorrow into something that walks and watches and waits.

Mira shifts in her sleep, a small sound escaping that might be distress or might be nothing, just the noise bodies make when consciousness loosens its grip. The movement causes her blanket to slip, revealing her shoulder, the pale curve of her neck, the vulnerability that sleep brings to even those who wear their waking hours like armor. Vincent rises from his bed with movements calculated for silence, his bare feet finding the spots on his floor that don't creak, muscle memory from years of late-night navigation when his parents still shared a house if not a marriage.

He kneels beside the futon, his good hand reaching for the blanket's edge. The fabric is thin, worn soft by too many washings, carrying the faint scent of his mother's detergent mixed with smoke from the fire that still clings to everything, everyone, marking them as witnesses to Duswood High's transformation from institution to ash. He pulls the blanket up carefully, covering Mira's exposed shoulder, the gesture feeling both intimate and necessary.

Her eyes open without transition, no slow flutter or gradual focus, just sudden complete awareness that makes Vincent's hand freeze mid-adjustment of the blanket. She doesn't startle, doesn't question why he's kneeling beside her, just looks at him with eyes that hold too much understanding for someone who just left sleep behind. The morning light catches in her dark irises, creating depths that seem to go further than anatomy should allow.

"Let's go," she says, not a question but acknowledgment of what they both know must happen today. Her voice carries the particular roughness of sleep mixed with something else, maybe determination to extract truths from a father who's been performing his own kind of burial for years.

Vincent nods, stands, offers his good hand which she takes without hesitation. Her grip is firm despite the early hour, despite everything, and he pulls her to sitting, then standing, the blanket falling away to pool on the futon like shed skin. They move through the morning routine with the efficiency of people who've learned that some days don't deserve ceremony. Vincent pulls on jeans that still smell of smoke, a shirt that's clean enough but wrinkled. Mira attempts to smooth her dress, gives up, accepts that today isn't about appearances but about excavation, about digging up what's been buried in the Thorn family's careful preservation.

They descend the stairs in synchronized quiet, each step placed to minimize sound though Vincent's mother's deep sleep could probably survive anything short of another explosion. The house feels hollow around them, not empty but drained, as if last night's revelations have extracted something essential from the walls themselves. Through the kitchen window, Duswood spreads in morning gray, the smoke from the still-smoldering school creating a haze that makes everything look like memory, like something already fading even as it happens.

Vincent opens the front door and they step into air that tastes of ash and morning dew. The sky presses down in uniform gray, no variation in the overcast that might suggest weather patterns or time of day, just consistent pressure that makes Vincent's tired eyes throb with barometric sensitivity.

They walk without touching but close enough that their movements create a shared rhythm, footsteps falling into sync without conscious thought. The streets stretch empty except for the occasional car passing slow, drivers craning necks to see the smoke column that still rises from where the high school used to be, that vertical monument to destruction that won't dissipate no matter how much wind tries to scatter it.

"We need to be direct," Mira says, her voice low but carrying in the morning quiet. "No more Lindy Hopping around truths. No more clinical deflection." Her hands clench and unclench at her sides, the only sign of the storm building inside her carefully controlled exterior. "I need to know exactly what happened. What he let happen."

Vincent wants to reach for her hand but doesn't, understanding that comfort right now might crack something she needs to keep solid until after they've confronted Elias. Instead, he matches her pace, her intensity, her determination to finally excavate the complete truth from a man who's made a profession of veneered exteriors.

"We ask about the ritual first," Vincent says. "The specific mechanics of it. What Rourke needed, what your father provided." The words feel too cold for the horror they're discussing, but cold might be what's needed, clinical distance to match Elias's own defensive strategies.

Mira's breath catches, and Vincent sees her jaw tighten, muscles standing out beneath skin that's gone pale with more than just morning's weak light. Mira's home rises before them, windows that seem to watch their approach.

The workshop sits behind the main building, a converted carriage house that Elias transformed into his private space, where the real work happens before patients see the polished front room, where discomfort is eased and small damages are quietly repaired. Vincent can see light through the windows, bright and steady, Elias already at work despite the early hour.

Mira stops at the workshop's door, her hand raised to knock but frozen in that position, caught between determination and dread. Vincent sees the tremor in her fingers, the way her breathing has gone shallow, quick, the physical manifestation of a daughter preparing to uncover her father's sins. He doesn't touch her, doesn't speak, just stands witness to this moment before everything changes again.

She knocks, three quick times that break the morning's quiet, and they wait for Elias to answer, to let them into his realm of clinical order where they'll dissect the past in their own way, laying open old choices and sacrifices, examining how love failed to prevent loss but might still be enough to stop more.

The door swings open smoothly, and Vincent follows Mira into air that smells sharply of antiseptic and mint, clean to the point of sterility. Relentless LED lights strikes polished countertops and spotless glass cabinets stocked with neatly organized dental tools, every surface gleaming as if wiped down just moments before. The scent of clove oil lingers beneath it all, layered with the faint sweetness of patient toothpaste samples and the sterile tang of disinfectant. Along the walls, metal trays and sealed packs of instruments sit in perfect order, a testament to Elias's relentless precision and the quiet ritual of keeping pain at bay.

Elias stands at the central table, his back to them, shoulders set in rigid lines. He wears a clean blue suit as if maintaining appearance might maintain control. His hands move across something Vincent can't see, methodical motions that could be work or could be distraction, the practiced movements of someone who needs to keep their hands busy to keep their mind from unraveling.

When he turns, his face holds the same professional composure it always does, that dentist's mask of calm and carefully neutral reassurance, offering comfort without giving anything away. His hands leave the counter, his fingers curling and uncurling as if searching for something akin to control, or maybe forgiveness, maybe just the right words to keep the truth where he thinks it should stay.

Elias's jaw works as if testing words before releasing them, his professional mask sliding back into place with effort. "You know I helped Rourke. That was a long time ago. It was dumb and so foolish."

Mira stands in the doorway, her voice trembling but sharp. "What else? What haven't you said, dad?"

Elias looks away, jaw tight. "Mira…"

"How did she die?" Mira's question cuts through his attempted deflection with the precision of one of his own drills, sharp enough to draw blood without immediately showing the wound.

Elias's stare lingers on Mira as if he's about to reveal something, but not quite. "Cardiac arrest," he says, the medical terminology falling from his lips with practiced ease. "The official cause was sudden cardiac death, likely from an undiagnosed arrhythmia. It happens more often than people realize. The heart simply stops maintaining its rhythm, and without immediate intervention…"

"Stop." Mira moves deeper into the workshop, her movement forcing Elias to turn, to track her progress past shelves of gleaming dental instruments, their packages stacked in perfect alignment.

Vincent notices Elias's hand settle on a dental mirror beside the tray, fingers tracing the smooth handle as if the familiar tool might steady him. It's an unconscious gesture, reaching for something that belongs to the ordered, logical world of his practice, a place where pain can be understood and eased, not carried in silence.

The gray morning light presses against the frosted windows, turning the room a muted silver. As the clouds shift outside, the overhead LEDs cast even, unwavering shadows across the spotless floor, lending the space a sterile stillness that feels almost too perfect and clinical, controlled, as if nothing unpredictable could ever happen here.

"Your mother had a weak heart," Elias says, but his voice has lost its clinical certainty, words coming out rough at the edges like they're scraping against something in his throat. "That part was true. The doctors confirmed it during the autopsy. A pre-existing condition that made her vulnerable to…"

"To what?" Mira's voice rises slightly, not quite shouting but carrying enough force to make the bottles on the shelves seem to vibrate, or maybe that's Vincent's vision responding to the tension that thickens the air like humidity before a storm. "What was she vulnerable to that you're not saying?"

Sweat beads on Elias's forehead despite the workshop's coolness, each drop catching light before he wipes them away with the back of his hand. The mirror clinks against the table-top, the metallic sound lingering in the bright, close air. Vincent catches the slight tremor in Elias's fingers as he lets it go.

"You were young," Elias tries again, but the words sound hollow even to him, Vincent can tell from the way his shoulders drop, defeated before the sentence completes. "There are things about that night, about what happened, that would only cause you more pain."

"Worse than what I already live with?" Mira's hands clench at her sides, and Vincent recognizes the gesture. "More pain than growing up in this sterile house without her, while you hide behind that calm and never let me see how much you hurt, too?"

The accusation lands like a physical blow. Elias rocks back slightly, his hip hitting the workbench's edge hard enough that several tools shift position, their careful arrangement disrupted. A plaque scrapper slides toward the edge, and

Vincent watches it teeter there, balanced between falling and staying.

"There were complications," Elias says, and now his voice has dropped to barely above a whisper, as if speaking louder might summon something that listens for confessions. "With Muldrath's binding. Eight years ago, the containment began to crack."

The admission hangs in the air like burning tooth dust, invisible but undeniable. Vincent feels Mira go still beside him, that particular stillness that precedes either collapse or explosion, and he shifts slightly closer, ready to catch her if she falls or hold her back if she lunges.

"The original ritual," Elias continues, his words coming faster now as if a dam has cracked and everything must flow out before he can rebuild it, "it required balance. Rourke understood that grief couldn't simply be contained, it had to be bound to something else, something that could hold its weight without breaking." His hands move to the ledgers on the workbench, fingers tracing entries Vincent can't read from this distance but that seem to give Elias something to focus on besides his daughter's face. "But bindings decay. Eight years ago, Muldrath began to show signs of... instability."

"So you performed another ritual," Mira says, not a question but a statement of fact.

"A reinforcement." Elias nods, the movement sharp and brief like he's trying to minimize it. "Rourke wrote the instructions. Detailed instructions for controlling containment." The sweat on his forehead has returned, running now in thin streams that follow the lines of his face like tears taking the wrong route. "The reinforcement required a different kind of sacrifice. Not grief this time, but its opposite."

Vincent watches understanding dawn on Mira's face, watches the pieces click together with almost audible precision. Her mother's weak heart. The timing eight years ago. The reinforcement ritual that required joy to balance sorrow.

"She volunteered," Elias says, and his voice cracks completely now, the clinical tone shattering. "When she understood what would happen if Muldrath's binding failed completely, when she saw what it would mean for the town, for you, she volunteered." His legs seem to give out, and he sinks onto a wooden stool that creaks under his weight, suddenly looking older than his years.

"Your mother was the joy that balanced an entire town's sorrow," he says, the words emerging broken, each one a small death. "She offered herself to reinforce the binding, knowing her heart couldn't survive the ritual's demands. She chose to become part of the structure that keeps Muldrath contained, that keeps it from becoming something worse than what it already is."

The silence stretches until Elias rises from the stool with the careful movements of someone whose joints have aged decades in minutes, each motion deliberate as if sudden movement might shatter something more than just the quiet. He crosses to a cabinet Vincent hasn't noticed before, built into the workshop's far corner where shadows pool thickest, its dark wood contrasts with the rest of the room's furniture.

The cabinet's doors open with a sound like exhaling, releasing air that's been trapped too long, and Elias reaches inside with the practiced certainty of someone who's retrieved these items before, maybe many times and when the weight of knowledge presses down like stone. His hands emerge clutching leather-bound journals whose covers show water damage, dark stains that spread across the leather in patterns that suggest submersion, recovery, secrets that survived drowning.

A worn leather case follows, soft with age and handling, the kind of container that might hold surgical instruments or communion wafers or something between sacred and profane. Elias sets both on the workbench with care that borders on reverence, or maybe fear.

"Rourke was brilliant," Elias says, his fingers hovering over the journals without quite touching them, as if contact might transfer something through the pages. "But brilliance without wisdom is how you tear holes in the world." He opens the first journal to reveal handwriting so precise it looks mechanical, each letter formed with obsessive consistency, the work of someone who believed that perfect form might create perfect function. "He thought he was binding grief, creating Muldrath as a container for the town's accumulated sorrow. But he was wrong."

The pages turn under Elias's careful fingers, revealing diagrams that hurt to follow with human eyes, geometries that suggest dimensions beyond the three that bodies navigate, symbols that seem to shift when Vincent looks at them directly, becoming stable only in peripheral vision. Mira hasn't moved from where she stands, her body rigid with the effort of processing her mother's sacrifice, but her eyes track the revealed pages with the intensity of someone memorizing evidence.

"We were serving something else," Elias continues, his voice dropping to barely above a whisper, as if volume might attract attention from whatever he's about to name. "Something that exists in the spaces between grief and rage, between memory and forgetting. Rourke called it many things in his journals, never the same name twice, as if naming it consistently would give it more power or maybe summon its attention."

He stops at a page covered in a single symbol drawn large, taking up the entire spread. Vincent feels his damaged hand throb in response, as if the symbol speaks to broken things, calls to them in frequencies only pain and violence can hear.

"You never look for him," Elias says, and the pronoun carries weight that makes the workshop's air feel suddenly thin, harder to breathe. "Because when you do, he looks back."

The words hang in the air like a curse being activated, and Vincent notices the temperature drop, not dramatically but enough that his breath becomes faintly visible, small clouds that dissipate quickly as if something's consuming them. The shadows in the corner where the cabinet stands seem darker now, deeper, suggesting depth to the room's dimensions that wasn't there before.

"Who?" Mira asks, though her voice suggests she might not want the answer, might already know it in that deep place where instinct lives, where the body knows truths the mind won't acknowledge.

Elias's hand shakes as he opens the leather case, revealing papers so old their edges crumble slightly at his touch, releasing particles that drift down like ancient snow. The papers are covered in symbols different from Rourke's journals, older, drawn with less precision but more certainty, as if whoever made them understood exactly what they were invoking and did it anyway.

"The Adversary," Elias says, the title emerging like something he's been holding in his throat for years. "The one who opposes, who corrupts, who transforms devotion into degradation." His fingers trace one of the symbols without quite touching it, maintaining a careful distance as if the ink might still burn. "Rourke thought he was using ancient knowledge to help Duswood, but he was being used. We all were."

From his coat pocket, Elias produces something that catches the clinical LEDs despite its age, a string of beads worn smooth by countless fingers. The Holy Face chaplet hangs from his grip, its small crucifix spinning slowly, revealing handwriting on the back so small Vincent can't read it from where he stands but knows must be significant from the way Mira's breath catches.

"Every night before the binding ritual," Elias says, his voice carrying the mechanical quality of confession, of words that must be said regardless of their effect, "I prayed that he might not see. 'Arise, O Lord, and let Your enemies be scattered, and let those that hate You flee before Your Face.' Over and over, like a ward, like armor made of words." He laughs, but the sound contains no humor. "I thought if I prayed hard enough, if I showed enough devotion to the opposite force, I might be overlooked. We might be overlooked. Might be deemed unworthy of The Adversary's attention."

He extends the chaplet toward Mira, his hand trembling with more than age or exhaustion. "This was your mother's. She understood better than any of us what we were really dealing with. She prayed for protection from evil that wears familiar faces." The beads transfer from his hand to Mira's, and Vincent sees her fingers close around them with the desperation of someone grasping for a lifeline in dark water.

"Her handwriting," Mira says, reading the tiny script on the crucifix's back, though she doesn't share what it says, keeps that last message from her mother private, sacred, her own.

"It's the only thing that ever made me feel unseen by that presence," Elias says, his now-empty hand dropping to his side like something severed. "When I held it, when I prayed with it, I could almost believe we weren't being watched, weren't being orchestrated like instruments in some cosmic violation."

He straightens, attempts to rebuild his professional composure, but the cracks remain visible, permanent now, fractures that will never properly heal. "I'll help you unbind Muldrath. Safely. Properly. Break the bond for good." His voice gains strength with purpose, with the possibility of redemption through action. "I know the ritual's structure, its weak points. We can dissolve it without releasing what it contains, without giving The Adversary what he wants."

Mira stands motionless for a moment that stretches like pulled taffy, her face cycling through expressions too quickly for Vincent to catalog them all—betrayal, grief, rage, understanding, refusal to understand. Then she turns with the mechanical precision of someone whose emotional capacity has been exceeded, who needs distance to process what can't be processed in proximity to its source.

She moves toward the door in silence, her mother's chaplet wrapped so tightly around her fingers that the beads leave small, pale marks in her palm. Her dark dress whispers against itself as she walks. The door opens beneath her touch, letting in a muted gray light that filters through the overcast sky that has no battle with shadow, just an even wash that makes everything look flat and cold. She crosses the threshold as if stepping from one reality into another.

CHAPTER
SEVENTEEN

Vincent follows Mira from the workshop into morning, her mother's chaplet wound so tight around her fingers that the beads disappear into her flesh, leaving only the chain visible. She walks with purpose that excludes him, each step taking her further into whatever internal landscape she's navigating, and Vincent maintains a careful distance. Her house recedes behind them, and with it Elias's confessions.

The residential streets of Duswood spread before them in their familiar grid, but familiarity ends with geography. They pass the public fountain at Elm Street's corner, where brown water spurts from the cherub's mouth in irregular pulses. Not rust-brown from old pipes but organic brown, thick with particulates that catch morning light like suspended decay. The water hits the fountain's basin with sounds too heavy for liquid, more like mud or something worse, and the smell reaches them from twenty feet away of sweet rot mixed with metal.

They turn onto Maple Street, and the absurdity multiplies. The Hendersons' front door stands open, not thrown wide but ajar enough to show the darkness inside. No movement within, no sound of television or conversation, just that particular stillness that speaks of absence rather than sleep. Three houses down, another door hangs open, this one revealing a hallway where family photos still line the walls but dust motes dance through empty air. Vincent counts five open doors on this block alone, each revealing interiors that look lived-in but feel abandoned, as if the families simply walked out mid-routine and didn't return.

Through one doorway, Vincent glimpses a kitchen table still set for breakfast, cereal bowls half-full of milk gone thick, toast left in the toaster, coffee pot still on but long since boiled dry. The normality of the scene makes its abandonment more disturbing, suggests not flight but disappearance that took them between one moment and the next.

Mira's pace doesn't slow, but Vincent sees her eyes track each empty house, cataloging absences with the clinical precision she learned from her father. Her free hand moves slightly, fingers twitching as if counting, and Vincent realizes she's noting which families are gone, creating a mental map of Duswood's quiet evacuation.

Whispers follow them like thrown stones, residents gathered in doorways of houses still occupied, their voices low but carrying in the morning stillness. Vincent catches fragments without trying: "...saw them walking toward the swamp at dawn..." and "...whole Peterson family, just gone..." and "...water's not been right since the fire..." The conversations stop when Vincent and Mira pass, faces turning away, but resume once they're deemed far enough.

An elderly man Vincent recognizes but can't name stands in his doorway wearing a bathrobe over yesterday's clothes, his eyes tracking their movement with the intensity of someone watching for signs, portents, confirmation of fears he won't voice. When Vincent meets his gaze, the man doesn't look away, doesn't pretend he wasn't staring, just nods once with the grim acknowledgment of someone who's given up pretending everything's fine.

The creek cuts through Duswood's center like a wound that won't heal, and today the wound weeps. The water that should run clear or at most carry the normal silt of September rain moves thick and dark, consistency not of water, too viscous, taking too long to flow over rocks that jut from the stream like bones. The smell hits them from the bridge's approach, organic rot mixed with something chemical.

Vincent leans over the bridge's railing, his damaged hand protesting the pressure, and watches something that might be a fish or might be something else move beneath the surface. The thing surfaces briefly, and Vincent sees it's fish-like, its scales sloughing off in sheets that drift downstream like discarded skin, revealing meat beneath.

"It's spreading," Mira says, her first words since leaving the workshop, voice rough from silence. "Whatever Muldrath is, whatever The Adversary wants, it's poisoning everything from the inside out."

Movement at the street corner catches Vincent's eye, and Jennifer Winter materializes from between buildings with her phone extended, camera capturing the creek's contaminated flow. Her blonde curls catch hidden sunlight that seems too bright for the gray morning, and her white jacket stands out like a beacon against Duswood's accelerating decay. She doesn't greet them, just continues recording.

"The whole town's water system is compromised," Jennifer says without lowering her phone, panning across the thick water, the dying fish, their watching faces. "Started this morning around four. Brown water from every tap, every fountain, every source that connects to the municipal system." She finally lowers the phone, and Vincent sees exhaustion beneath her professional composure, the weight of being the only one willing to document what others refuse to see.

"Wendell has information," Jennifer continues, her voice

dropping to barely above a whisper as a couple passes, their faces carefully blank, deliberately not hearing. "About the binding ritual. The original documentation Rourke used to create Muldrath." She glances at Mira, the fresh grief etched in her features. "He's been hiding it in the Press archives for thirty years, waiting for someone brave enough or desperate enough to need it."

She turns without waiting for response, her heels clicking against pavement with that familiar determination. Vincent looks at Mira, sees her nod once, decision made, and they follow Jennifer toward the Press office.

The door sticks when Jennifer pushes it, swollen wood protesting against frame, requiring her shoulder against it before it gives way with a sound like breaking. They enter into air thick with ink and old paper, into the constant buzz of failing fluorescent tubes that strobe reality into segments, into static that rises and falls like breathing from a radio.

Wendell Lynch stands behind his desk, coffee-stained shirt hanging loose on his frame, thick glasses reflecting the stuttering fluorescent light in patterns that make his eyes unreadable. The office spreads around him in organized chaos, filing cabinets with drawers that don't quite close, stacks of newspapers dating back decades, and that persistent radio static emanating from a receiver that hasn't been touched in years.

Jayce sits perched on a filing cabinet near the window, his leg bouncing with mechanical persistence, creating a rhythm that competes with the fluorescent's buzz. His notebook lies open across his lap with symbols Vincent doesn't recognize, patterns that might be Jayce's attempt to make sense of senselessness. Rene occupies a corner table, her sketchbook already open, pencil moving across paper with the fluid certainty of someone translating visions that arrive faster than hands can capture them.

"About time," Wendell says, his voice carrying that particular gruffness that comes from decades of cigarettes and disappointment. "Been expecting you since the water turned. Nothing stays secret in Duswood except the secrets that matter, and those stay secret until they can't anymore." He moves to a filing cabinet older than the others, its metal surface pocked with rust.

The lock on the cabinet requires three different keys, each pulled from different hiding spots around the office—one from behind a framed front page about the elementary school fire in sixty-three, another from inside a coffee can full of pencil stubs, the third from Wendell's shoe where it's been hidden so long the leather bears its impression. The drawer opens with a grinding protest that makes everyone wince, metal on metal creating frequencies that seem to make the radio static fluctuate in response.

"Thirty years I've been sitting on this," Wendell says, pulling out a water-stained manila folder. "Thirty years of knowing what Rourke did, what this town let him do, what we all agreed to forget because forgetting seemed safer than remembering."

He spreads the pages across his desk with careful movements, as if they might crumble or ignite or transform into something else entirely. The papers are yellowed, torn in places, some sections missing entirely, creating gaps in the text that feel deliberate, as if someone removed specific information to prevent the ritual's replication. Vincent leans closer, and the smell of old paper fills his nostrils, mixed with something else he can't quite place.

The ritual diagrams are intricate, drawn with the obsessive precision of someone who believed that exact angles and measurements could bind the unbindable. Circles within circles, symbols that hurt to look at directly, notations in Latin mixed with something older, something that predates written language but somehow exists on the page anyway. Vincent traces the air above one symbol, not touching but feeling heat or cold or something between radiating from the aged ink.

"It's incomplete," Jennifer says, her phone out again, capturing images of each page with methodical precision. "The binding circle is here, the initial invocations, but the actual mechanism for creating Muldrath, the part that transforms grief into form, that's missing."

"Someone tore those pages out," Wendell confirms, adjusting his glasses to peer at the torn edges. "My guess is Rourke himself, after the binding was complete. Didn't want anyone else attempting what he'd done. Or maybe he was trying to protect us from knowing the full price."

The door opens without warning, no knock, no announcement, just sudden movement that makes everyone turn. Elias Thorn stands in the doorway holding a leather folder that matches the water stains on Wendell's papers, as if both documents survived the same flood, the same attempt at destruction that failed to erase what shouldn't exist. His blue suit looks more formal than usual, pressed with the care of someone attending their own funeral, and his face carries an expression of resignation mixed with determination, the look of someone who's made a decision they can't unmake.

The silence stretches like pulled wire. Mira stands frozen beside Vincent and he feels the tremor that runs through her at her father's appearance, the physical manifestation of emotions too complex for simple labels like anger or grief.

"You're not the only one with archives," Elias says, his voice maintaining that clinical tone but underneath it something else, something that might be fear or might be hope or might be exhaustion. He crosses to Wendell's desk with measured steps, each footfall deliberate, considered, and places his folder beside the incomplete ritual.

The pages he reveals are the missing sections, torn edges matching perfectly with Wendell's documents like puzzle pieces separated for three decades finally reuniting. The room seems to contract around this moment, the fluorescent lights stuttering more violently, the radio static rising in pitch as if responding to the ritual's completion.

"You had these all along," Wendell says, not an accusation but acknowledgment of something he maybe always suspected. "You and Rourke, you kept the halves separate in case..."

"In case someone needed to undo what we did," Elias finishes, his hands steady as he aligns the pages, torn edges meeting with precision that suggests they want to be whole again, were always meant to be whole. "I helped create this. It's my responsibility to help destroy it."

Vincent and Jennifer bend over the completed documents, their heads close enough that Vincent can smell Jennifer's perfume mixing with the musty scent of old documentation. The missing pages reveal the transformation process, the exact method by which grief becomes solid, sorrow becomes stone. The notations are dense, mixing scientific terminology with occult symbolism, as if Rourke was trying to apply physics to metaphysics, chemistry to emotion.

"This is..." Jennifer starts, then stops, her finger hovering over a particular passage. "This says the binding requires an anchor. A living person who serves as the bridge between Muldrath and the grief it's meant to contain."

"The anchor maintains the binding," Vincent reads, his voice catching on the implications. "Without the anchor's continued existence, the binding deteriorates." He looks up at Elias, understanding arriving cold and complete. "Rourke was the anchor. That's why no one could find him. He had to stay hidden, stay alive, or Muldrath would..."

"Become unbound," Elias confirms. "But eight years ago, when the binding began to fail, when your mother..." He stops, glances at Mira who hasn't moved, hasn't spoken, just stands absorbing information. "The reinforcement created a secondary anchor. Distributed the burden."

Jayce pushes off from the filing cabinet, his pacing taking

him between the tall metal structures in a pattern that seems random but might be deliberate. His pen taps against his leg in rhythms that match neither the fluorescent buzz nor the radio static, creating a third frequency that makes the very air feel unstable.

In her corner, Rene's pencil moves across paper with increasing speed, her hand shaking slightly but her lines remaining precise, as if something else guides the graphite, uses her as a conduit for documentation that needs to exist. Vincent glimpses her drawing the ritual circle rendered in perfect proportion, but around it, in the margins, other things. Faces that might be human or might be stone. Water that flows upward. A figure that stands at the circle's center, arms spread wide, but whether in welcome or warning, Vincent can't tell.

The radio static suddenly sharpens into something almost like words, syllables that don't quite form meaning but suggest it, and everyone freezes, listening to nothing speak in tongues that predate language. Then it fades back to white noise.

Elias spreads his hands across the completed ritual pages, his fingers finding specific symbols with the muscle memory of someone who's traced these patterns in nightmares for decades. The fluorescent lights above continue their stuttering rhythm, casting his face in alternating moments of harsh illumination and shadow, making him look like two different people occupying the same space.

"The unbinding must happen where the original binding occurred," he says, his voice returning to that professional tone that distances him from the horror of what he's describing. "The rocky hilltop overlooking the cedar swamp, where the town's founders once built their first cemetery before realizing the ground wouldn't hold the dead, kept pushing them back up like the earth itself was refusing them." His finger traces a location on the ritual diagram, a point where multiple circles intersect." Rourke chose it because the boundary between solid and liquid, earth and water, life and death is thinnest there. The stone formations create natural amplification for the kind of energies the ritual requires."

Vincent remembers the hilltop from childhood explorations before parents started warning children away, before the missing pets and strange sounds made it a place to avoid. The rocks there form patterns that seem almost deliberate, circles within circles that mirror the ritual diagrams.

"The unbinding is more complex than the original binding," Elias continues, pulling out a second set of papers, these ones newer, covered in his own precise handwriting. "The binding created Muldrath through accumulation, gathering grief over time until it reached critical mass. But unbinding requires precision, like surgery. We need to sever the connections in the right order, or the release of energy could..." He pauses, searching for words that won't cause panic. "Could cause significant collateral damage."

"How significant?" Jennifer asks, her phone recording everything, creating documentation that might matter if they fail, if someone else needs to understand what they attempted.

"The grief of thirty years, released all at once?" Elias's hands tremble slightly as they hover over the papers. "It would be like a psychic explosion. Everyone in Duswood would feel every loss, every sorrow, as if it were their own. The mind isn't built to survive that. Best case, everyone dies. Worst case…grief would drive us all mad. People wouldn't be able to tell their pain from their neighbor's. No one would have anything left to live for. The whole town would tear itself apart, trapped in sorrow that folds into itself exponentially and never ends."

The room fills with the weight of that possibility, everyone imagining what it would mean to feel thirty years of loss in a single moment. Wendell reaches for his coffee mug, finds it empty, sets it back down with a hollow ceramic sound that seems too loud in the silence.

"But that's only if we do it wrong," Elias says quickly, trying to salvage hope from the horror he's just described. "If we follow the proper sequence, if we have the right elements in place, we can dissolve the binding gradually, like letting air out of a balloon instead of popping it."

"What elements?" Jayce asks from his position by the window.

Elias's jaw tightens, the muscle jumping beneath skin that's gone pale despite the warm fluorescent light. "We need something to draw Muldrath to the hilltop. It won't come just because we call. It responds to genuine emotional triggers, to authentic pain or fear or loss. We need..." He stops, swallows, tries again. "We need bait."

The word hangs in the air like a physical thing, ugly and necessary. Vincent feels the room's attention shift, everyone arriving at the same conclusion through different paths of logic. They need someone Muldrath will follow, someone whose emotional signature is strong enough to override whatever other commands it might be following.

"I'll do it," Wendell says, surprising everyone. "I've been complicit in this town's lies for thirty years. Let me finally do something honest."

"Your guilt isn't strong enough," Elias says with clinical brutality. "Muldrath responds to fresh grief, active sorrow, not old regrets that have calcified into routine."

"Then who?" Jennifer demands, though Vincent suspects she already knows, can see it in the way her eyes keep darting to Mira, who's been silent through this entire exchange.

The debate erupts with voices overlapping, each person offering themselves or explaining why someone else would be better suited. Jayce suggests they could use recordings of CJ's voice, the missing boy whose phone they found in Muldrath's possession. Rene, still drawing in her corner, quietly offers that she's been having dreams, that maybe her connection to whatever speaks through static would be enough.

Through it all, Mira stands perfectly still, the chaplet wound around her fingers catching the stuttering light in brief flashes of silver. She watches her father with eyes that hold too much understanding, and Vincent sees the moment she makes her decision, sees it in the way her shoulders set, her chin lifts slightly, her whole body shifting from passive observation to active choice.

"I'll be the bait," Mira says, her voice cutting through the debate with the finality of a blade through silk. The room goes silent.

"I'm the only one with a direct link," she continues before anyone can protest. "My mother's sacrifice eight years ago, it created a connection between me and Muldrath whether I wanted it or not. The reinforcement ritual used her joy, her love for me, as the binding agent. That makes me the strongest emotional trigger available."

Elias moves with speed that belies his usual measured pace, crossing to his daughter in two strides, his hands reaching for her shoulders but stopping just short of contact, hovering in the space between protection and possession. "No," he says, and for the first time since Vincent has known him, Elias Thorn's voice breaks into a sound so raw it barely resembles speech, revealing the caring father beneath the professional facade. "I won't lose you too. I can't."

"You don't get to make that choice," Mira says, and there's steel in her voice that Vincent has never heard before, strength that's been forged in the furnace of recent revelations. "You made choices for me my whole life. Chose to hide the truth about Mother. Chose to let me grow up in ignorance while the thing that killed her walked through our town. Chose to protect me from knowledge instead of giving me the tools to protect myself."

She steps back from his hovering hands, creating distance that's more than physical. "This isn't your choice to make."

The confrontation stretches between them, father and daughter separated by more than space, by years of careful lies and protected truths, by love that manifested as concealment and concealment that curdled into something neither of them wanted. Vincent watches Elias age in real time, his shoulders dropping, his carefully maintained posture crumbling into something more honest, more human.

"She would never forgive me if I let something happen to you," Elias says, but the fight has gone out of his voice, replaced by exhaustion that runs bone-deep.

"She already forgave you," Mira says. "She knew what you were doing, why you were doing it. She made her own choice. Now I'm making mine."

The acceptance spreads through the room like water finding its level, everyone understanding that this is how it has to be, that Mira's connection makes her not just the best choice but the only choice that makes sense. Elias nods once, sharp and painful, then turns to the desk where he begins listing what they'll need with the mechanical precision of someone focusing on logistics to avoid drowning in emotion.

"Chalk for the containment circles," he says, his voice steady again through visible effort. "Sea salt for the boundary lines. Table salt won't work, it needs to be unrefined, carrying its original mineral complexity. Candles, white, unscented, at least twelve. And..." He pauses, looks at the chaplet still wound around Mira's fingers. "And that. Your mother's prayers might be the only thing that keeps The Adversary from noticing what we're doing until it's too late to stop us."

They move through the office gathering supplies from unexpected places: chalk from a drawer full of old school supplies, salt from Wendell's emergency kit that he's kept since the seventies when people still believed in civil defense, candles from a box labeled "Power Outage Supplies" that hasn't been opened in years. Each item carries its own weight of normalcy being repurposed for the decidedly abnormal, everyday objects becoming ritual components.

Rene tears the drawing of the ritual circle from her sketchbook, folds it carefully, and hands it to Vincent. Her fingers brush his as the paper transfers between them, and he feels them trembling, not from fear but from something else, maybe exhaustion from channeling visions that arrive unbidden, maybe anticipation of finally acting instead of just observing.

They file out of the office into afternoon that's arrived without anyone noticing, the day having progressed despite the morning's revelations. The street stretches empty in both directions, that particular stillness that Duswood has perfected. Vincent steps onto the sidewalk last, letting the others move ahead, and that's when he notices it.

Across the street, in the narrow alley between the hardware store and the long-closed bakery, a figure stands perfectly still. Too still. The kind of stillness that human bodies don't naturally achieve, that requires either death or something pretending to be human but forgetting the small movements that living requires. The figure is tall, thin, wearing what might be a coat or might be shadows that have taken solid form. Where its face should be, Vincent sees only darkness, not the absence of features but the presence of void. Nothing.

He blinks, starts to call out to the others, but in that fraction of a second between closing and opening his eyes, the figure dissolves. Not disappearing but actually dissolving, becoming fog that dissipates into the afternoon air, leaving only the memory of observation, the certainty that they've been watched, that someone or something knows their plans.

Vincent catches up to the group, the question burning in his throat but remaining unspoken. Are they walking into a trap that's been set specifically for them? Or is something even darker than Muldrath waiting at the ritual site, something that's been patient for thirty years and has finally found the perfect confluence of desperation and determination to achieve its own purposes?

The hilltop waits beyond the town's edge, rocks that remember the first failed cemetery, ground that refused the dead, and Vincent wonders if they're about to discover why the earth there rejected burial, what lies beneath stone that even death couldn't penetrate.

CHAPTER
EIGHTEEN

The path to the hilltop winds through dying grass that crunches beneath Vincent's feet like small bones breaking. The incline pulls at his calves as they climb toward stone formations that jut from the earth like broken teeth. Behind him, Jayce's breathing comes quick and shallow. Rene moves in her characteristic drift, somehow finding footing on the uneven ground without seeming to look where she steps. Jennifer has stayed behind in town, documenting what she calls "the baseline" before everything changes.

The hilltop spreads before them as they crest the final rise, a plateau of exposed rock and sparse vegetation. The stones here don't follow natural patterns. They rise in suggestions of circles, half-formed spirals that nature doesn't make on its own. Vincent recognizes the formations from Rene's drawings, from the ritual diagrams. Three twisted pines stand sentinel at the plateau's edge, their branches grown horizontal from decades of wind.

Wendell drops his bag with a grunt that echoes off the rocks, the sound carrying in the still air. "Used to come here as kids," he says, pulling out chalk and salt and candles with the efficiency of someone who's thought through every motion.

"Before we knew better. Before the stories got specific enough to be warnings instead of legends."

Elias moves among the natural stone formations with purpose, his hands finding specific rocks, testing their placement, making minute adjustments that only he understands. His blue suit looks wrong against the wild landscape, too formal for scrambling over rough stone, but he doesn't seem to notice or care. Vincent watches him work and sees not the composed doctor but someone revisiting a crime scene, reliving choices that led to this moment.

"The original binding happened here," Elias says, his voice carrying that clinical tone that distances him from emotion. "Rourke chose this place because the boundary conditions were already weak. The failed cemetery from the 1800s, the underground water that surfaces in the swamp, the mineral composition of these rocks. Everything conspired to make this ground reject the natural order."

He kneels beside a flat stone larger than the others, its surface worn smooth by weather or use. His fingers trace patterns invisible to everyone else, muscle memory of symbols drawn thirty years ago. "We thought we were so clever. Thought we could transform Duswood's accumulated grief into something useful, something that would serve the town instead of drowning it."

Vincent helps position stones according to the diagram Rene drew, each placement requiring precision that feels both mathematical and instinctive. The rocks are heavier than they look, dense with something more than mineral weight. When he sets one in place, it seems to settle deeper than gravity alone would pull it, as if the earth recognizes these arrangements and accepts them, or maybe fears them.

"Rourke's disappearance," Elias continues, standing now, brushing dirt from his knees with automatic movements, "wasn't a disappearance at all. He became something else. The ritual didn't just create Muldrath. It changed him, made him part of the binding itself. He's been here all along, existing in the spaces between what we see and what we refuse to see."

The revelation settles over the group like fog, cold and encompassing. Vincent notices that there is no wind. None at all.

"Eight years ago," Elias says, and he shifts slightly when noting the timeline that marks his wife's death, "the reinforcement ritual didn't just stabilize Muldrath's binding. It deepened it. Made the connection between the creature and the town's grief permanent. Symbiotic. Muldrath doesn't just contain our sorrow anymore. It feeds on it. And we feed on its containment, our ability to forget, to function despite loss."

Mira stands at the circle's edge where the prepared stones form their ancient pattern, her back to them all, facing the darkening sky. The chaplet wraps around her right hand so tightly that Vincent can see the marks it leaves even from distance, each bead pressing into flesh like she's trying to anchor herself through pain.

Elias approaches his daughter with the careful movements of someone approaching a wild animal. His hands shake as he reaches for her shoulders, and Vincent sees the effort it takes for him to make contact, to bridge the distance that recent revelations have created between them.

"Your mother stood here," Elias says, and the words emerge broken, each one a small confession. "Right where you're standing. She held that same chaplet. Prayed the same prayers you learned as a child but never understood the urgency of."

Mira doesn't turn, doesn't acknowledge his touch, but Vincent sees the subtle shift in her posture, the way she leans back slightly, not quite accepting comfort but not rejecting it either.

"It will keep The Adversary's eyes off you," Elias continues, his voice fracturing on the entity's title. "Your mother believed that. Had to believe it. The prayers, the blessed beads, they create a kind of blindness in whatever watches through Muldrath's eyes. Make you invisible to the thing that feeds on recognition."

Now the wind picks up as full darkness claims the hilltop, and with it comes the smell of the swamp below, thick and organic, decay mixed with something else, something that smells like anticipation. The prepared circle of stones seems to pulse in Vincent's peripheral vision.

Vincent looks at the others, sees his own apprehension reflected in their faces. Jayce clutches his flashlight like a weapon. Rene stands perfectly still, her eyes closed, lips moving in what might be practice for the chant.

The ritual space is ready. The players are in position. All that remains is to begin, to speak the words that will summon Muldrath, that will attempt to unbind thirty years of accumulated grief without releasing it all at once, without destroying everyone in Duswood with the psychic weight of their collective sorrow.

Vincent wonders if they're about to save the town or complete its destruction, if there's even a difference anymore between salvation and ending when the thing being saved has been sick for so long it's forgotten what health feels like.

Rene moves to the north point of the circle with fluid certainty, her feet finding the exact spot where stone meets earth. Her sketchbook lies abandoned beside Wendell's bag. She raises her hands, not dramatically but with the simple purpose of someone opening a door.

The first words from Rourke's journal emerge from her throat in a voice that doesn't quite sound like hers, pitched lower, carrying resonance that makes Vincent's neck tighten. The language isn't Latin or any tongue he recognizes, but something that predates written record, sounds that human throats shouldn't shape but hers does. Each syllable falls into the space between the stones like water finding its level, filling gaps Vincent didn't know existed.

"*Mor-dun ath vey'ale,*" Rene chants, and the words seem to pull themselves from her rather than being pushed out. "*Keth'ran du mor'ale synthes.*" Her voice trembles on the first repetition, a girl speaking words that want to be spoken by something older, something that understands their weight. But with each cycle, her tone strengthens, finds its register, transforms from recitation to invocation.

Vincent feels the words in his chest, each syllable creating vibrations that don't match his heartbeat, that impose their own rhythm on his body. A low throbbing in his head begins to pulse in time with the chant.

Elias takes his position at the southern point, directly opposite Rene, his dark blue suit making him almost invisible except for his pale face floating in the darkness. He pulls a small leather book from his jacket, its pages soft with age and handling, and Vincent recognizes a psalter, the kind priests used before modern translations made ancient words accessible.

"Let God arise," Elias begins, his voice even and precise, shaped by years of calming anxious patients and finding order in discomfort, giving structure to pain too over-whelming for words. "Let his enemies be scattered, and let all who hate him flee from before his face."

The Latin follows, "*Exsurgat Deus et dissipentur inimici eius et fugiant qui oderunt eum a facie eius,*" and Vincent hears how it layers over Rene's chant, not competing but weaving through it, creating harmonics that shouldn't exist between such different languages. The two voices create a sound that's neither speech nor song but something between, something that makes the air itself seem to thicken, become medium rather than absence.

The others move without verbal coordination, taking posi-tions around the circle's perimeter. Vincent finds himself closest to where Mira stands, close enough to reach her if needed but far enough to not break whatever boundary the stones create. Jayce positions himself to Vincent's left, his flashlight beam dancing across the ground in nervous arcs, creating shadows that move independent of the light that casts them. Wendell stands opposite, his bulk a reassuring solidity.

Mira turns from her position at the circle's edge, and Vincent sees her face properly for the first time since the ritual began. Her expression carries the same determination he saw when she kissed him by the swamp, when she chose to know truth rather than comfort, but now there's something else, a peace. The calm of someone who's already made their peace with whatever comes next.

She steps over the boundary of stones with the deliberation of someone entering water they know is cold, committing fully rather than prolonging the anticipation. The moment her foot crosses into the circle's interior, the air changes with the subtlety of that moment when birds stop singing because they sense something humans don't.

The chaplet unwinds from her hand as she walks to the circle's center, the beads catching some faint little light, creating brief constellations of reflection that don't match any light source Vincent can identify. She holds it loosely now, familiar with its weight but not its meaning.

Rene's chant continues, growing stronger, and Elias's psalm layers over it in rhythms that create something that sounds almost like music if music could be made from grief and hope in equal measure. The words fill the space within the circle, invisible but present, like humidity that can be felt but not seen.

Mira raises her face to the dark sky, her throat exposed in a gesture of vulnerability that makes Vincent's protective instincts spike. He shifts forward slightly, catching himself before he breaks the circle's boundary, understanding that interference now would destroy more than the ritual.

"Lunara Thorn," Mira calls out, her mother's name emerging not as a shout but as something more penetrating, words that don't need volume because they carry weight that transcends sound. "Lunara Morrigan Thorn."

The name hangs in the air like struck bronze, resonating long after speech should fade. Vincent feels it in his bones. The twisted pines at the plateau's edge creak despite the wind having died completely, their branches moving in response to something other than weather.

"I carry your blood," Mira continues, her voice steady but thick with emotion Vincent has never heard from her before. "I carry your sacrifice. I carry your love." The words aren't part of any ritual Vincent knows, aren't from Rourke's journal or Elias's preparations. They're Mira's own, spontaneous and necessary, the words of a daughter calling to a mother who died to protect her.

The stones of the circle respond.

It starts as the faintest suggestion of light, like phosphorescence in deep water, barely visible and possibly imagined. But as Mira continues to speak her mother's name, to invoke their connection, the glow strengthens. Blue light, cold and beautiful, seeps from the stones as if they're remembering some ancient illumination.

The air within the circle thickens visibly, not with smoke or fog but with presence, with the weight of something arriving or maybe something that was always here becoming visible. Vincent's head throbs with increasing intensity, and he realizes the pain has synchronized with the pulse of light from the stones, his body becoming part of the ritual's rhythm without his permission.

The temperature drops, not gradually but in a sudden plunge that makes Vincent's breath visible, small clouds that dissipate quickly as if something's consuming them. The smell from the swamp intensifies, but now it carries something else, a sweetness that might be flowers or might be the particular scent of things that grow in places light doesn't reach.

Thunder rolls across the clear sky, sound without source, and Vincent understands they've crossed some threshold, moved from preparation to invocation, from possibility to inevitability. Whatever they've called, whatever Mira's voice has awakened, it's coming.

NINETEEN

The treeline breaks first with sound rather than sight, branches snapping with the deliberate rhythm of something too large for stealth, too patient for haste. Vincent's attention snaps from the glowing circle to the darkness between the twisted pines, where shadows have begun to move independent of any light source. The sound builds, not just breaking wood but something deeper, a grinding that might be stone against stone or might be the earth itself protesting weight it was never meant to bear.

Muldrath emerges like a wound in reality.

Its form defies consistent observation, shifting between states of matter as if it can't decide what it wants to be. The base structure suggests humanoid intention, two legs, two arms, something that might be a head, but the execution differs in every way that matters. Stone comprises its core, but not clean stone. This is aggregate, compressed layers of different minerals, creating patterns in its surface, that suggest meaning just beyond comprehension.

Roots wind through the stone like veins, some dead and brittle, others impossibly green, pulsing with sap that glows faintly in the circle's blue light. Soil fills the gaps between stone and root, dark and rich, too fertile, as if it's been fed things that make even death nervous. The soil shifts constantly, small avalanches that reveal and conceal the underlying structure, making Muldrath appear to breathe despite having no lungs.

Insects cascade from its joints with each movement, beetles and centipedes and things that crawl and skitter, all falling like living rain before burrowing immediately into the ground as if fleeing something worse than death. The insects leave trails in the dirt that form patterns, symbols that exist just long enough to almost mean something before other feet destroy them.

The face is the worst part because sometimes it's not there at all, just a smooth expanse of stone that reflects nothing, and sometimes it's too there, too human, features that might belong to a dozen different people all trying to exist in the same space. Vincent catches glimpses of faces he almost recognizes, citizens of Duswood who disappeared over the years, their features preserved in stone and sorrow.

The creature moves toward the circle, each step deliberate and inevitable. The ground beneath its feet doesn't just compress but transforms, grass dying instantly, soil turning the gray of old ash. It leaves footprints that steam in the cold air.

Twenty feet from the circle, Muldrath stops. Its head tilts with an almost curious gesture, like a dog hearing a frequency humans can't detect. The blue light from the stones reflects off its surface, creating colors that don't have names, that exist in the space between what eyes can see and what brains can process.

Mira stands in the circle's center, the chaplet raised in her hand like an offering or a weapon, Vincent can't tell which. The beads catch the blue light and throw it back changed, transformed into something that makes Muldrath hesitate. The creature's form shifts more rapidly now, stone becoming soil becoming root becoming stone again, as if the sight of the chaplet causes some kind of internal conflict, a war between what it is and what it was meant to be.

The moment stretches, predator and prey locked in acknowledgment that transcends their roles, and Vincent realizes Muldrath recognizes the chaplet, remembers it, maybe remembers the woman who held it eight years ago when she offered herself to reinforce its binding.

Then the darkness beside the twisted pines explodes into motion.

Silas Rourke bursts from shadows that shouldn't have been able to conceal him. His limbs bend in too many places, as if he has extra joints, or as if his bones have gone soft and only muscle memory keeps him approximately human-shaped. His skin has the gray-white of ash mixed with milk, stretched too tight in some places, hanging loose in others, like a suit that doesn't fit but can't be removed.

"Stop!" His voice tears from his throat with harmonics that sound like it came from more than a single voice, high and low frequencies layered like multiple people speaking in forced unison. "You don't understand what you're doing! It cannot be done!"

Vincent sees Rourke's eyes as he rushes toward the circle, and there's something bad about them; pupils too large, irises the color of old copper that's begun to green. But it's the intelligence behind them that's truly terrifying, not mad or absent but present in a way that suggests he sees everything, understands everything, has been watching.

"The binding is all that holds worse things back!" Rourke shouts, his words carrying that otherworldly resonance. "Break it and you break the barrier between what is and what waits!"

Elias moves faster than Vincent would have thought possible for a man his age, intercepting Rourke before he can reach the circle's edge. Their bodies collide with a sound that's both organic and mineral, flesh meeting whatever Rourke has become. Elias's hands find Rourke's shoulders, and Vincent sees him recoil slightly at the contact before forcing himself to maintain his grip.

Rourke's skin feels course under Elias's hands, cold and papery like something that died but kept moving, or like bark that's learned to approximate flesh. The texture shifts constantly, sometimes smooth, sometimes rough, as if Rourke's body can't maintain consistent form without conscious effort, and all his consciousness is focused on his warning.

"Silas," Elias says, his voice cutting through Rourke's continued shouts with the authority of someone who's dealt with hysteria before, who knows how to project calm even when feeling none. "We know what we're doing. We're finishing what should never have been started."

"You know nothing!" Rourke's body contorts in Elias's grip, movements that would break normal bones but seem to cause him no pain. "The Adversary showed me, made me see. Muldrath isn't the prison. It's the guard. It's the only thing keeping the true hunger away!"

Wind that has been dead suddenly howls across the hilltop, carrying the scent of things burning, stone and water and concepts made physical. The glowing stones flicker, their light struggling against something that wants darkness, needs darkness, feeds on the absence of illumination.

Vincent starts forward to help Elias, Jayce moving with him in rare synchronization, but Elias waves them back with violent gestures that brook no argument. "Maintain the circle!" he shouts over the wind. "Don't break the boundary!"

Rourke tries to twist free, his body moving in ways that suggest his skeleton has become optional, but Elias adjusts his grip, finding purchase on something more solid beneath Rourke's transformed flesh. They struggle at the edge of the light cast by the stones, two figures locked in combat that's both physical and metaphysical, each trying to impose their version of reality on the other.

"Listen to me," Rourke's voice drops to something almost human, almost the man he used to be before the ritual changed him. "I've seen what lies beneath. I've been its witness for thirty years. The grief we bound into Muldrath, it's nothing compared to what waits if the binding fails."

His eyes find Mira in the circle, and something like recognition passes across his inhuman features. "Your mother understood. She saw what I saw when she offered herself. The necessity of suffering to prevent worse suffering."

Elias's hands tighten on Rourke's shoulders, and Vincent hears something crack, though whether it's bone or stone or something between, he can't tell. "My wife died because of your arrogance," Elias says, his clinical composure finally cracking, revealing the raw father beneath. "You convinced us we could engineer salvation through sacrifice. But all we did was feed something that should have been allowed to starve."

Rene's chant continues through the chaos, her voice somehow steady despite the wind trying to steal her words. The ancient syllables rise and fall in patterns that create their own momentum, their own gravity that pulls everything toward completion. Elias's psalm layers over it, Latin phrases that sound like weapons in the darkness, each word a small act of defiance against whatever Rourke has become, whatever him and Muldrath serve.

Muldrath watches from its position twenty feet away, neither advancing nor retreating, caught between imperatives, waiting for something that will tip the balance. Its form continues to shift, faces appearing and disappearing in its stone surface, and Vincent swears he sees Lunara Thorn's features for just a moment, peaceful and patient and entirely too aware.

Muldrath's attention shifts with the slow certainty of a planet changing orbit, its eyeless face turning from Mira to where Rourke struggles in Elias's grip. The movement creates a sound like millstones grinding, stone against stone in frequencies not heard before. The creature's form solidifies slightly, the constant shifting between states slowing as if it needs all its substance for what comes next.

Vincent watches recognition dawn on Rourke's transformed features, his too-large pupils dilating further until they're just black holes in his ash-pale face. "No," he says, but the word fails him, split into jagged voices denying in unison. "Do you forget who we serve? He'll unleash everything!"

Muldrath moves forward with purpose now, no longer the patient approach of before but something decisive, final. Each step leaves deeper impressions in the ground, as if the creature is gathering mass from somewhere, becoming more real, more present, more undeniable. The insects that cascade from its joints increase their flow, a waterfall of chittering life that forms a carpet of writhing bodies.

Elias releases Rourke and steps back, his movements careful and deliberate, understanding that something beyond human intervention is about to occur. Rourke staggers, his fluid grace gone, replaced by the jerky movements of someone whose body no longer responds properly to mental commands. He turns to run, but his legs bend, dropping him to his knees in the dirt.

Muldrath reaches him in two strides. Its massive form looms over Rourke, blocking the light from the glowing stones, creating a shadow that seems to have weight, presence, intent. The creature's arms, thick amalgamations of stone and root and something that might be bone, reach down with no hesitation.

The wiry roots wrap around Rourke's torso, and Vincent hears him gasp, a sound that's entirely human, entirely vulnerable. For a moment, Rourke looks like the man he must have been before the ritual, before thirty years of serving as anchor to an abomination, before The Adversary whispered promises that turned to prison sentences.

"Please," Rourke says, and this time his voice is singular, clean, just a man begging. "I only wanted to help. I thought I could fix Duswood's pain."

Muldrath lifts him without effort. The roots now forming hand-like structures. Rourke's legs dangle, kicking weakly at air, his transformed body suddenly looking fragile. The creature holds him face to face.

Vincent thinks Muldrath might speak, might offer some judgment or acknowledgment, but the creature remains silent as it always has, communication through action rather than words. Its grip tightens, petrified fingers compressing with the patient force of geology, of time itself made manifest and impatient.

The first crack sounds like a branch breaking, sharp and definitive. Then more, a cascade of breaking sounds that Vincent realizes are Rourke's bones giving way under a millennia of pressure. Rourke's screams start human but transform into something else, frequencies that suggest his vocal cords are changing, reorganizing, trying to find a shape that can express this particular agony.

Dark fluid seeps between Muldrath's fingers, not quite blood, too thick, too dark, carrying a luminescence that suggests it once held power, once served as the medium between human and inhuman. The fluid drips to the ground and immediately the earth rejects it, soil pulling away, creating small craters that fill with the strange substance before it sinks deeper.

Rourke's screams cut off mid-note, his body going limp with the sudden completeness of death. His form folds in ways that make Vincent look away, geometry that offends the eye's understanding of how bodies should behave.

Muldrath drops him without ceremony, and Rourke's remains hit the ground with a sound both wet and dry, organic and mineral. The body doesn't look human anymore, doesn't look like anything that ever lived, just a collection of perverse angles and leaked fluids that the earth is already beginning to claim, pulling it down.

The wind dies instantly, completely. The absence of sound feels larger than the chaos that preceded it, a silence that has weight, that presses against eardrums with the pressure of depths. Even Rene's chant has stopped, though Vincent didn't notice when.

In this crystalline silence, Muldrath turns back to Mira.

The creature's movements have changed, no longer decisive but uncertain, almost tentative. Each step toward the circle comes with hesitation, as if Rourke's death has severed some essential control that kept it focused. The faces in its stone surface appear more frequently now, staying longer, and Vincent recognizes more of them. Citizens of Duswood who died over the years, their features preserved in aggregate and sorrow.

The insects have stopped falling from its joints, the last of them burrowing quickly into the disturbed earth. Without their constant cascade, Muldrath seems more solid but also more vulnerable, like something essential has been exhausted. Its form shifts less, settling into something that's almost consistently humanoid.

Mira hasn't moved from the circle's center, hasn't flinched during Rourke's destruction, stands now with the chaplet held loosely in her hand like she's forgotten she's holding it. Her face carries an expression Vincent has never seen on her before, not peace exactly but acceptance, the look of someone who understands what comes next and has made their peace with it.

Muldrath stops at the circle's edge, and Vincent realizes it can't cross, not won't but can't, the glowing stones creating a barrier that even its massive form respects. The creature stands there, waiting, and Vincent understands that this is Mira's choice now, her moment to decide how this ends.

She steps forward, moving through the blue light of the stones like walking through water, each step deliberate and certain. The chaplet swings from her hand, the beads emanating a soft orange light from within them now, not reflected but generated, as if her mother's prayers have accumulated enough power over eight years to become luminous.

At the circle's edge, separated from Muldrath by perhaps three feet of ordinary ground, Mira stops. She raises the chaplet, not threatening but offering, and speaks words Vincent can barely hear, meant for the creature alone.

"She forgave you," Mira says, and her voice carries the certainty of someone who knows this truth deeper than knowledge. "My mother. She forgave you even as you took her. She understood you were as trapped as anyone."

Muldrath's form shudders, a movement that runs through its entire structure. The faces in its stone surface all turn toward Mira, dozens of dead eyes focusing on her with expressions that might be gratitude or might be grief or might be both.

Mira steps out of the circle, closing the distance between them, and presses the chaplet into Muldrath's chest. The moment of contact creates a sound like a bell rung underwater, muffled but carrying frequencies that bypass the ears and resonate directly in bone.

For a moment, Muldrath's face becomes fully human, not a collection of features but a single, coherent face that carries peace Vincent didn't think stone could express. The features are familiar but not quite anyone's, as if all the faces that have appeared in its surface have averaged into something new.

Then the creature begins to crumble.

Not violently, not with the destructive force of its formation, but with the gentle dissolution of something whose time has come. The stone becomes sand that becomes dust that becomes nothing, each particle carrying away a fragment of bound grief, releasing it not all at once but in manageable doses that dissipate into the night air like morning fog touched by sun.

The roots withdraw into the earth with sounds like sighing, disappearing into soil that immediately looks healthier, more natural. The ground beneath where Muldrath stood shows no sign of its presence, grass already beginning to straighten, to reach toward stars that seem brighter now, closer, more interested in this small hilltop where something significant has ended.

The dissolution takes less than a minute but feels like hours, like watching thirty years of accumulated sorrow finally given permission to disperse, to stop being monument and become memory, to stop being weight and become wind.

When the last of Muldrath fades, carried away on air that smells now of pine and earth and nothing else, Mira's legs give out. She doesn't fall so much as fold, her body deciding it's done standing, done being strong, done holding the weight of her mother's sacrifice and her father's guilt and her town's willful ignorance.

Elias catches her before she hits the ground, his arms wrapping around his daughter with the desperate grip of someone who's already lost too much. He whispers something Vincent can't hear, words meant only for her, apologies or promises or both. Then, softly, barely more than a breath, he says, "It's done."

Vincent kneels beside them, his good hand finding Mira's. Their fingers brush, and she turns her head slightly, eyes finding his with effort that speaks of exhaustion beyond physical. But she manages the smallest smile, barely a movement of lips but carrying more meaning than words could convey. A promise that they've survived this, that morning will come, that some things broken can be rebuilt if not repaired.

The blue light from the stones fades gradually, like eyes

closing, leaving them in darkness lit only by stars. The hilltop feels clean now, purged, ready to be just a place where children play again instead of a wound in the world where grief pooled and festered.

Vincent's hand brushes Mira's again, intentional this time, and she shifts her fingers to interlace with his. Not a grasp but a connection, light and certain and carrying the promise of conversations to come, of truth told in daylight instead of whispered in darkness, of a Duswood that might finally learn to mourn properly instead of binding its sorrow into shapes that should never walk.

CHAPTER
TWENTY

Kipling Avenue stretches before Vincent, shopfronts gleaming with fresh paint. His hand, freed from its wrapping three days ago, still aches when the weather shifts, knuckles bearing scars that look like a map of some old country. The morning carries that particular October clarity that makes everything look sharper.

The hardware store's new window reflects his passage, and he catches himself checking for shadows. Old habits from those weeks when Duswood's reality went soft at the edges. Mrs. Henderson emerges from the pharmacy clutching a white paper bag, sees Vincent, and her smile seems soft. She nods, he nods back, and they pass without words because what would they say? Nice weather for forgetting our town hosted a creature made of bound grief?

The creek bisects Kipling Avenue via a small bridge that is a favorite spot for teenagers to gather. Now it flows clear again, or clear enough from the week when it moved like syrup and smelled of decay. Vincent leans against the railing, watching minnows dart.

Two women pass behind him, their conversation deliberately bright. "Sarah's boy is doing so well in Little League," one says, her voice pitched with pride. The other responds with equal determination to discuss anything but what made Sarah's boy sleep with his parents for three weeks straight, what made him wake screaming about stone faces in his dreams.

Cedar Lagoon Pizzeria squats at the street's far end, its neon sign dark in daylight but still managing to suggest promises of normalcy through grease and melted cheese. Above the door, Joe's new sign catches Vincent's eye, hand-painted letters in aggressive yellow: "No Golems, No Weirdos, No Refunds." The humor feels forced but necessary, Joe's way of acknowledging what happened while refusing to let it define his business.

Vincent pushes through the door into air thick with garlic. The booths stretch empty despite lunch hour approaching, their vinyl surfaces reflecting overhead lights. The kitchen exhales its familiar symphony of sizzling and refrigerator hum.

Joe emerges from the kitchen, dish towel slung over his shoulder, his gray buzz cut catching the aggressive fluorescents. His eyes find Vincent's, hold them for a moment that acknowledges shared knowledge, then slide away to focus on wiping down a counter that's already clean. "Slice?" he asks, the single word. Nothing more.

"Nah. Maybe after school," Vincent says, and Joe nods like he expected this answer. The empty booths watch Vincent leave, their silence louder than any crowd could be.

School exists now in a row of battered trailers parked on the burnt-out asphalt where the building once stood. Narrow corridors of rubber mats replace linoleum, and Vincent's sneakers squeak on them just as insistently. He passes the door of the art trailer, its little window streaked with soot and rain; inside, a cluster of folding tables has been set up, and the chair where Rene used to sit stays conspicuously empty.

His fingers dive into the narrow drawer of his rescue-desk, past broken erasers and stubby pencils, until they close around a folded scrap of paper. He pulls out one of Rene's sketches, smudged at the creases. In the corner her signature curls like a promise she never got to keep. Vincent refolds it carefully, tucks it between pages of half-forgotten calculus, a subject whose tidy answers now feel obscene. The bell crackles through the trailer-park PA—too loud and too hollow—sending students spilling out onto the scarred pavement. Vincent moves with them.

The parking lot spreads under afternoon sun. Jennifer Winter's white sports car gleams like an accusation against the ordinary sedans and pickups, too clean, too purposeful, already half-gone despite sitting still. She leans against the driver's door, designer sunglasses making her expression unreadable, but her posture speaks of decision made, bridges pre-burned for convenience.

Kent occupies the passenger seat, visible through the windshield as a patient shadow. He nods at Vincent through the glass, acknowledgment between people who barely knew each other's last names.

"You came," Jennifer says, pushing her sunglasses up to rest in her blonde curls. She reaches into the car, retrieves a manila envelope thick with what feels like responsibility when she extends it toward Vincent. "Everything I documented. Everything Wendell wouldn't print. Everything the state papers wouldn't touch because it sounds insane, which it is."

The envelope weighs more than paper should, dense with photographs and testimonies and timelines that map impossibility into something approaching sense. Vincent's scarred knuckles protest as his fingers close around it, the gesture of acceptance meaning more than just taking custody of records.

"In case it starts again," Jennifer says, the words landing between them like dropped stones into still water. "In case someone needs to know that it happened before, that it can happen, that Duswood's built on a foundation that people tend to forget how strong it can be."

"You think it will?" Vincent asks, though he knows her answer from the way she's already turned slightly toward the car, body language telegraphing departure.

"I think this town's got a taste for forgetting that's stronger than its memory," she says, pulling her sunglasses back down, becoming professionally distant again. "And things that get forgotten have a way of returning when they're least expected."

"You leaving town?" Vincent asks, nodding at the car.

Jennifer smiles, but it's thin. "Yeah. Time to get away from here for a while. Kent and I might check out Missouri. Neither of us have ever been. Maybe it'll stay quiet out there."

She slides into the driver's seat with the fluid motion of someone who's practiced leaving, who's made an art of departure. The engine starts with a purr that speaks of proper maintenance and elsewhere intentions. Kent says something that makes her almost smile, and they pull away from the curb with the careful speed of people who won't be coming back to check what they left behind.

Vincent stands in the parking lot holding evidence of impossibility, watching Jennifer's car shrink toward the horizon. The envelope's weight redistributes as he shifts it under his arm, papers settling into new configurations. The afternoon continues its aggressive brightness.

The cemetery sprawls across the hillside's southern slope in organized terraces and manageable like grief can be contained in neat rows if you just plan the spacing right. Vincent follows the gravel path between headstones that range from fresh-carved granite to markers so old the names have worn to suggestions, entire lives reduced to smooth stone and speculation. October air carries the smell of turned earth from a new plot three rows over.

Jayce walks beside him but not quite with him, maintaining that careful distance of people who share destination, but don't mean to get there together. His hands stay buried in his denim jacket's pockets, shoulders hunched against a brisk wind.

Carl's grave occupies a spot beneath a maple that's just beginning its autumn performance, leaves shifting from green to gold to red in gradients that would be beautiful if they weren't marking time above someone who won't see another season change. The headstone itself is simple gray granite, rough-cut at the edges but polished smooth where Carl's name runs in letters that still look too fresh, too sharp.

Small stones cluster at the headstone's base, accumulated offerings from visits Vincent has made alone, visits Jayce has made alone, never together until now. Some are smooth river rocks, others jagged pieces of quartz or granite, each one a physical marker of presence, of remembering, of the Jewish tradition Carl's grandmother taught them about leaving something that lasts longer than flowers, longer than words, maybe longer than memory itself.

The moss has begun its patient claim on the stone's lower edges, soft green that makes the granite look less foreign against the earth. Vincent kneels, his scarred knuckles protesting the movement, and his fingers find the carved letters of Carl's name. The stone feels warm despite the October chill.

The inscription reads:

Loved fiercely, laughed loudly,
Never backed down.

Jayce crouches beside the grave's opposite corner. From his jacket he produces a handful of wildflowers that look like he picked them on the walk here, stems crushed from being carried in a pocket but blooms still defiant, purple and yellow and white mixed without design. He arranges them against the headstone with more precision than the gesture seems to require, each bloom positioned and repositioned until they create something that isn't quite pattern but isn't quite random either.

"Remember when he tried to convince us that gas station coffee was just as good as the stuff from that fancy place downtown?" Jayce says, the words emerging sudden and unexpected. "Spent twenty minutes defending it with like, economic theory he made up on the spot."

Vincent's hand stills on the carved name, a smile pulling at his mouth. "He drew graphs," Vincent adds, remembering Carl's notebook filled with supposedly scientific proof that convenience store coffee represented the apex of cost-to-satisfaction ratio. "Actual graphs with axes labeled and everything."

"And then Miller asked him to actually drink some to prove his point," Jayce continues, his own smile audible in his voice, "and Carl just stood there with this cup of absolute motor oil, trying not to gag while insisting it was delicious."

The memory hangs between them, warming the space around the grave like Carl himself is participating, adding his own defensive arguments about acquired tastes and cultural coffee snobbery. Vincent's fingers trace the dates beneath Carl's name, numbers that bracket a life shorter than it should have been.

"It's true. He never backed down from anything," Vincent says, settling back to sit properly on the grass, accepting the dampness that seeps through his jeans as the price of being present. "Even when he was obviously wrong. Especially when he was obviously wrong."

Jayce shifts from his crouch to sit as well, creating a mirror of Vincent's position across the grave, two points of a triangle with Carl's stone as the third. "The dance," he says, and doesn't need to specify which one because they both know, both remember that particular disaster with the clarity that only comes from witnessing a friend's spectacular failure.

"Freshman year," Vincent confirms, already feeling the

laughter building in his chest despite the setting. "Chelsea Marshall."

"He practiced his asking-her-out speech on us for a week," Jayce says, his fingers absently straightening the wildflowers that don't need straightening. "Had note cards. Color-coded note cards with conversation trees mapped out for every possible response."

"Except for the response he actually got," Vincent adds, remembering Carl's face when Chelsea had simply said yes immediately, destroying his entire prepared dialogue structure in a single syllable.

"And then the dance itself," Jayce continues, his shoulders shaking slightly with suppressed laughter. "When he tried to do that spin move he saw in some movie..."

"And clotheslined her with his own arm," Vincent finishes, the laughter escaping now, inappropriate and necessary and exactly what Carl would want. "The sound she made. Like a squeaky toy being stepped on."

They're both laughing now, not polite cemetery chuckles but real laughter that echoes off neighboring headstones and probably disturbs whoever's visiting the grave four rows over. But it feels right, feels like the kind of tribute Carl would appreciate more than flowers or stones or solemn silence. He never wanted people feeling sorry for him when he was alive, probably doesn't want it now that he's not.

"She still danced with him after," Jayce says when the laughter subsides to manageable levels, wiping his eyes with the back of his hand. "Three more songs, even though her neck was already bruising."

"Because that was Carl," Vincent says, understanding arriving with the words. "People forgave him everything because he was so genuinely himself all the time. Never pretended to be cooler or smarter or better than he was."

"I miss him," Jayce says, words simple and devastating in

their honesty. "I miss having someone around who made failing seem like just another kind of winning."

Vincent nods, his throat tight with emotion that's not quite grief anymore but something more complex, grief mixed with gratitude mixed with the understanding that missing someone doesn't always have to hurt, sometimes it can just be acknowledgment of absence without the weight of loss.

They sit in comfortable silence for a while, the October afternoon wrapping around them with the kind of perfect temperature that makes you forget winter's coming, that makes everything seem possible even in a cemetery where possibility has clear borders. Vincent finds a small piece of granite in his pocket, rough-edged and unremarkable except for the way it fits perfectly in his palm. He places it carefully with the other stones at the headstone's base, adding his presence to the accumulation.

"Same time next week?" Jayce asks as they stand, brushing grass and earth from their jeans with movements that mirror each other without intention.

"Yeah," Vincent agrees, understanding that this is how healing happens, not all at once but in regular doses, in shared remembering that transforms loss into something bearable, maybe even something beautiful in its own broken way.

They walk back through the cemetery together, their footsteps falling into synchronization without effort, two people who've found their rhythm through shared loss and unexpected laughter. The maple tree releases more leaves as they pass beneath it, gold and red cascading like nature's confetti, and Vincent thinks Carl would appreciate the gesture.

The cemetery gate closes behind them with a soft click that sounds like punctuation, ending this visit but promising others, regular as seasons, reliable as Carl's terrible jokes, necessary as breathing.

Dusk transforms Duswood's residential streets into something softer than their daylight honesty, shadows filling the spaces between houses like dark water rising, streetlights flickering to life in sequence as if following Vincent and Mira's path home. Vincent walks close enough to feel the warmth radiating from her dark dress, close enough that their hands might brush if either of them had the courage to let that happen, but they maintain that careful distance of people who've shared too much to be casual but haven't figured out what that makes them to each other.

Another streetlight buzzes to life just as they pass beneath it, casting their shadows long and thin behind them, and Mira glances up at the synchronicity with an expression that might be amusement or might be something more watchful. Since Muldrath's dissolution, she notices patterns everywhere, coincidences that might not be, the universe's small gestures that suggest it's paying attention even when it seems indifferent.

"The lights have been doing that all week," she says, her voice carrying that particular quality it's developed since the hilltop, not quite whisper but something that doesn't want to disturb whatever might be listening. "Following me."

The Holy Face chaplet wraps around her wrist where it's lived since that night, beads worn smooth by her mother's fingers now wearing smooth again under Mira's constant touch. She fidgets with it as they walk, an unconscious rotation, her way of processing thoughts too large for words. Vincent has memorized the gesture, the way her thumb finds each bead in sequence, the slight pause at the crucifix before beginning again.

Three more streetlights bloom to life ahead of them, perfectly timed to their approach, and Vincent feels the hair on his arms rise with something that isn't quite fear but isn't quite not fear either. The lights seem brighter than usual, or maybe it's just that the darkness between them seems darker, more substantial, like it has intention.

They turn onto Mira's street where her home squats at the

corner, windows dark except for the perpetual light in Elias's workshop, that unnaturally bright glow that means he's working late again. The house itself looks different in this liminal light, less forbidding and more resigned.

The porch light is already on when they arrive, that single yellow bulb that makes everything beneath it look like it exists in sepia, in memory, in some past that's happening right now. They stop at the base of the steps, neither moving to ascend nor to separate, caught in that moment when goodbye should happen but doesn't want to.

Mira's fingers find the chaplet again, but this time she unwraps it partially, revealing the red marks it's left on her wrist, perfect impressions of each bead like Braille spelling out something only skin can read. "It's heavy for what it is," she says, not looking at Vincent but at the marks, at the evidence of weight that physics can't quite explain. "Not just the beads. The history. What my mother did with it. What it means that I'm wearing it now."

She rewraps it quickly, like exposure makes it vulnerable to something, and Vincent wants to reach out, to touch her hand or her shoulder or anywhere that might provide comfort, but he understands that sometimes comfort makes things harder, makes the weight more real by acknowledging it exists.

"She wore it during the reinforcement ritual," Mira continues, climbing the porch steps slowly, Vincent following, both of them moving like they're approaching something that might spook if they're too sudden. "My father told me. She held it while she offered herself, while she became the joy to balance thirty years of sorrow. And now I carry it, and sometimes I feel her in it. Not like a ghost. Like an echo. Like the memory of someone being brave when being brave was the only option left."

"Do you regret knowing?" Vincent asks, the question emerging without planning, pulled from him by the intimacy of the moment, by the way the porch light makes them feel separate from the world, contained in their own small sphere of illumination.

Mira exhales. "I regret that knowledge came through loss," she says finally. "That understanding required sacrifice. That truth cost what it cost." She pauses, looks directly at Vincent for the first time since they started walking. "But not knowing? That would be worse. Living above a foundation of lies, no matter how kindly meant, that's not living. That's just existing."

The front door opens without warning, Elias's silhouette filling the frame in that way he has of appearing exactly when conversations reach the point where they might reveal too much. His black suit makes him nearly invisible except for his face and hands, pale objects floating in the doorway's darkness. He doesn't speak immediately, just observes them with those clinical eyes.

"You should come inside, Mira," he says finally, but his tone suggests invitation rather than command, a father who's learning to suggest rather than decree. His gaze shifts to Vincent, and something in his expression softens slightly, not quite approval but acknowledgment that Vincent has earned his place in their strange orbit.

"Vincent should know," Mira says, not asking permission but informing her father of a decision already made. "About what you said. About what might be coming."

Elias steps onto the porch proper, closing the door behind him with the careful movements of someone ensuring privacy. The yellow light makes his face look older, or maybe just more honest, showing the exhaustion that his professional composure usually hides. "The Adversary isn't gone," he says, his voice low enough that Vincent has to lean in to hear. "He's only lost his grip on this place. On Duswood specifically. But entities like that, they don't just disappear.

They find other foundations to corrupt, other griefs and emotions to exploit."

"You think he'll come back?" Vincent asks, though the question feels naive even as he speaks it. Of course something like that comes back. That's what makes it adversarial.

"I think he never truly leaves," Elias says, his hand finding the doorframe for support that might be physical or might be psychological. "He just becomes less immediate, less present. But he watches. Waits for the moment when vigilance becomes complacency, when the binding's dissolution creates new vulnerabilities."

"The chaplet," Mira says, raising her wrist slightly. "That's why you wanted me to keep wearing it."

"Your mother believed it created a kind of blindness," Elias confirms. "Made the wearer harder to perceive for things that exist outside normal perception. Not invisible, but... unremarkable. Easy to overlook."

The conversation might continue, might reveal more about what Elias knows or suspects, but the smell arrives without warning, rolling across the porch like a physical presence. It's overwhelming stench, organic rot mixed with something chemical, like roadkill that's been marinating in industrial waste, sweet and sharp and hostile all at once. Vincent's eyes water immediately, his throat closing against the assault, and he sees Mira's hand shoot to cover her nose and mouth.

The smell intensifies, becomes almost visible in the dim porch light, a thickness to the air. It carries heat despite the cool evening, fevered warmth that speaks of infection, of things finding a way to grow, feeding on what they shouldn't. Vincent tastes it, bile rising in his throat, his body rejecting the very presence of whatever produces this stench.

Then, as suddenly as it arrived, it's gone. Not fading but vanishing, like something decided to stop exhaling in their direction. The normal evening air rushes back, carrying wood smoke from someone's fireplace and the last roses of the season, ordinary scents that feel like salvation after that assault.

Elias has gone rigid, his fingers white where they grip the doorframe, his face showing the kind of recognition that comes with repeated experience. "Inside," he says, the single word carrying enough authority that Mira moves without question, though she glances back at Vincent with eyes that promise this conversation isn't over, that there are things she needs to tell him that can't be said in doorways or under yellow lights where unknown things might listen.

Vincent backs away from the porch, his legs unsteady from the smell's aftermath, his stomach still churning. "Tomorrow?" he calls up to Mira, who stands just inside the doorway now, her father's protective presence behind her.

She nods. Her hand rises to wave or beckon or just acknowledge that tomorrow exists.

COMING SOON: QUIET BLOOM (BOOK 2)

Quiet Bloom - As of October 2025, Quiet Bloom is in post-production. Tentative release in December. Look for updates on Instagram and in my newsletter.

ABOUT THE AUTHOR

N.B. Cross writes quiet horror and dark fiction rooted in small towns, haunted landscapes, and the shadows that live between memory and grief. His short story collection, *Static Between the Trees*, introduced readers to his blend of atmosphere and unease. Hollow Stone is the first book in the Stonebound trilogy.

Learn more at nbcrossauthor.com and join the Signals from the Static newsletter for behind-the-scenes notes, new stories, and early updates.

Follow at instagram.com/n.b.cross/

ALSO BY N.B. CROSS

Static Between the Trees (short story collection)

www.ingramcontent.com/pod-product-compliance
Lightning Source LLC
Chambersburg PA
CBHW061249310726

48971CB00007B/2281